CALAMITIES AND MIRACLES

Family Feared Lost

RICHARD PAUL WARREN

A true story based on the original journal written by Ruth M. Foell

PublishAmerica
Baltimore

First printing

PublishAmerica has allowed this work to remain exactly as the author intended, verbatim, without editorial input.

ISBN: 1-60474-041-8
PUBLISHED BY PUBLISHAMERICA, LLLP
www.publishamerica.com
Baltimore

Printed in the United States of America

DEDICATION

This book is dedicated to Ruth Mary Foell, nurse, gourmet chef, author, poet, listener, counselor, loving wife and mother.

To Renée and Albert,
My best wishes!
Richard Paul Warren

ACKNOWLEDGEMENTS

I wish to express my appreciation to the following people who helped to make this book a reality:

My wife, Connie, for her patience, encouragement, and her many hours of professional assistance proof-reading and editing.

Libby Berndt, publisher of *The Sidney Herald*, for assisting with background information about the Sidney, Montana area.

Sandra L. Turner and the volunteers at *The MonDak Heritage Center* in Sidney, Montana for providing research data from their archives.

If you look up, there are no limits.
—Japanese Proverb

PROLOGUE

When two earthen dams in the hills above Sidney, Montana collapsed in the middle of a cold winter night, they unleashed millions of gallons of water and gigantic blocks of ice that hurtled downhill into the unsuspecting town as most of its inhabitants lay asleep. The sudden, horrendous flood inundated 85% of Sidney. Miraculously, the only apparent fatalities were members of one family, the family of Herman and Ruth Foell who lived "underground" in a basement home on the edge of town nearest to the dams. Their home was totally destroyed, transformed into an underwater tomb in a matter of minutes. Rescuers had little doubt that the entire Foell family was trapped there beneath the icy floodwaters.

This is a true story about that family, gleaned from the pages of Ruth Mary Foell's own journal that was recovered after her untimely death. A copy of her unfinished manuscript contained entries up to only three or four weeks prior to the dramatic catastrophe that nearly swept their small town into oblivion.

I visited with Ruth's sister, Helen Nelson, around 1985. I found her in Santa Barbara, California where she worked in a well-known collector's book shop until she was at least 80. I had known Helen and her family in Montana because my family lived in Sidney awhile when I was a youngster, so I could relate to the town and to that period of time. Helen was there "when the dams broke"—and so we talked. Although my family wasn't living in Sidney when the dams collapsed, I do remember my folks talking about the horrible disaster that struck our former home town, so I had a personal interest in that event.

Inheriting Ruth's manuscript stirred my curiosity once again about what really happened that night, so I eventually found the time to start digging for the facts.

In most cases, I have used the actual names of real people as I learned about them, except where a true name might cause embarrassment or discomfort for an individual or the person's family. I have changed the names of the owner and the ranch operations manager of the ranch where the breached dams were located primarily because their dialogues in Chapter Eighteen are not actually quotations. I fabricated their conversations as I imagined they would have taken place in order to better describe the event as it actually unfolded. The ranch manager was the only eye witness who saw the dams collapse before his very eyes.

As I transcribed and edited her journal when putting this book together, I appreciated the fact that Ruth Foell did not have the advantages of electronic word processing, spell check or the speed of a computer keyboard. In a Forward she had prepared for her future book, Ruth explained that she used an old second-hand, manual typewriter—hunt-and-peck method. Her writing was no doubt an arduous, sometimes frustrating accomplishment, and it would have been tragic if that effort were wasted. It is time now to finally share her story and her thoughts with the survivors of her family, and with others who still believe in the immeasurable sustaining power and strength provided by faith, a sense of humor, and a loving family.

Richard Paul Warren

LOVE IN OUR HOME

by Ruth M. Foell
(Published in *The Montana Woman*, December 1950)

The love in our home is God's presence there.
Never feel you're alone with no one to care.
Love is everywhere you chance to look,
The smile in your loved one's eyes,
In the pages of the Good Book.

Home is made of simple things,
Available to us all...
The growing plants in the window,
The pictures on the wall.

The homey odor of baking bread,
And the traditions it imparts,
A table 'round which we gather,
With bowed heads and grateful hearts.

The slamming of the door, with
"Are you in here, Mom?"
The cookie jar on the shelf,
The simplest of fare.
All this speaks of love
And where our hearts sing.

More happy homes, more smiles on our faces
Would give more peace to homes in faraway places.
For it is faith in God and love in everyday life,
Which will make nations strong and free from all strife.

Mrs. H. A. Foell, President
Sidney Woman's Club

CHAPTER ONE
Aftermath of the Great Sidney Flood

In the predawn hours of a cold winter night on Monday, March 26, 1951, two earthen dams in the hills above Sidney, Montana collapsed. Their reservoirs retained more than 800 acre-feet of water and were filled beyond capacity. When the dams ruptured, first the upper dam and then the lower, they unleashed millions of gallons of water and ice that hurtled downhill into the little town as it lay sleeping. The terrifying, frigid onslaught crashed into the valley like a deadly tsunami, crushing buildings and bridges, sweeping away animals, automobiles, roadways and power lines, destroying everything in its path. If the force of the ravaging floodwater wasn't destructive enough, it carried with it gigantic blocks of ice weighing several tons that performed as missiles and battering rams. The thundering, devastating wave wiped out a sizeable portion of Sidney and seriously damaged the rest of the little town.

Miraculously, the only apparent fatalities were members of one family, the family of Herman and Ruth Foell who lived "underground" with their three young sons in a basement home on the west edge of town—nearest to the dams. Their home at 121 North Sunset Boulevard was one of the first dwellings to be struck by the initial wave and was totally destroyed. The window wells and the only exit were blocked by tons of ice, making escape impossible. The entire Foell family was believed to be trapped in that dark, submerged tomb beneath the icy floodwaters. No other deaths were reported.

Sidney is normally a pleasant, peaceful little town nestled in the Yellowstone River Valley, ten miles west of the North Dakota border; but the damage caused by the flood ran into hundreds of thousands and perhaps millions of dollars, affecting the lives of nearly everyone in the valley. When Vivian Baker stopped by to visit Helen Nelson nearly a week after the Great Flood, she had tears in her eyes. Helen invited her in and offered her a cup of coffee. "Oh Helen," she sobbed, "I'm so sorry... so terribly sorry."

Vivian could barely talk, because she began sobbing so hard. Helen hugged her and they clung to each other for a long time, consoling each other. Then Helen led Vivian back to the big farmhouse kitchen, poured two cups of coffee and nodded toward the table. She noticed the lady had a flat package tucked under her arm, wrapped in brown paper. Vivian laid the packet on the table, pulled out a chair and sat down. Helen waited for the older woman to compose herself. After carefully sipping at the hot coffee for several minutes, Vivian began to speak again, slowly, haltingly at first.

"I... I just heard yesterday about what happened to your sister, and I... I just don't know what to say. Ruth was such a good woman! Everybody loved her. We all loved them... the whole family... Ruth and Herman and the boys. There are lots of us who are really gonna be sad not seeing 'em around here anymore, God bless 'em!"

Vivian was the epitome of everybody's sweet, loving grandmother, with her gray hair drawn back from her care-worn face into a tidy bun, and a neat row of bangs softening her furrowed brow that made her appear a bit more youthful. Helen was very fond of the woman who had befriended her younger sister since the first day Ruth and her family began attending Vivian's church after moving to Sidney.

"I... I brought this along for you, Helen," Vivian continued, handing the package to Helen. "Ruth loaned it to me just a few weeks ago and I didn't get a chance to get it back to her before they... before she..." Again she broke down, taking a minute or so to regain control. "I'm so sorry. This all just happened so sudden and I know it was so awful for them. I feel so bad. I just don't know what to do. I miss them so much already."

Helen leaned across the table and put her hand on Vivian's arm, trying to soothe her. "There, there, dear, we must believe that Ruth has moved on to a better place where she can hopefully find peace and be happier. These last three years here in Montana have been just one trial after another for her and Herman and the boys. She truly needed a change, although this was certainly not the way they planned it. You know, they started having water problems at their place again not very long before the dams went out."

"They did? Ya know, I did hear something about that... but then I was ill for a time and missed church for a couple of Sundays, so I didn't see Ruth for a while. I didn't hear no details... just that the water finally got to 'em and... and now they're gone," Vivian answered weakly, almost choking on the last few words. Then leaning forward hesitantly, she asked, "What happened, Helen? Sorry. I expect you don't much feel like talking about it right now. Ruth and Herman certainly had more than their share of troubles with too much water on that piece of land."

"Yeah, they sure did, and it looked like it was going to start all over again, even after dumping 30 truckloads of fill around the basement and sloping it all away from the house. Oh dear," Helen exclaimed, interrupting herself and seeming a bit flustered. "Where are my manners? Would you care for a homemade ginger cookie, Viv? As I was saying, that stretch with the warm winds during the daytime started an early thaw, and the water was starting to build up again... really scary! Herman got up about four o'clock one morning and tried to dig some drainage ditches to carry more water away from the house; and when he went back inside, he passed out cold! Ruth said he just tipped off the chair and hit the floor like a sack of cement!"

"Land sakes!" Vivian gasped, putting her hands to her wide-open mouth! "I hadn't heard none of this! Was it a heart attack or what? Herman was such a nice man! Ruth was always braggin' about her husband, and I don't wonder."

"Well, Doc Harper rushed right out and looked him over pretty good and said it was just exhaustion. Who can say? But it scared Ruth something awful. Herman too, I guess. She called me later and told me they were seriously thinking about pulling up stakes and moving out before something really drastic happened. She said she had this strong, ominous feeling that they needed to get out of there very soon. She felt something dreadful was coming… something terribly dreadful. It was like the Lord tried to warn her before any of us knew what was going to happen."

Helen Nelson was the eldest of three sisters. Ruth was the middle one. Helen always seemed to be the strongest, the most stable, the sister who could face any storm and survive with a hint of a smile and knowing eyes that seemed to have discovered the secrets of endurance. She was reminiscent of the determined pioneer spirit possessed by the strong-willed, wiry women of the Great Plains only a couple of generations before Helen. Her lean but sturdy frame herded her five children in directions they often didn't wish to go, but they knew their mother was a force to be reckoned with. Though Helen was generally a stoic woman of few complaints and always reluctant to offer advice, Ruth sometimes came to her older sister to draw from her strength when she was discouraged or troubled. And now, Helen already missed Ruth greatly. They had lived so far from each other much of their adult lives, that it had been wonderful having her in the same town for almost three years. Helen poured a second cup of coffee for each of them and set out more cookies. They continued exchanging stories about the flood for nearly an hour.

"Did you hear about Becker's big new house just down the road from you," Vivian blurted out with a snort, "the one with its own bowling alley in the basement? I know it's not funny, but… oh Lord… they're probably not gonna be bowling much for a while now!" Both ladies broke down laughing. They couldn't help themselves. Somehow, when wealthy people suffer some property damage, it just doesn't seem so tragic compared to the losses of other people who are struggling to survive. In the midst of disaster and misery, it seemed healing to be able to giggle like schoolgirls sharing gossip.

"I guess Nels Bach lost about 50 head of sheep. Most ranchers in the valley didn't get hurt too bad, though. It could have been a lot worse, but I heard that some of them got an early warning on Sunday that one of the dams had a bad leak or something, so they moved their stock to higher ground away from Lone Tree Creek. We were sure lucky here," Helen sighed and looked heavenward with a silent thank you. "I'm glad we built this place on high ground. If we were still living in that old farmhouse closer to town, we'd have been washed away for sure. Tell me, Vivian, how did you and Ed fare during the flood?"

"Oh, we had a good bit of damage, but we were really very fortunate compared to lots of folks in town. Our yard is ruint—such a mess—and the basement filled with about four feet of water and mud. But we finally got the basement pumped out and the furnace is working again. Sure was cold in the house for quite a spell there. Still got a lot of cleanup work to do though. I swear, you couldn't beg, borrow or steal a pump anywhere in town, since they was kinda scarce and everybody needin' them all at the same time. You know they rushed to ship in all the pumps they could find from down in Glendive and up to Williston. Don't know yet how much stuff was ruint down there in our basement, but it ain't nothing compared to folks who lived in basement homes like... oh my God ... like Ruth and Herman! Oh Helen, I feel so awful about them!" Vivian started sobbing all over again.

Helen drank a swallow of coffee, took a deep breath and continued. "You're sure right about that, Vivian. People living in basement homes—and we have a bunch of them built in this town since the war—those folks really got wiped out. Like the Morrison's nice basement home out there on Lambert Road. They were awakened by the loud roar of the water and ice, threw on their robes and raced up the stairs and out of their house. By the time they got out to their car, the water was over a foot deep; so Gordon drove over to the highway where they waited until the floodwaters went down. And when they were finally able to make it back to their basement, guess what? They found three sides of it caved in! One big wall slab of concrete was pushed over and crushed the bed where they were sleeping just before the water hit!!"

Vivian gasped in horror. "Land sakes! At least they escaped with their lives."

"Yes," Helen continued, her voice trembling a bit "with their lives at least. But they weren't able to save anything else. Their furniture, appliances, all their clothes... completely ruined. We're talking about thousands of dollars here. Same story with Johnny Smith and his wife. They also had a basement home on Lambert Road... wiped out. My church is trying to help those folks... plus the Red Cross."

"Me and Ed drove out to see the fair grounds the other day and the highway goes right past Ruth's place, of course. Lord have mercy, Helen... there's nothing left to save there either! And the fair grounds? Almost totally wiped out! It's all so unbelievable."

"Yes, I saw it," Helen sighed with resignation.

"I read in the paper where Don Nutter said they was still gonna have the County Fair this year, but they'd have to kinda cut back on account of the damage and all. Nutter... wasn't he the man that donated his blood that saved Ruth's boy's life?"

"Yes, that was almost a year ago now. It was Dickie, Ruth's middle boy. They almost lost him then for sure!"

"That reminds me," Vivian butted in. "Did you hear about the Newells over on South Roosevelt? Their two little boys have a room in their basement, and the older boy came through the water and upstairs with his puppy in his arms to wake up Charlie and his wife. The boy told them there was lots of water in the basement and they had better go down and get his brother because the other little guy was still on his bed, afraid to step into the deep water. Well, Mrs. Newell rushes down to rescue her other son, and wades through knee-deep water to get to him. By the time she carried him back to the stairs, the water was already up to her chest, and she could barely make it herself."

"My word," Helen exclaimed, shaking her head. There was no end to all of the fearsome stories. "How frightening that must have been! And what about Andy Nault and his family? They all rushed out to his truck in front of their house to try to get to higher ground, but the engine wouldn't start. All wet or something. Before they knew it, the water was up over the seat and they had to climb up on top of the cab! Well, then the Moores next door got forced out of their house, too, and they climbed onto the truck and tried to scramble up on the cab's roof, too, but there wasn't enough room for all of them. The Moores have a four year-old and a little baby, so try to picture the four of them trying to crowd on top of the pickup truck's roof with the three Naults. So, Andy and his wife grabbed some branches overhead and climbed up into a tree. No shoes, no coats... just all of them shivering in the darkness, 'cause you remember all the lights went out, too. They all got rescued a couple hours later by the police in a boat."

"Yeah, how 'bout all them boats!" Vivian wondered out loud. "Where did we suddenly get so many boats in Sidney, Montana? It's like they came out of nowhere! And thank goodness, too, because Doc Peterson's family had to crawl up on the roof of their house and were marooned there for hours until somebody came by in a boat to help them. Of course, they live down on the south side that got hit the worst." Vivian let out a long sigh, shaking her head sadly. "Lots of folks hurtin' right now. I guess the Red Cross is just swamped with calls for help."

"And you know what else?" Helen interjected. "Land values! It isn't just the physical damage alone. It's what's going to happen with land values. As you know, my husband Bill runs the State Experimental Farm here, and he knows all about irrigation. He says with those reservoirs gone now, thousands of acres of irrigated land are going to run dry... almost worthless. What kind of crops can you grow on dry land? More wheat? No shortage of wheat I know of. So there goes our sugar beet industry!""

"Oh Lord A'mighty, Helen, I hadn't even thought about that! Do you suppose they'll rebuild the dams?"

"I suppose they're going to have to... eventually. But I expect the folks in this town are going to want some strong assurances that any new dams better be damned safe! Um... sorry. Didn't mean that to come out like a pun." Helen wanted to change the subject anyway. She was weary of talking about the flood. "What's in the package, Vivian? You say you borrowed it from my sister?"

"Oh, yes. You know that book Ruth has been writing? Sort of like a diary or a journal about her family's experiences here in Montana.

Well, Ruth gave a reading from parts of it for the Women's Club last month, and I was unable to attend that meeting. Many of the ladies told me I missed a wonderful program and just raved about her book and how funny it was and how lovingly she writes! I felt terrible about missing her reading, and I told her so when I saw her in church the next Sunday. So about three weeks ago, she loaned me her carbon copy of the manuscript so I could read it. I couldn't hardly put it down until I read all of it. It's not all finished yet, but I just loved what she has already done! And since she's... since she's not... uh... not here anymore, I thought I should bring it out to you."

After Vivian left, Helen poured yet another cup of coffee and sat down at the kitchen table, staring at the flat, plainly wrapped package in front of her, thinking of her recently departed sister. The house was deathly quiet. Her husband, Bill, and the three older kids were out helping flood victims trying to salvage their remaining possessions from the thick, cold muck of the receding floodwaters. Little Judy was at a playmate's house and Bobby was taking a long afternoon nap. Although she had heard a great deal about Ruth's book and listened to parts of it that her sister read to her, Helen had never actually read any of the stories from its pages. She removed the brown wrapping from the carbon copy of her sister's typed manuscript, caressed the cover lovingly and began to read.

CHAPTER TWO
Ruth's Story—Coming of Age

If you think married life is dull and monotonous, I can't agree with you. Sometimes it appears that way, I know, but if you'll only pause for a moment now and then to reflect on the various episodes of your wedded life, you'll find many rich memories that no one can ever take from you. I have been blessed with many of these treasures, gaining a little something from each. In my reveries, when I recall some of my marital experiences, I find that I can smile and often chuckle about even those episodes that were disheartening at the time, and sometimes a bit tragic. The good Lord has endowed us all with a sense of humor. We only have to make use of it to add sunshine to our paths. To be certain, there are clouds in every one's life, but if you add a little sunshine from your heart to the mist of your disappointments, you'll always find a rainbow.

After devoting most of my childhood in Wisconsin to "grownup" responsibilities, my perspective of married life was not too favorable. I decided to avoid any marital entanglements as long as possible. My mother was absorbed by the business world, partly because we needed the extra income and partly because she was naturally clever in business affairs. She enjoyed her work, but was also looking to the future and the pretty new home we would have one day. That dream never materialized. I have learned that too many of us are blind to *today's blessings and happiness* because we are so busy looking impatiently into the future for what it may hold, or looking back with regrets over our past errors.

With mother working every day, the full burden of the housework was placed on the shoulders of my older sister, Helen, and me. By the time I was twelve, I was already baking bread, pies, doughnuts and a few of my own concoctions. The chores around the house took most of our spare time, leaving little for study or recreation. After graduating from high school, I knew that college was out of the question for me, so I decided to go somewhere "on my own" to enjoy some of the things I felt I had been deprived of. Since my mother was a secretary to a railroad executive, passes were available to our family at any time. My older sister became the manager of a gift shop owned by the railroad in West Yellowstone. After a serious family conference, I was allowed to join Helen for the summer. Clutching my precious pass to freedom, I boarded a train and headed west to Wyoming with the promise of a job in the gift shop.

I'll never forget that exciting season in the summer of 1927, the new friendships, the beautiful mountains and the thrill of having only myself to take care of. I remember the trainloads of tourists coming to Yellowstone Park, clamorous and excited. When I wasn't working, I often joined them on horseback, riding up into the canyons to be enveloped by the beautiful panoramas of nature. The mountains were breathtaking as they rose majestically over the lush green forests, canyons and tumbling, ice-cold streams. I was actually born in Greeley, Colorado, but I was so young when we moved to Wisconsin that I had no recollection of the grandeur of the Rocky Mountains. Still, I felt like the "call of the West" was always in my blood. That wonderful summer was an extraordinary contrast to the life I had been leading most of my first eighteen years. Every day as my goblet was filled to overflowing, I drank deeply of the sweetness of my new experiences and independence. I was exhilarated by each adventure that came my way, determined to live and love each day to the fullest. Before getting married and having to settle down to what I imagined would be a dreary life filled with housework and children, I wanted to enjoy every minute of my autonomous young life. I have learned since that the institution of marriage need not be confining and dreary at all, unless you make it so. But I was very young then and could judge married life only from my own personal family experience and limited observations.

All too soon, that summer came to an end. The tourists left, the college students who worked at Yellowstone Park returned to school, and my sister was ready to return to her winter job in Wisconsin. But I wasn't ready to return home, so I decided to visit Grandma Hibbard in Seattle. It was there that I became impressed by the huge hospital that revived my secret desire to become a nurse. Suddenly, my hazy future took form and I wanted very much to enter nurse's training. With my folk's permission and Grandma's promise to watch over me, I entered nursing school at the big Swedish Hospital.

The following months were filled with hard but gratifying work. I attended the University of Washington part-time, a privilege I had never dared to hope for. I believe nursing is one of the noblest professions a woman can enter. Even though I didn't complete my training, the knowledge and experience I gained was never lost, and served me well in later years. I kept myself too busy to suffer much from homesickness. We worked long hours during the flu epidemic that attacked so intensely that winter, and in my fatigued condition, I fell victim to pneumonia. During the long, lonely convalescence that followed, I realized how far from home I really was. With the types of transportation available in the late 1920's, Seattle was a long, long way from Wisconsin, and it had been quite awhile since I had seen my family. I knew then that I really did miss them, and vowed to return home to Wisconsin as soon as I was well enough to travel. I regretted leaving my training, but had achieved enough valuable education as a practical nurse that I was able to apply it to many occasions in my everyday life, and certainly when I raised my children and cared for my husband. Still, I have wished many times that I had completed my medical studies to become a registered nurse, or at least an LPN. The additional income would have been appreciated in the lean years that were to follow.

The amount of nursing training I did manage to complete soon paid off. I secured a very nice position as a governess as a direct result of my references from the hospital in Seattle. The next seven years of my life were somewhat governed by my job, but I was generously compensated financially and with travel opportunities. Through all those years, I was the constant companion of a sweet little girl, the only daughter of a wealthy Milwaukee family. I remember days that were trying for me and lonely sometimes, but many wonderful trips made up for such days. We always traveled first class, and visited such marvelous places I might not otherwise have seen on my own, like Mexico, Arizona, all over the West, and even spent several months in the Ojai Valley in California. But eventually, after I had spent seven years of my life devoted to this lovable family, I realized that travel and money alone would never satisfy my need for personal happiness. I wanted my own family and my own little home.

During the period this family employed me, I met Herman at a party. We were attracted to each other from the first time we met. It was love at first sight and we kept "steady company" from that time on. Due to my family's strenuous objections, we were separated several times but not for long. You see, Herman was a German immigrant, and even though Milwaukee is heavily populated with citizens and descendants from Germany and Poland, "foreigners" or people with accents are not to be trusted, especially if your family is purely of English descent as mine is. I've been told my ancestors arrived in America shortly after the *Mayflower* folks, so my parents felt much more American than Herman's folks could feel. There was another major obstacle—the Depression. Herman was one of the many unemployed. When he came to the United States a few years before I met him, he had planned to attend the Milwaukee School of Engineering. His German education qualified him as an industrial engineering draftsman and tool designer, but he wanted to become a full-fledged engineer. The Depression killed that dream. All of his money was spent for room and board as he searched in vain for employment.

Herman did any kind of work he could find to sustain himself, and he still believed he was very fortunate to be in this wonderful country. After many years of struggle and near starvation in Germany, he felt he was actually quite well off in his new world. He recalled how he stood in line as a child for hours, even days, for a little pail of skim milk, a bit of bread and some cheese. We've often tried to impress our young family with this story so they would appreciate their food more, but it never went over very big. They have never been hungry, so they don't comprehend the meaning of hunger. Herman finally landed a job and it wasn't long before we could afford to be married. His salary was small, but we had both learned to get along on very little. We required practically no recreational expense, because we found so much happiness in simple pleasures. We have proved that old adage, "The best things in life are free!" We enjoyed good music. We loved to hike, and we spent many hours window-shopping. After seventeen years of married life now, our love is seventeen times better because we have never become jaded. That strength has carried us through many tough times.

One adjustment I needed to cope with was my new last name. For 25 years, I was Ruth Wilson, easy enough to pronounce. My married surname became "Foell", an anglicized version of "Föll". Almost no one pronounces it right the first time they see it spelled. I have heard "Foal, Fo-ell, Fuel, Foil, Fool", and even "Foul". But I've learned to smile sweetly and say, "It's pronounced 'Fell'... like down the stairs." That helps them to remember it the next time... maybe. In later years, we told our sons that when they grow up and get into the business or professional world, they are welcome to legally change the spelling of their name to "Fell" so people would know how to pronounce it correctly. Dickie insists that he will be so famous that people will just know how to say it right. Hmmm... I wouldn't be surprised. But I'm getting ahead of myself a bit.

In spite of our plans not to start a family for three years, our first little boy, Jack, arrived a few weeks before our first wedding anniversary. We quickly discovered that our little one-room apartment was no longer large enough. Amazingly, Herman's small paycheck had taken care of us pretty well, with some careful management. Those were the days when you could go shopping with a dollar and come home with a big bag of groceries. After some exhaustive searching, we located a rear entrance flat in a nice location, only half a block from the largest city park. Our new home needed some paint and a bit of fixing up, but it had good possibilities and we could afford the rent. That's the big secret about being able to handle whatever comes your way: Always look for the possibilities and opportunities.

What little furniture we moved from our tiny apartment looked lost in this five-room flat! But, with the expenses attending the new baby, we had no extra money for furniture. Friends told us about a furniture store with very lenient terms. They also stocked second-hand furniture, so we lost no time investigating. The proprietor proved to be a very sympathetic, understanding man, and convinced us that we could furnish our little flat for very little expense. Every piece of furniture we selected was "pre-owned", but we were proud of it, and prouder still of the bargains we chose. We bought all we needed except for an icebox. We rationalized that with winter just around the corner, we could manage without one. The truth was that we couldn't afford to buy enough food at one time that required cold storage anyway. Evenings and weekends, Herman and I enjoyed many hours together, "touching up" and refinishing our newly acquired possessions until they looked like new. Herman is a master with those kinds of skills, and I follow directions quite well. The furniture became beautiful and personal, and it all belonged to US! We felt very rich indeed, and very proud of our harmonious life in the midst of a troubled, depressed world. We had both deprived ourselves of so many things for so long that it took very little to make us happy. We treasured each day together, and each day we were happier and more in love. Before we knew it, Christmas had arrived and our baby was nearly three months old, fascinated by all the bright, colorful lights.

That winter passed quickly and joyfully for us, and we fared quite well in spite of the Depression. Suddenly, the warmth of spring arrived and our need for an icebox became very apparent. So, off we marched again to our good-hearted furniture dealer.

All the way across the city, we kept reminding ourselves that we were going to get the cheapest, most practical box we could find. We discovered that the supply of used iceboxes was very limited, so we wandered hesitantly over to the new refrigerators so beautifully displayed nearby. After listening to an impressive sales pitch, we wound up buying, not an icebox, but the master-deluxe refrigerator model because the quality of such an essential appliance was crucial to the health and welfare of our growing, young family... of course. Well, we didn't exactly *buy* the super-master-deluxe fridge. We made a down payment on it. To celebrate the sale, the dealer took us to the neighboring tavern for a glass of beer. The possibility that neither of us cared for a beer never entered the man's mind. So, rather than offend the man's kind gesture, we went along with it. As the beers were set down before us, we were horrified to see a raw egg wallowing in the bottom of each glass mug, apparently a custom in this neighborhood. Herman and I both forced a smile, shuddered ever so slightly, closed our eyes and attempted to down the concoction. We both left the mugs half emptied with the excuse that we weren't terribly thirsty. The extravagance of our purchase was momentarily forgotten as we laughed about the "treat" on the way home, but we sobered up soon enough when we began to discuss the budgeting we would have to do to make the monthly payments on the refrigerator.

"... we were horrified to see a raw egg wallowing in the bottom of each glass mug..."

The following week, we established new records for economizing when Herman's working hours were suddenly cut. Instead of working five days a week, his job was cut to *three* days, making a substantial difference in his pay envelope! Our struggle with the budget suddenly got very serious. My shopping experience from the so-called "lean" days when I was in high school came in very handy. We cut a lot of corners, but we soon ran out of corners to cut... and that was a problem! Our new refrigerator was one of those conspicuous big-ticket items, but of course we hadn't anticipated the big reduction in income. We did without a *lot* of things for quite awhile, but we somehow managed to make that burdensome payment every month. Would you believe that after seventeen years, we still are using that same refrigerator we bought back in the Depression? Incredible, but worth every one of those hard earned pennies, and we haven't had one repair bill on that old box either! It still looks good too, even compared to the more modern ones.

We never mentioned our almost foodless days to my folks, but they must have guessed because Dad Wilson would just "happen to pass by" every so often with an armful of groceries. He'll never know how beautiful those sacks of flour and sugar looked to me. After such a visit, I usually baked, and the smell of homemade bread, cookies and coffee cake filled the air again. Besides fulfilling our hunger needs, it sure gave us the moral support we needed.

In the next few years, we had two more baby boys, Dick and Lynn. Jackie was thrilled with his new brothers, but put in a request for a baby sister. Lynn was destined to be our last baby, and we had been positive he would be a little girl. I had quite a heated discussion with the nurse as I was recovering from the ether, insisting the baby's name was "Marilynn". Months earlier, we had chosen the name of a friend who was very close to us. I finally compromised when the doctor confirmed that I had given birth to another boy. I cut off the "Mari-", leaving "Lynn", a mighty lovable little boy. Actually, I'm still surprised that Lynn has such a nice disposition. From the time he was conceived, he was the subject of much controversy. It took me six months to convince my good doctor that I was pregnant.

I'm sure that my case is one that doctor would rather forget. You see, he was relying on the "rabbit test" which was in vogue at that time, and my test results were repeatedly negative, so I couldn't possibly have been in a "delicate condition". He tried to persuade me that it must be my imagination. In the next two or three months, my "imagination" continued to grow, so I went back to the medical wizard. Again, the rabbit said "no", so back I'd go to the doctor's office, imagining everything from tumors to equally unattractive alternatives. Because a medical "expert" said I wasn't pregnant, and an ignorant rabbit said I wasn't pregnant, I simply wasn't! Well, the baby "that wasn't" started becoming very active in my womb, and finally my husband was convinced when my tummy nearly booted him out of bed one night. Once more, we returned to the doctor, who almost groaned when he saw me again. I was in a very unhappy frame of mind, and I declared upon entering the office that I would not leave until both the doctor and the rabbit came over to my way of thinking! By this time, my emotional dam burst and tears of nervous frustration began pouring out.

The doctor took one look at my tear-streaked face and said, "You poor kid. To hell with the rabbit! Come on in here." After a brief examination, he sat down muttering, "I'll be damned! A six month pregnancy and I didn't even know it... after practicing medicine for twenty years!"

I might add that I had the questionable honor of being in a special medical advisory bulletin in Milwaukee at that time. I guess I was one patient out of a million that the rabbit lied about. The "never-fail" test failed... repeatedly! I haven't trusted a rabbit since!

"You poor kid. To hell with the rabbit! Come on in here."

CHAPTER THREE
Leaving Big City Life Behind

Fortunately, when the third baby joined the family, Herman was employed full time and steadily, but wasn't very happy with the working conditions. He accepted his lot stoically, because many people didn't have jobs at all, so he felt he had no right to complain. His precious patience was rewarded when my brother informed me that the company he worked for was desperately in need of men. The factory was apparently doing quite well, producing economical cookware that was in demand, depression or not. It was located in a small town some distance from Milwaukee, so Herman made a special trip out there for an interview. He returned home with the exciting news that he'd landed a good job with better pay. West Bend was one of the prettiest, most progressive towns in the state and had a growing reputation throughout the Midwest.

Housing in 1940 was just as scarce as it is now, ten years later. We made innumerable trips out to the little town before we discovered a good prospect. We spotted a partially built, two-story house, and tracked down the owner. We were a bit afraid our little family of three boys would queer any possibility of renting a brand new home. You never realize how unpopular children are until you go house hunting. But Mr. Hall was wonderful! When we explained our desperate need for a home, he simply said, "Well, you've got one right now!" When I blurted out that we had three little boys, Herman and I held our breaths until our new landlord replied, "So what? I happen to like children, so that's no reason not to have a house to live in! And call me

'Walter'. I think nice folks like you will raise your boys just fine." We both could have hugged Mr. Hall, and I'm sorry we didn't. He would have loved it. He never regretted renting to us, and some of the happiest days of our lives were spent in that two-story stucco home. There was only one small hitch in the deal. The house wouldn't be completed until late fall, and this was only early July. But our road was paved right on the spot, because Mr. Hall knew of a cottage for rent on a nearby lake. We could get it for a fairly modest rent if we took it for the whole season.

We lost no time in looking at the place. It was on one of Wisconsin's lovely lakes, only two or three miles from town. There was no electricity. It had kerosene lamps and a kerosene stove, but also boasted a glassed-in porch overlooking the lake. It had a huge kitchen, dining room and living room downstairs, with three bedrooms upstairs. It appeared to be an old farmhouse, sturdy, in good repair, and without too many inconveniences. One of the inconveniences was the "little house" in the woods more than a hundred feet away from the cottage, because the only indoor plumbing was the pump at the kitchen sink. That would take a bit of getting used to, particularly with the little boys. The place was beautifully located on the side of a hill in a heavily wooded area, completely surrounded by tall pines and overlooking the large, tranquil lake to complete an appealing picture of serenity.

In short order, we made the move from the city, stored our furniture in a warehouse of Mr. Hall's, and began "camping out" at the cottage for the duration. Mr. Hall seemed to have a solution for our most pressing problems, bless his generous heart. At this point, Jack was almost five; Dick was two, and little Lynn was just a little more than one month old. The first couple of months were adventurous. I suppose it was even sort of fun in spite of a few hardships, one of which was laundry. I had to wash every day, by hand, in rainwater we captured in an old barrel. But it wasn't so bad, once we adjusted to the primitive routines... and a few surprises. For example, Dick will always remember that path to the outhouse. At night, the two older boys used a potty chair that had a "chamber pot" with a cover on it; because it was more convenient. But, during the day, I encouraged them to use the "little house". I usually had to accompany Dickie on that long trek to the privy and hold onto him while he did his business, because he was terrified of falling through that big hole into the "basement". On the way to the outhouse one day, with Dick's little hand in mine, enjoying the fresh, warm breeze and the singing birds, we were both startled by a long snake that slithered across the path only a couple of feet in front of us! I screamed, and Dick reacted in a manner that made it unnecessary to continue our trip to the outhouse. He was already finished with whatever he needed to do right there on the spot. It may have only been a harmless garter snake, but to my way of thinking, there is no such thing as a harmless snake!

Except for weekenders, we didn't have any close neighbors, but I was too busy to get lonely during the week. The boy's early bedtime granted Herman and me many long, delightful evenings together. Even with three children, we still acted like newlyweds. It was so peaceful and lovely as we watched the sun slowly setting until it slipped out of sight, leaving a beautiful rose-colored sky reflected in the calm of the lake. The mosquitoes, however, were so terrible toward evening that Herman would whistle loudly to signal his presence at the top of the hill where he left the car upon arriving home. The purpose of the signal was to prepare us to open the door at just the right moment as he made his hundred-yard dash down the hill, toting the daily block of ice for the icebox. The door was open and shut with precision timing after a week or so of practice. I'll never forget that drill, or Herman's frantic sprint through the squadrons of mosquitoes so fast they didn't have time to light upon him, and then the immediate use of insect spray as an extra measure of protection. Our first few nights at the cottage were such an incredible contrast from the noisy nights in the city, with its sounds of traffic and restless people. It was so quiet at the lake that the silence kept us awake. With no electricity, we didn't even have a radio to play. I swear you could hear a twig drop or a bird move in its nest. Herman used to laugh and tell me he could even hear a mouse peeing on a leaf fifty meters away. The squirrels scurrying across the roof startled me badly at first until Herman explained what they were.

One of the funniest sights I still remember was our nightly mosquito hunt. It became a ritual. We would just get all relaxed and comfortable after our busy days, and settle into the not too uncomfortable old beds. Then, out of nowhere came that hauntingly familiar theme song of the mosquito. For a while we would try to ignore it, but Herman would be pestered beyond endurance. Suddenly, he would leap out of bed with a frantic yell, "I can't stand it anymore!" And the hunt was on! I'd grab the flashlight and spot the intruder; Herman would stalk him with the flyswatter. There would be no peace until after the kill, and I can't remember a single night that we didn't repeat that same performance... all summer long.

There would be no peace until after the kill...

We kept our supply of kerosene in a can in the "outhouse". One day, I went out to get the can to refill my stove. Usually Herman took care of that particular chore for me, but somehow he had forgotten. So I brought the fuel can into the cottage and carefully filled the glass container on the end of the old stove myself, then started heating a pot of good old homemade beef stew. With the stove working, I could now also heat up my old fashioned irons and get my ironing out of the way while dinner was cooking. I must admit to feeling somewhat proud of the way I had adapted to this Spartan life, devoid of modern conveniences. It was tolerable because I knew I wouldn't be a pioneer housewife for very long, and would appreciate the new home we would be moving into all the more. Jack and Dick were playing on the porch, and the baby was sleeping in his little bed not far away from the ironing board. All of a sudden, the stove started making a strange noise, followed by a series of small sputtering, popping explosions accompanied by nasty puffs of black smoke! I grabbed a pail of water and the baby, and stood guard on the porch while Jackie ran to find the nearest neighbor who lived a few hundred yards down the lakeshore. I thought my son would never return, and silently prayed that he wouldn't be sidetracked by some fascinating distraction. Evidently, I had frightened him into hurrying, because it wasn't very long before our good neighbor came on the run. He calmly took the fuel tank off the stove and had everything under control in a matter of minutes. He picked up the can I'd used and asked if that was what I'd poured into the stove's fuel tank. I nodded hesitantly, and he inquired, "Since when have you been using gasoline in the kerosene stove?" My face turned as red with embarrassment as the color of the gas can. I had grabbed the wrong fuel container and hadn't even noticed what was written on it in big, bold letters. It wasn't going to be easy to tell Herman about the stupid thing I had done, but I would have to confess when he came home. I had learned that if I didn't report the day's happenings to him, the boys would. They gave (and still do) a detailed current events report to their father every night. Many times I have wished they weren't quite so thorough with the details.

With the arrival of the cold, rainy fall weather, I became anxious to move into town. It was lonely at the lake when the vacation season ended, and I felt isolated. I soon discovered that the small wood stove wasn't adequate to warm the cottage on those damp, chilly days when the wind swept across the lake and infiltrated the old house. Finally, at the end of September 1940, we moved into town. We sure were getting some good training on adaptability. Within a four-month period, we had moved from big city living to a remote, antiquated cottage to a brand new, modern home in a small town. I liked to think of it as survival school training. The experience and lessons learned would sure be useful for all of us in the years to come. Fortunately, most of us don't have the power to see into our futures, or the faint hearted would drop in their tracks. I know I will never again appreciate a house in the same way I felt about that new home at 603 Indiana Avenue. You cannot imagine the thrill I felt when I pushed a button and there was light! I plugged in our table model radio, turned it on, and there was music! I ran upstairs and flushed the you-know-what, and there were tears of joy filling my eyes. I flushed it twice just to enjoy a cheap moment of ecstasy! And to put the frosting on the cake, we plugged in our treasured super-master-deluxe refrigerator right there in our new kitchen with the built-in gas stove and electric lights and faucets on the sink and smooth clean counters. My goodness, the cabinets even had doors on them! That first night after work, Herman brought home a block of ice, just out of habit. I didn't say a word; just watched. He got the silliest look on his face when he opened the refrigerator door, saw the light turn on and felt the cool reality strike him right in the face. We both burst out laughing with joy and a profound feeling of gratitude for our good fortune. Modern conveniences are so taken for granted today. If more of us were deprived of all the modern gadgets this age offers, we would be less spoiled and would appreciate the simple things like electricity and running water. Switching on a radio and turning the dial brings us a variety of music or comedy or a good mystery drama, pulled from some sort of invisible energy right out of the air! So much is available to all of us today, and we become distracted by all the emphasis placed on luxuries.

December 7, 1941, that terrible day of the shocking attack on Pearl Harbor, suddenly changed the lives of millions of people all over the world. It certainly had an impact on our small town! For Herman, it meant longer hours at the factory, for they had been assigned government contracts to manufacture war materials. Instead of making spouts for coffee pots, their machines had to be re-tooled to turn out shell casings for our big naval guns. And there were other military products that Herman wasn't allowed to talk about. As several factories in our town converted to the production of military supplies, high fences quickly surrounded them, fences patrolled by armed soldiers and gates manned by unfriendly guards with cold, suspicious stares.

The sudden wartime manufacturing boom created a desperate need for toolmakers and designers. Herman saw this as a real opportunity, so at the end of his long day, he drove into Milwaukee to attend night courses at Marquette University where he studied advanced tool design and industrial engineering. Not surprising to me, he did outstanding work and brought home papers that were always graded with an "A", sometimes even with a smiley face drawn on them by his delighted professors. My husband is truly a very brilliant man, and I am always so very proud of him! Herman never had time to sit down and eat before he left for school, so he would eat a sandwich I fixed for him on the way into the city. The days when he didn't have a night class were long days, too, because he would work at the plant until midnight and sometimes later. He began to look drawn and pale, and when I commented on it, he said it was very little to do for the country he had adopted and loved so much.

One day, an incident occurred at the factory that nearly broke Herman's heart and almost destroyed his faith in his fellow Americans. He came home that night looking very dejected, unusually quiet. After a while of thoughtful silence, he told me what had happened. He was almost in tears, half from rage and half from disappointment. A man who held a position just above Herman was apparently an overzealous "patriot", and had decided that Herman needed to be watched because he was born in Germany. The ironic part of the story is that this man's parents were both German immigrants! But *he* was born in the United States. Herman had not been aware that he was being watched. Such a thought never entered his mind. He was told later by friends in the shop that the spying had been going on for some time, and they could not figure out the reason for this peculiar, daily occurrence. By chance one day, Herman looked up from his work and noticed a man standing a short distance away, arms folded, just watching him. He caught the same man observing him several times that day, and each day through the following week. He began to feel very uncomfortable, suddenly realizing that he was actually under suspicion for something. Were they afraid that he might be a thief, or worse yet, a saboteur? It was unbelievable, an insult to his decency, dedication and patriotism. Finally, when there was no question in Herman's mind as to the man's purpose, Herman responded by laying his tools down, folding his arms and returning the stare every time he spotted the man watching him. It wasn't very long before Herman was summoned to his supervisor's office where he came face to face with the unpleasant source of the suspicions, Mr. Schmidt. He asked Herman why he frequently stopped working. Herman replied that whenever he was spied upon for no reason, he would refuse to work. With that answer, the man erupted into a hysterical tirade, denouncing Herman as a "damned foreigner", an imposter and a number of other choice defamations. Herman said the maniac raved on senselessly for a long time, blaming the war on people like Herman, and how stupid and dangerous it was for the company to hire foreigners, and other pent up bits of hateful ugliness that spewed like venom from the man's bigoted brain. Finally, the great American, Mr. Schmidt, concluded by saying that his son was "overseas fighting the Nazis while a goddam Kraut like *you* is playing it safe here in America!" That did it!

Herman had sat patiently, not saying a word, listening to that mental midget unload his warped, vicious monolog at him. Finally Herman said he could take no more. He jumped to his feet, clenching his fists in anger, and told Schmidt, "Now *you* listen to *me*, and listen well! I came to this country by choice because I *wanted* to. America stood for everything I'd never been privileged to have in Germany: free speech, religious freedom, opportunity to become whatever I'm capable of becoming, more education, freedom from having my loyalties questioned, and a better world to raise my family in! America offered me friendship, better food and the fulfillment of ideals that were almost destroyed in me in Europe. I came to this country in 1929, became a naturalized American citizen and married an American girl in 1934, and I'm raising three fine American boys!"

Herman told me the man just sat there gaping at him, too stunned by Herman's unexpected passionate retort to utter a sound, so he continued. "You didn't have to choose your country," he shouted. "You were born here, although I'm told your parents came here from Germany. But from what you have said to me today, you two-faced, hateful hypocrite, you have proved to me that I am a better American than you are, or ever will be! Good day, sir!"

With that, Herman turned on his heel and stormed out of the office. Attracted by all the shouting in Schmidt's office, a small group of men had gathered outside the door and overheard the conversation. He was shocked to be greeted by applause and cheers and hands reaching out to shake his. Herman told them he needed to clear his name, but they all said it wasn't necessary. They believed in him. Nevertheless, he marched upstairs to the company president's office with his head held high and demanded to see the top boss immediately. After all, this was America! The astonished secretary said that the executive was at home, and Herman said, "Well, call him up and tell him to get down here right away! We have an urgent matter to discuss!"

She took one look at Herman's face and reached for the phone. In less than twenty minutes, this good man arrived and greeted Herman with a handshake. "What's going on here, Herman? You look deeply troubled. Are you feeling sick? What happened? Come on into my office and we'll talk about it." He told his secretary he didn't want to be interrupted.

Mr. Zieglar had known Herman personally and respected him. They'd had many informative, friendly conversations in the past. He was impressed with Herman's inventiveness and brilliant ideas, and had even incorporated some of Herman's suggestions into their production lines. The time it took for Mr. Zieglar to drive down to the plant had taken the edge off of Herman's anger, and left him instead with a feeling of humiliation that was written all over his face. He told his story from the beginning to the patient chief executive, who listened with understanding and indignation. He promised Herman that Mr. Schmidt would never degrade him again, and he kept his word. The president's office issued a public apology about the incident throughout the plant, and it was Mr. Schmidt who became the disgraced party in the end. Herman made more friends than ever before, and won the respect he had truly earned. In spite of the happy ending, we will always remember that nasty little affair, and have learned that there are many different faces to prejudice.

One other anti-immigrant incident happened shortly after Herman's disturbance at work, only this time it occurred at home. I discovered a large swastika marked on the sidewalk leading up to our front porch early one Saturday morning. It was a cowardly act of ignorance, like most graffiti, committed under the cover of darkness during the night. Fortunately, the patriotic mental cretin had used chalk, but the message was received nevertheless. I had hoped to scrub it off before my sweet hubby saw it, so soon after the hurtful episode at the factory. Unfortunately, he peeked out the living room window and saw me on hands and knees with a pail of soapy water, scrubbing something off the sidewalk. When he came outside to see what I was doing, enough of the image was still showing that he knew what it was. I looked up at him, trying to read his face to determine what he was thinking, because he didn't say a word. He just stared at the chalky symbol partly washed away. The muscles in his jaws knotted as he clenched his teeth, and his eyes seemed a bit glassy as if he were suppressing his tears, but he made not a sound. As a boy, Herman learned many years ago to suffer pain in silence. After what seemed like a long period of time when even the light breeze was halted to await his reaction, he cleared his throat and said softly, "Stupid kids! They drew it backwards. That is an old American Indian symbol for peace and good luck. I don't think that's what they intended."

His face softened and he smiled ever so slightly. He told me he had a quick errand to run and he would be right back. Then he drove off without another word. By the time he returned a short while later, I had scrubbed the reversed swastika from the sidewalk, and nothing further was ever mentioned about it. I watched him go into the garage and come back out with the wheelbarrow and some tools, but he didn't explain anything. I had learned during the eight years we were married at that point not to ask questions when he was in his silent mode. He would tell me what he was up to soon enough, so I went into the house to get the boys busy with their Saturday chores. Once, when I glanced out the front window briefly, I saw him digging a hole in the middle of the front lawn. I had a brief, foolish notion in my head that Herman had caught the mischief-maker and was engaged in a burial. Somehow, that image didn't quite fit the gentle man I knew so well. It wasn't very long before Herman came into the house, washed his hands and calmly said, "I believe I will have that second cup of coffee now. It's finished, if you want to take a look."

After pouring his coffee, we stepped out on the front porch to inspect his handiwork. From the center of the front yard rose a sturdy white flagpole twelve feet high, braced until the concrete would harden and cure at the base. I looked up at him, and his eyes were misty again... but this time with pride. The next Monday morning, I looked out front after Herman had left for work. A beautiful, brand new American flag was waving gently in the soft breeze. We never saw another swastika on our sidewalk.

The strain of working long hours, the trips to Milwaukee for classes at night, the little extra duties he attended to as the volunteer air raid block warden, and fixing things around the house were all beginning to take their toll on his endurance, and it showed on Herman's face. The unpleasant episode at the plant also helped to take its toll on his endurance. There was very little time for family life or recreation, as was the case in many homes those days. The boys didn't see their dad for days at a time because they were usually asleep when he was home. But he always went into their room and kissed each one of them before he went to bed, and kissed them again in the early morning before he left for work. I made sure the boys knew that their dad was there for them, even if they didn't always see him. They needed to know he was busting his butt for his family and should be their hero. We were lucky to be together as a whole family in those trying times, when so many homes were missing a father or sons who were sent off to war.

I made a special effort to see that the "home front" ran smoothly, and even managed to do some Red Cross volunteer work, as well as some other civic duties. When Herman came home late and bone weary, there was always a hot drink waiting for him, along with his newspaper that he seldom read anymore. A six-hour sleep was an unusually good night for him. One night as I reached over and turned off the bed lamp, I asked him a question. He didn't answer. I knew he was still awake, so I repeated my question... still no reply. I told him I didn't think it was funny if he was playing a joke on me, and he only laughed a strange, unfamiliar laugh, the kind of sound a deranged person might make. It frightened me and I pleaded with him to stop acting silly. His only response was that same scary, maniacal cackle. It raised a crop of "goose bumps" on my skin the size of golf balls and I jumped out of bed. I was beginning to think the man in bed with me wasn't my husband.

I turned on the light and stared at him. Herman looked all right except for an odd, bewildered look in his eyes. I touched his face to see if he was feverish, but he was cool. He just looked at me in a puzzling way and started that ghastly, idiotic laugh again. I whimpered that I had warned him about working too hard and pushing the limit, and that he had obviously cracked under the strain. He let loose another nutty laugh cackle and I headed downstairs to call the doctor. Herman frantically signaled for me to come back, and motioned to me with sign language to bring him a pencil and paper. Meanwhile, he calmly reached for a magazine on the bedside table and began to read. By this time, he too was probably sure he had lost his faculties. On a pad of paper, Herman scribbled that he could read and reason, but he just couldn't talk. I wasted no more time before calling the doctor.

When the good doctor finally answered the phone, I started crying, womanlike, and told him that Herman was babbling like an idiot. The doctor told me it was a heck of a time to call him up just to tell him that. Finally, I calmed down enough to explain the symptoms. To my surprise, he knew immediately what it was. He described it as a cold virus that settles into the tongue muscles, particularly if the patient is suffering from fatigue, and that he had just treated a similar case. He directed me to apply hot compresses to Herman's throat every half hour during the night, and to call him in the morning if there was no improvement. I went into action immediately, and continued the treatments all night while Herman slept like a baby. Toward morning, I slipped into a brief nap, but awakened with a start to hear my husband say, "Good morning, darling!" I hadn't heard a sweeter sound for many a day. He was perfectly recovered with no sign of the affliction he'd suffered just the night before. We seem to have a real knack for encountering weird new experiences.

All things considered, those were happy days, those days on Indiana Avenue. In spite of the stress and the war and Herman's long hours of work, I remember a lot of good times, too. When I think about that segment of our life, I immediately picture three little tricycles, graduated in size, or three small sleds lined up at the back door. We started early in the boys' lives to impress them with the fact that living involves more than play; it involves responsibilities they are required to assume. Responsibility was a big word for them, but they knew what it meant, and they grew up taking good care of their possessions just out of habit. Come to think of it, they were more conscientious when they were five or thereabout than they are now. They still have responsibilities now, but they seem to need a little more reminding than they did then.

The boys all accepted our disciplinary measures with good grace. Oh, I will admit to a little healthy rebellion now and then, but it never reached the complete mutiny stage. Dick was a little difficult to reach sometimes, and still is. I have never been able to figure out if it is stubbornness, or just a little "experiment" on his side to see how far he can go before we lose patience. I'm afraid that's a little unfinished business his wife will inherit. Bedtime was the most challenging time, for us as well as the children. Putting three little boys in the same room and expecting them to go to sleep without disturbance was asking too much. The long, drawn out "good nights" seemed endless, especially at the close of a tiring day. On one particular evening, we had sent the boys to bed and given them the limited time to settle down. Dick decided he just wasn't ready to comply. He was told in no uncertain terms that he would not be reminded again! This obviously made no impression, so Herman dropped his newspaper, and marched upstairs. I followed to observe. Herman yanked open the door and said with an icy calm voice, "Hello, Dick!"

Dick replied with a cheerful, "Hi, Daddy!" He was caught standing in the middle of the bedroom in his entertainment mode, still fully dressed while his brothers were in pajamas and in bed. His father's voice lowered and darkened like an impending storm when he asked his impish little son if he had decided that he was too old to take orders from his parents anymore. Dickie stared back at his dad in a sort of hypnotic trance for a moment, and whether intentional or not, he slowly nodded his head, yes.

"All right," Herman responded sternly, "you just go into the closet, get your zipper bag and pack your things! You may leave. You are old enough to be on your own now!"

This didn't have the effect on Dick that we expected. We were certain he would break down and cry or show some sort of remorse for his behavior. But, no ... not Dickie! He calmly walked to the closet, got the battered little overnight bag, and put in his pajamas and two beat-up, favorite toy cars. At Herman's suggestion, he added a pair of socks and went to the bathroom to get his toothbrush. At this point in the bedroom drama, the air was so thick with tension that everything seemed to move in slow motion. The whole matter was developing into a very sticky problem, and I couldn't see what the outcome was going to be. I wasn't too sure that Herman was on top of it either. Not this time.

My anxiety grew as this half-pint little boy stoically walked over to the beds and kissed his brothers goodbye. They promptly burst into tears. Without another word, he marched down the stairs. I asked Herman in a whisper what he was going to do. He replied, "I can carry the bluff just as far as that little squirt can!"

At the front door, Dickie turned and kissed us both. The big tears rolling down his cheeks were dead giveaways of his real feelings in the matter, and we thought at last he was responding the way we wanted him to. On the contrary, the little man went out the door and walked into the moonless autumn night. He was four years old! Yes, as it sometimes happens, our disciplinary strategy boomeranged! We stood there for a moment, stunned, staring at each other with that helpless "Now what?" look on our faces. I went to pieces completely and started after him, but Herman was already ahead of me. The little twerp was almost an entire block away by the time Herman caught up to him. The faces on both father and son were strained and pale as they walked back to the house, hand in hand. I restrained myself from picking Dickie up and giving him a big hug, and refrained from saying anything at all. That part was easy. I didn't know what to say anyway. Herman and I never interfered with or contradicted each other's discipline of the kids. When Herman asked the fledgling, would-be runaway if he was ready to cooperate and obey his parents, Dickie answered, sobbing, "Oh yes, Daddy!"

...the little man went out the door into the moonless autumn night.

Both Lynn and Jack were still crying when we got back upstairs, and it took all the self-control I could muster not to join in the sobbing chorus. I wanted so much to tell them how much we loved them, and that we would never let them go. All Herman said was, "Good night, boys. Go right to sleep," as if nothing had happened. We listened to their prayers very conscientiously that night, shut the bedroom door, and went downstairs. For a few moments, we sat on the davenport in silent contemplation. After bravely trying to fight back his tears, Herman finally turned to me and took me in his arms, sobbing, "Ohhhhh, Honey!" We both had a good cry! Now, I ask you: Who do you think suffered most at this event?

Another episode we experienced was really more common with many families. We decided that the boys should have a dog. Actually it was Herman and the boys who made the decision. I wasn't too enthused about the idea, realizing that it would be one more responsibility I would end up taking over. We saw a little black puppy for sale and bought him on the spur of the moment. He wasn't really very little, as I recall now. He was a mixture of spaniel, setter and horse, if you'd have asked me. At first, he wasn't allowed inside the house, but we later compromised and let him sleep in the basement at night or in bad weather. He was intelligent enough to realize that he couldn't come into the house's living area, but he was awfully dumb about his personal habits. He received numerous spankings, nose rubbings and scolding, but he never quite became housebroken. Consequently, I added the broom and shovel routine to my housework schedule. We named him "Blackie", which was not too original, but it fit. I had a few choice names of my own for him, which were never spoken out loud ... that is, not in anyone's presence.

It was hard to convince the deliverymen that he was just a puppy. They would take one look at the coal black animal with the conspicuous white fangs, quickly leave their packages outside the door, and beat a hasty retreat to their trucks without any conversation whatsoever. The boys loved Blackie, but that love dwindled as soon as there was any work required that involved him. After months of patient coaching and "training", the dog still displayed little interest in cooperation. He seemed to plead ignorance whenever that suited him. He ran away at every opportunity, and came back only when he was good and ready to return—or hungry. I could stand a few feet away from him and call him, and he would just stand there at a safe distance and stare at me defiantly. Following many months of wild goose chases and messy basements, we decided that Blackie would be much happier on a farm. I was elated at the prospect! It took days to obtain the boys agreement, but when Blackie developed his nasty little habit of nipping, they came around to our side in a hurry. And that was the end of pet ownership ... for the time being anyway.

We did have a little canary for a while. His name was Tuffy. For some reason, Tuffy became depressed and stopped singing for us altogether. We thought he might be getting ready to die or something, so we sent him out to our friends' farm where Blackie had taken up residence. Tuffy didn't die for a long, long time. They put him in a cage with two female canaries and Tuffy not only sang many fine concerts, he provided other services as well. They said he bred little canaries as fast as rabbits. I still don't like rabbits either.

Our four years on Indiana Avenue passed rapidly and my boys grew like weeds. The war continued relentlessly in Europe and in the Pacific. It was the main topic of conversation whenever we talked with other people, and we would trade stories and news that we had heard. My brother, Jack, was an infantry lieutenant in the Pacific islands somewhere. We never knew where he was, but Mother would share his letters with me whenever she received any. She had a beautiful embroidered blue star hanging in the front window for him, and we prayed for his safety every day. The boys included their uncle in their bedtime prayers every night too. He was their hero. Mrs. Wendleborne across the street had two blue stars in her front window. Both of her sons were serving in the navy, fresh out of high school. One dreadful day, one of the blue stars was changed to a gold star. One of her sons was killed in action. Everybody up and down the street cried for that boy. The war had come to visit our neighborhood in a very personal way. He was the first, but there would be others to follow that we knew personally.

Finally, the tide of war began to turn against our enemies. The radio brought us news of more and more victories in battle, and we began to feel safer at home. We noticed fewer air raid drills, but we still had to keep the blackout shades on our windows at night, and we continued to farm the huge "victory garden" in the vacant lot next door that we shared with our neighbors. Those years were crowded with some serious medical problems and surgeries, the frightening polio plague, the shortages and the rationing programs; but we managed to survive intact and with gratitude for our many blessings.

CHAPTER FOUR
The Old Homestead

For some time, I had played with the idea of opening a classy, homey little dining establishment. I never dreamed that I would ever have a chance to try my "tea room" plan. Herman was very much in favor of my idea after he saw how serious I was, and that I had thought the whole plan out pretty carefully. After many rides around our pretty little town looking for a house that could be both a business and living quarters, we found just what we wanted at 530 Walnut Street. It was a very large, old doctor's home. He had moved to Florida and had put this place up for sale. The price was reasonable, but there was certainly a lot of repair work and remodeling to do. After some careful estimates and calculations, we figured we could swing the deal by doing most of the work ourselves.

It was a stately looking house, a small mansion built very solidly just after the turn of the century. Just a coat of paint on the outside alone would easily transform it into a vision of beauty. On the first two floors, twelve big rooms showed great potential. The large basement with walls built from blocks of granite rock provided plenty of storage room, and the huge attic was spacious and airy with dormer windows. From the attic, one could climb through a hatch to a "widow's walk" at the very top of the house, from which you could see all over town. When I first entered the house, the wood paneled entry hall and the huge, curved stairway with heavy oak banisters took my breath away. My imagination ran wild with all the possibilities I could envision. I felt like I was in the middle of a beautiful dream.

Herman's wonderful boss helped us considerably along the way, even with the legal aspects. He said he enjoyed helping anyone who was willing to work for what they wanted. We bought the house in the spring of 1944 and planned to hold our grand opening in the fall. There was much more work to be done than we had guessed, but we rolled up our sleeves and got busy. Some of the furnishings were claimed by the owner, and the remaining things were put up for auction. As we cleared out the doctor's former office and what appeared to be an examination room, we ran across some strange looking glass containers with "souvenirs" from surgical operations. We quickly disposed of the repulsive "preserves" by putting them in refuse cans. When the trash collectors came, we made a point of being on hand to watch, out of sight of course. It was comical to behold their puzzled expressions and gestures as they examined the bottles, trying to figure out what they contained.

We quickly disposed of the repulsive preserves...

The old doctor who had lived and worked in that house for many years was obviously a little eccentric, and there was ample proof of that all over the place. One of our discoveries was a set of huge water tanks up in the attic. They were so large that they evidently had been carted up there in sections. Long before the town had a water system, well water had been pumped up to those tanks and distributed from there to the various taps around the house. Herman said it was to provide water pressure. The obsolete, antique pump was still mounted in the basement. It took hours to dismantle and carry out the heavy cast iron pieces. After receiving estimates from plumbers, painters, carpenters and electricians, we found the total remodeling cost so staggering that we had no choice but to do it all ourselves. Herman figured that by taking time off from work, he could still save enough money on all these jobs to make it worthwhile, even with some loss of wages.

My dad's work hadn't been very steady, and he and Mom had been having a tough time financially. We begged my folks to come and live with us and help us with our new venture. Dad had a lot of experience as a finish carpenter and contractor, and Mom was an expert in the kitchen, as well as having good business skills, so they really felt needed and had a lot to contribute. Dad knocked out walls where they weren't needed, and built new partitions where we did need them. Herman worked on the plumbing and the electrical circuits. Together, they built two new restrooms for our customers. My job? I painted, and I painted and painted some more! Sanding and finishing all the hardwood floors on the first and second levels kept Herman and me up until the wee hours, taking turns with the rented sanding machine. That's when we really began to realize just how big those rooms were!

Dad was working in a room on the first floor one day when he discovered a very unusual type of construction, a "floating floor"! It was new to us, but upon inquiry to one of the older local contractors, we discovered there actually was such a flooring system, and that it was very difficult and expensive to construct. We also discovered that the exterior frame walls were very thick, with wide, closely spaced studs, and heavily insulated with a material that looked like seaweed. Afraid that it was highly flammable, we grabbed a handful of the mossy looking stuff and tried to light it with a match. It wouldn't burn—not even smolder! It was exhilarating to find our "new" home so well insulated and so solidly built.

Herman needed to open up the thick, concrete basement floor to lay more pipes. Using only a pick axe, he said it was the toughest job he had encountered in the whole house—sort of like trying to crack granite with a tack hammer. He also had to help me paint a few of the difficult high ceilings, and wallpaper our upstairs living room and the folks' two-room "apartment". To complete the project, we hired a roofing contractor to install all new shingles to replace the wood shakes, hired out the exterior painting (white with brown trim), and completed most of the final touches inside. The transformation was amazing! At last, we had our beautiful Tea Room, far prettier than I'd ever envisioned in my fondest dreams. The old house was quite picturesque and rather elegant, and the people of West Bend seemed as pleased with the results as we were. With great pride, we were thrilled to hang the big sign above the steps to that huge wrap-around front porch, "The Old Homestead", a very appropriate name.

... we were thrilled to hang that big sign above the front steps

Opening Day was predictably like most typical opening days. We advertised a baked ham dinner, homemade rolls and homemade pies, but our ovens and stoves weren't connected until late the night before. We opened the doors at twelve noon on a Sunday, and Herman was still laying tile until an hour before we served! The hired help was all lined up and ready, the food was ready—barely—and I had the worst case of jitters I've ever experienced. I had never done anything like this in my entire life before, except in my dreams. We received flowers from practically every business in town wishing us well. It was the first time in my life, and the last, that I've ever received too many flowers! They were gorgeous, but overwhelmed every spare corner of the dining rooms, parlor and entry hall of the Tea Room.

Fifty people arrived all about the same time, and they all expected to be served immediately. Most were patient, but one particular party threw the proverbial "monkey wrench" into the midst of the confusion. The woman kept repeating in a very loud voice that she had reservations, and demanded to be taken care of at once! Actually, *everyone* had reservations because we served dinner by reservation only. Herman looked like he was ready to oblige her, but not in the way she expected. Others were equally disgusted with the obnoxious woman and told us out loud to take our time; they had all day to relax and enjoy. That eased matters considerably, and the rude woman piped down.

Poor Herman! One minute he was told to help Dad out front to greet our guests (Dad enjoyed playing the host), and the next minute, he got an S.O.S. from the kitchen to help with the dishes. Our dishwasher proved to be an easygoing woman ... a *very* easygoing woman ... who worked with a cigarette hanging out of one corner of her mouth. Mother loved that! I made a silent vow to take care of that little matter later. I never got the chance. She ate a hearty dinner, collected her pay, and left. She told me she just wanted to work that one day to get a new dress because she was leaving town the next day. We were off to a great start!

My "right hand" was a wonderful, mellow gal by the name of Rose. Her only fault that I knew of was her appetite. She loved good food, especially noodles, and she was definitely not the type who should eat too many noodles. She was very heavy and had trouble with her feet trying to support all that weight. But, we all loved "Rosie" and will never forget her steady, easy disposition and unfaltering loyalty. Her presence pulled me through many a hard, long day, especially her ability to work without being told what needed doing every two minutes.

The children were in "seventh heaven". They loved the novelty of being able to order their meals every day. When I realized they were plowing recklessly through the menu, I took matters in hand and ordered *for* them ahead of time—to save them the trouble of having to make so many difficult decisions, of course. The waitresses thought I was very strict with my cute little boys, and were willing to give them anything their little hearts desired. The boys naturally ate that up, literally, until I stepped in again. Moms are such spoil sports.

My mother and I baked until we were exhausted. We had tried to assign some of the baking to kitchen employees, but the results were disastrous; so we carried on alone. Our reputation was built on everything being "home-cooked" and "home-baked", including the crescent rolls, pies, tortes and pastries. Besides this responsibility, I had all the planning, ordering and managing to do. When the laundress failed me, I had that chore to take over as well. The continual supply of fresh linen napkins and tablecloths had to be met. So, I was busy on most days from five in the morning until midnight, six days a week. We were closed on Mondays, which became my favorite day of the week. Wartime food rationing was not only irritating, but created an almost overwhelming task of menu planning and juggling supplies.

Our guest book was soon filled with names from nearly every state and several foreign countries. This astounded us because West Bend isn't exactly close to any major east-west or north-south routes of travel. In fact, one might say it was sort of "off the beaten track." Also, we couldn't afford to pay for very much advertising, so this remarkable patronage was a true testament for "word-of-mouth advertising"! One of our precious customers was a business man who frequently traveled back and forth between Los Angeles and New York City by train. He often planned a deliberate interruption in his trip at Chicago so he could treat himself to a train ride up to West Bend. From the depot, he took a taxi to the Olde Homestead, enjoyed a delightful dinner and visit, then returned to Chicago to pick up where he left off on his journey. He told us he always looked forward to that slightly extravagant side trip and it was worth every extra mile.

Our reputation for delicious home-cooked food wasn't the only drawing card. It was the atmosphere of refinement, the lovely semi-classical music in the background, and the gracious service they received. I had an old record player in the upper hallway that played soft, sweet music continuously. It produced a soothing magical effect as it drifted down the old open stairway and into the parlor and dining rooms. Lunch and dinner were served by reservation only, Tuesday through Sunday, and we were always filled to capacity every day. Someday, I would like to undertake a similar venture, but without the enforced rationing and the responsibility of small children. After more than two years of fun and excitement at the Old Homestead Tea Room, the strain proved to be too much for me. I couldn't continue being manager, cook, laundress, hostess, buyer and mother all at once, and the burdens finally took their toll. I suffered a serious nervous breakdown brought on by stress and extreme exhaustion, and that put an end to that little dream.

In early 1947, we sold our beautiful old mansion on doctor's orders, and auctioned off all the restaurant equipment. Dr. Frankow suggested we consider a complete change in our living pattern, so we decided to travel west to try our fortune at something totally new. We didn't know what. For about a week, we just wandered, visiting sights the boys had never seen before, such as Mount Rushmore, the Badlands, and my precious Yellowstone Park where I had spent that magical summer as a young girl twenty years earlier. My sister, Helen, lived in eastern Montana then, in a little town called Sidney. We accepted her invitation to stay with her for awhile, deciding what our next move should be. She had five children, three girls and two boys, so we had quite a tribe when combined with our family. Fortunately, they lived in a huge house with four bedrooms, and we were able to do some double-bunking. The boys' cousins didn't seem to mind at all, for it was the first time they had met each other. It was the best medicine I could have taken, thanks to my wonderful husband for going along with it. The "vacation" was a complete change of pace for us. The people were wonderful, and the contrast in scenery was exactly what I needed to recover. One of the town's large tractor and road equipment dealers offered Herman a position in their service department should we decide to settle in their community. They were very impressed with his knowledge of machinery and engines, and told him they had a job waiting for him any time he decided to move out there. The job showed promise for a rosy future, and he realized how happy I was in this new atmosphere, so he accepted the offer. When I first met my husband, I was amazed by the way his mind works. He continues to amaze me to this day. My doctor advised me to turn over a new leaf. It looked as though we were about to turn the whole tree upside down!

The boys approved instantly, especially when they heard that Grandpa and Grandma Wilson were also planning to move out west to live in Sidney. My dad was lured by a demand for finish carpenters and cabinet makers in the little town. For that matter, there seemed to be a shortage of skilled workers in many of the trades. Suddenly, our lives had taken a dramatically new direction. Perhaps this wasn't the path we should have traveled. Who can say for certain? We couldn't just sit home and wait for destiny to show us another way. The Foells are the kind of people who can enjoy the scenery even on a detour; so we thought it was better to take even the wrong road than to just sit and wonder what direction to take, and go nowhere at all. We rationalized that the experience, new lessons to learn, and new friends that we would make along the way would surely make the adventure worthwhile. The boys, Herman and I have always enjoyed the outdoors. Believe me, Montana has *lots* of outdoors! We loved the West and its wide open spaces. It appealed strongly to all of us. It beckoned to us—so we answered the call.

CHAPTER FIVE
Montana, Here We Come

My younger sister Florence and her husband, who were still living in West Bend, and all of our Wisconsin friends thought we were "tetched" in the head for just pulling up stakes and making such a drastic change. From every direction, we heard, "Why? How can you leave people you've known most of your life for such an uncertain future?" We just smiled and explained that we had considered all the angles and knew what we were doing, which was quite naive as we would discover in the months to come. We were soon to learn about a few "angles" that we had never imagined, never mind what we had overlooked in our hasty planning.

We had faith in our future, and in our ability to deal with it. With such firm convictions in mind, we weathered the questioning from our worried friends. It was necessary to return to Wisconsin after our Montana exploration and vacation to wind up a few unsettled business matters, not the least of which was selling the small Cape Cod house we had just bought the previous year and packing up our worldly possessions. It took us much longer than we had planned, but we patiently waded through it all, our minds focused on the adventurous direction we had chosen for our future. Herman placed a long distance call to the tractor and equipment company that wanted to hire him and yes, they still had a job opening for him. Finally, we placed our furniture in storage with the moving company and decided to leave it there on hold until we found a place to live in Montana. After many parties and farewells, we were off at last.

From the sale of our Tea Room the year before, and the little house on Wolcott Street where we only lived one year, we had more cash than we'd ever known. So, with a few bucks in the bank and high hopes in our hearts, we left very early one morning right after Labor Day, 1948. At this time, Lynn was eight, a mighty lovable little blackberry-eyed boy. Dick was a small, quick, freckle-faced ten year old with very blonde hair and bright blue eyes. Jack was lanky, thirteen and slow as molasses. He was the serious one, but as good as he was "pokey". I've never seen brothers as different in temperament and looks as my three boys are. I've often wondered how teachers are able to deal with a whole room full of different characters and temperaments. Discipline, for one thing, has to be individually applied at our house.

The stars of the night were fading and a gray dawn was breaking as we drove out of the little town that had been our home for eight years. We had driven past our house once more, and twice past "the old homestead", filling our eyes and hearts with the memories of homes that were no longer ours. It was good to leave so early, avoiding any more heart-breaking and tearful good byes.

... we drove out of the little town that had been our home for eight years.

Our '39 Dodge was showing its age, but it had done itself proud on all of our trips so far. We prayed that it would continue to do so, at least until we reached Montana. On this particular morning, it was loaded to capacity, quite possibly *beyond* its capacity. The carrier rack on top of the car was packed to its limit, and Herman had loaded the

trunk "scientifically", so the car really carried more in just the trunk alone than I am sure it was designed for. But that's my husband! People should watch him lay out a cheese and bologna sandwich. It's fascinating and entertaining! The cheese and lunch meat are pieced together like a jigsaw puzzle for maximum coverage. There is no waste and no overhangs around the edges of the bread slices. Everything fits to perfection! I'm surprised that he actually eats it and demolishes such flawless construction. Well, that's the same meticulous way Herman loaded the car for our journey. Later, when looking in the back of the trunk for "something", I discovered that the trunk was really packed, or I should say "compacted" as two loads into one space. I don't seem to remember what I was hunting for, but I do remember that Herman didn't appreciate my little disarranging search methods. He had packed the car practically with mathematical precision, and I apparently disturbed the delicate balance during my clumsy quest. The articles we wouldn't need on the trip were fitted and pieced into every nook and cranny of the trunk, the same way he laid out a cheese sandwich, I suppose. The immediate necessities were packed within easy reach. Why didn't I know that?

The pep our car displayed on that historic morning equaled the enthusiasm of the entire family. It had a slight reluctance to hurry. It could have been the dampness of the early morning air, or a slight uncertainty about the success of the trip ahead; but more likely, it was the record-breaking load it was carrying. We were only a few miles out when I looked back in the car to see Dickie stretched out over his two brothers' laps, shoes off, comic book in hand, and monopolizing all available space and pillows. To this day, I cannot understand how anyone so indifferent to the passing scenic beauty could write such a glowing report later to his Montana teacher and classmates. He gave a very detailed report on all the highlights of the entire trip! The ability of the average child to observe, unobserved, and remember what he saw has long been underestimated.

It was a beautiful morning, and we sang together as we drove through one sleepy, awakening town after another. The miraculous autumn changes performed by nature were in full progress. The fields displayed fat, golden pumpkins and shocks of corn. The beautiful forests were a breathless panorama of scarlet, brown, gold and yellow. Little did we know how much we would eventually hunger for such sights as these on the treeless Great Plains.

A few clouds we hadn't noticed earlier began to accumulate and build in the sky. One huge, dark, billowy cloud seemed to suddenly appear right above the car, where it proceeded to burst open and pour all over us. We have never taken a trip yet that it didn't rain. This was no easy drizzle, but a drenching downpour that partially obliterated the road ahead. A little veil of evil smelling smoke wafted out from under the dashboard. After my timid observation that I smelled smoke was completely ignored, I yelled "FIRE!" The results of that outburst were almost frightening as Herman brought the car to a screeching halt. I should mention that I had said "I think I smell something burning in the car" so often that no one paid any attention to me anymore. The rain grew heavier, coming down in thick sheets of water, and the smoke was getting a little thicker, pouring out from some mysterious recesses under the dash panel. Ordinarily this would be a minor repair job for Herman, according to my mechanical minded spouse; but on the muddy shoulder of a country road, in a blinding rain storm, this would become a major repair job. We lost a little of our exuberance as we slowly and cautiously proceeded to the next town.

Upon entering the little village, we quickly discovered that we were the only "early birds", and we wasted one precious hour waiting for the local garage man to show up for work. When he and his helpers did arrive, they were quick to inform us that they were too busy to take care of us until the latter part of the morning. After a persuasive conversation, Herman somehow coaxed the man into loaning him some tools and some space to do the job himself. Don't ask me how. All of us piled out of the broken car. The recess gave us an opportunity to take care of a few personal matters and have some hot coffee. Well, we took care of the immediate business, but failed to see any eating place that was open. Maybe they didn't serve food in that village until brunch.

... he assumed the role of contortionist, practically standing on his head...

Herman had the car repaired in a short time. While doing the awkward job, he assumed the role of contortionist, practically standing on his head, twisting his torso around the steering wheel, and dangling his feet out the door. I suggested that he might have some difficulty untangling himself, but he very indignantly said he wouldn't. While in the process of extricating himself from this painful pose, another tourist stepped up and asked if he would work on his car next. Herman quickly informed the man that he certainly would not, much to the garage proprietor's amusement. Outside of a lame back, a testy disposition, dirty clothes and grimy hands, he suffered no other serious after effects. However, because we weren't too sure that Daddy was in good humor, we were all on the quiet side as we hit the road again. Everyone was content to relax and be grateful that the old car seemed none the worse for the experience. The rain-washed air was fresh and invigorating, reviving our spirits once more.

Toward noon, we all got hungry about the same time. We had eaten very early that morning, and had covered a good many miles, so our appetites were sharp. Contrary to standard procedure used on former trips, I had packed a lunch. In fact, I had spent considerable time on planning and preparing it. I had individually packaged and labeled each one's favorite sandwich and their specialty, such as deviled eggs with Dick's sandwich, pickles and olives for Lynn's, peanut butter sandwich for Jack, and corned beef for Herman and me. Yes, I was pretty proud of that lunch box.

We pulled off into one of those pretty little roadside parks that very few states can boast of. There should be many, many more like these across the United States, with the heavy tourist travel we now have these days. With dismay, I discovered that the boys had placed the lunch box directly over where the hot exhaust pipe runs under the car floor. They put it at that particular spot because it provided a nice foot rest, which only added to my frustration and earned them a good scolding. The heat had certainly played havoc with our picnic. With the first bites, we all displayed the same expression, yechhhh, as one nose after the other turned up. The lettuce had wilted; the cold meat was unpleasantly warm, and the tomatoes in the sandwiches were stewed. The lovely lunch took a fast trip to the trash barrel, and we headed out for the nearest hamburger stand.

The lovely drive along the Mississippi River was uneventful for the first few hours. The wide expanse of water, the steamboats with their churning paddlewheels, and the locks and dams always fascinate my young family, as well as Herman and me. The beautiful wooded bluffs overshadowing the river are breathtaking with their massive height. Inspired by all the beauty, I quickly decided to use our movie camera for the first time. I'd had a few short lessons on the use of this modern marvel, so I filmed scene after scene. Months later, to my chagrin, I discovered that the film had *ex*pired while I was *in*spired. Miles of picture taking resulted in nothing more than the stern wheel of a steamboat and a brief shot of a windshield wiper. So much for Ruth's movie-making skills.

Toward evening, the rains came … again. Once started, the wind and rain grew steadily more ferocious by the minute! The electrical storms along the upper Mississippi valley have a nasty reputation.

Thunder and lightning, with all its impressive display, is not and never will be appreciated by yours truly. Three pop-eyed little boys and one pop-eyed mama witnessed a tremendous storm that we traveled through for several hours without an intermission! The lightning was almost continuous, flash after flash, and the thunder rolling down the river valley was almost deafening, echoing back and forth between the high bluffs rising above the river. The man of the family expressed no opinion one way or the other at the time, and his set face revealed nothing. He just stared straight ahead, concentrating on the road. Later, when it was all over, he confessed that it was the worst electrical storm he had ever witnessed, much less driven through.

The storm even seemed to frighten the car into a temporary breakdown. It began to rebel with an ominous moan, then screech with a terrible din that we could hear clearly between the horrendous peals of thunder. All that noise surrounding us, shattered by the blinding flashes of lightning, was almost too much for my delicate nervous system. I will never know how Herman was able to maintain such an outward display of calm, with that "everything's-under-control" look, while his car was loudly screeching at him with rude complaints. I am sure, however, that his unfaltering manner is the only thing that kept me from screaming my fool head off, and kept the boys from becoming hysterical. We heard a muted clunk, and my knowledgeable husband determined that the fan belt had broken. It was very dark by then, past midnight, and we were still another ten miles or more from the next town. We wondered if the car's battery would keep the engine running, much less keep the headlights bright enough to even find the next town.

"Never mind. I have a spare belt in the trunk," Herman said reassuringly. "For once, I'm prepared for the right emergency!" We found a safe place to pull off the road, slanting downhill just in case. Herman grabbed a flashlight to search for the life-saving belt. In a short while, he climbed back into the driver's seat, slammed the door shut, and sat quietly for a moment. In a barely audible voice, I heard him say, "I must have left it hanging on the wall back in our old garage."

In the wee hours of the morning, a hot car jerked and limped into the little Minnesota town with an even hotter papa behind the wheel. The town's only hotel was a small but neat frame building. As we entered, the sleepy clerk raised his bushy eyebrows at the weary, bedraggled family that trooped in. The first lap of our journey had been just a bit hectic, but our distress was soon forgotten at the sight of the clean, comfortable beds.

After a sound, refreshing sleep, we awoke the next morning with our spirits restored in anticipation of a new day promising new adventures. Herman walked down the street lined with only a few stores, but soon returned with a fan belt nevertheless. He installed it very quickly, and the three sleepy boys crawled into the car and took their positions. The sun was bright and the sky was clear and beautiful, assuring us a lovely day. I sat in the car waiting for Herman to put our big suitcases in the trunk, and to make his routine inspection of the tires. He leisurely appeared at my side of the car and said, "Wouldn't this be a beautiful morning to have a flat tire?"

We laughed and laughed. Sometimes my husband has such a wonderful sense of humor. Still chuckling, he continued, "Well, we *do* have a flat tire, and the really funny joke is that the spare is way back in the trunk behind all that luggage!"

As I watched the street behind our car filling up with suitcases, assorted boxes and miscellaneous bundles, my former opinion about his logical, scientific method of packing suffered a great setback. I was now of the opinion that neither one of us should brag about our intelligence nor cleverness just yet. The head of the household spoke not a word, but went straight to his work. After all, what could he say … with the children present? This was one of those moments when one understands why silence is golden. Need I mention that the spare tire was then placed in a more accessible location? One of the many nice things I've admired about Herman through the years is his commendable ability to whistle sweetly when I, and the even the good Lord above, might expect him to let loose with at least one cuss word. If the boys inherit that good trait, it will carry them through many a difficult time.

When we were once more on our way, I sincerely hoped that we had experienced all the hardships that were in store for us. I prefer getting it all out of the way up front rather than stringing it out through the whole journey. I did my share of the driving, as was our custom, and drove a hundred mile stretch once in a while to give Herman a chance to rest. When I drove, Herman would lie in the back seat and the boys would be redistributed. This always flattered me, because I felt it was a compliment to my driving. Of course, it could also have meant that he didn't want to see what was going to happen ... if anything *should* happen. It might be better not knowing. One by one, the boys fell asleep, too. Why was it that when Herman was driving and I started to doze off, the whole family would come to life? There would be harmonious singing, jarring the back of my seat, and sometimes an accidental clunk in the head from someone's elbow or a carelessly swung book. The scene I liked the best was the one where I would just be drifting off into a much needed nap, and one of the boys would yell "MOM" right in my ear, so loud that I would sit bolt upright and say, "What? Wh-what happened?" Usually it was a question they wanted to ask that could very well have waited. This was clearly an unfair sabotage of my rest period!

By some weird coincidence, every time I took the wheel ... and I mean **every** time ... a detour would materialize out of nowhere, or I would at least be challenged by a very rough road. And that's only part of the story. Children are known to be unpredictable. That certainly proved to be true on this trip! The boys all got carsick for the first time in their lives, in spite of all the previous traveling experience they had! It was continuous, one after the other, especially when I was driving. It was as though they saved it up just for me. As soon as I took the wheel, at the sharpest curve, the narrowest road or the steepest hill, I would hear that desperately urgent command, "STOP!" The boys usually managed to wait until they got out of the car, but I was afraid that luck wouldn't last. All three displayed such green, unhappy faces that we felt sorry for them, but were completely helpless to do anything for them.

Had Grandma Wilson (my mother) been on the trip with us, we would have had some help. Whether she took the train, bus or car, she always had motion sickness, so she had some medication with her at all times just for that purpose. Grandpa (my dad) still loves to tell about the boat trip they took on one of the new Great Lakes steamships. My grandfather edited a small town newspaper, and in the society column, he wrote: "Mrs. Wilson enjoyed her boat trip across Lake Michigan. She spent most of the time at the railing, feeding the fishes." My mother was so embarrassed that she wouldn't talk to him for a week. Had the boys' grandmother been with us on this trip, she would have dragged out her box of saltine crackers and her bottle of Dramamine. On previous car rides, Grandma handed out the crackers the minute she got into the car, much to Herman's annoyance. Everyone had to have one ... just in case. Cracker crumbs would litter the whole car, but the children thought it was a wonderful idea and succeeded in putting away quite a few.

I had read somewhere that paper bags were wonderful for such emergencies. After the first bout of carsickness, we stopped at the next town and looked in vain for the bags. With the post-war paper shortage still prevalent, we couldn't find any. Instead, we settled for some flimsy cartons. Confident that we were at least partially prepared for the next "stop" session, we proceeded with our journey. It was my turn to drive again, and I felt more at ease with the untimely emergency stops basically eliminated. It wasn't too long before I heard one of the familiar moans, and Herman grabbed the handy little carton. He held Lynn's head over the cardboard box while I kept my eyes on the highway with some difficulty, wondering how the new emergency barf box was working out.

Herman said, "This works swell, honey. Everything is under control." With that, he opened the window and tossed the mess out into the passing scenery, saying, "Just like that, and away we go!" A sudden gust of wind played the dirtiest trick one could imagine on Herman! It picked up the obnoxious little carton and threw it right back at him, striking him squarely in the face! One more patient was abruptly added to the temporary sick list, and I almost joined him, too.

The poor dear. After all the sick babies and nasty messes, he still became nauseous and helpless at times like this. I had difficulty smothering some giggles because of the complete absurdity of the whole scene. That would *not* have contributed to a congenial atmosphere for the remaining trip. But the flabbergasted expression on Herman's face, together with the stunned look of surprise he gave me was almost more comical than I could bear. A short recess was in order for a very necessary cleanup period. That little experiment had failed miserably, so we made a point of stopping at the next hardware store we could find and bought a covered enamel pan. Ironically, that ended the siege of car sickness!

I should clarify that our long ride had not been all flat tires, mechanical breakdowns, detours and car sickness. On the contrary, we spent many happy hours singing and just feeling carefree. I thought our harmony was pretty good, and it was one period of time when we felt unrestrained. We could even shout if we wanted to, for there were no nervous neighbors to complain. In our family, a car ride was always an occasion for a song or two, and everyone joined in simultaneously.

We made periodic stops at filling stations for gas or for the use of their restrooms, mostly for the latter. I could almost hear the attendant groan as we all piled out and headed for the "relief" station. The four males of the family lined up in the tiny station waiting for their turn, while I usually had free sailing. You see, there are some advantages in being the only woman in the party. I wonder if the greater percentage of filling station customers come to "rest" in the restrooms or just get cokes and free air. At one stop in the Dakotas, modern plumbing was not in style yet. It boasted the typical arrangement, a small duplex with the signs "His" and "Hers". Naturally all conversation was available to both sides. I heard my youngest remark that some careless people had left their nice Sears catalog in that smelly old house. That remark showed me up for the "old timer" that I am. I knew why the catalog was there!

At the beginning of our trip west, we had offered the boys a small reward as incentive for spotting the first animal, a deer, a prairie dog, or even a jack rabbit. All along the way, we had all looked in vain for anything that resembled a wild animal. Toward the end of our journey, a little gopher calmly ambled across the road. Jack spotted him and won the fabulous prize money, two bits. We all laughed when the award was made for the first sighting of our first wild animal in the wild and wooly west!

The scenes in the rugged Big Horn Mountains are pictures I'll never forget. The almost dangerously steep climbs of the roadway, the winding mountain highways, and the potential danger of large fallen rocks hidden on the road just around each sharp curve kept us breathless. Frequently, the little pickup trucks driven by the highway department men inspecting road conditions whizzed by us, darting in and out of lanes of tourist traffic without a care. Maybe this mountain driving was a little nerve jarring for us, but not to those old hands. They would pull up at the side of the road onto a narrow dirt shoulder bordering a drop of hundreds of feet, and jump out on the very edge! The butterflies in our stomachs would do a speedy tap dance routine at the sight of so brash a display of boldness. It was probably such old stuff to them that they weren't even conscious of the stir their exhibition was causing in the approaching cars.

One of the highlights of this segment of the trip was our encounter with a real "wise guy" vacation driver with Illinois plates. He was a "weaver", one of those reckless drivers who just have to pass, no matter what. At the foot of a steep incline, his horn was going continuously as he weaved in and out of traffic impatiently, disregarding all consideration of safety. We lost track of him as he pulled way ahead of us and out of sight for a time. As we neared the summit of the mountain and approached a very narrow, sharp curve, workmen were doing some very hazardous road repair work, and it was there that we caught up to our "show off" motorist. He was holding up traffic as he walked up ahead of his car and literally measured the width of the roadway to see if his beautiful big Packard could make it through! He was mopping his brow with a big handkerchief as the perspiration ran down his face even in the cool mountain air, and he looked as if he would give his right arm for wings at that moment. At the rate he was driving, he would earn his wings anyway, probably sooner rather than later.

Herman and I were so impressed by the gorgeous view from atop those mountains. As we peered down at the steep slopes and sheer cliffs from our high perch, the towering pines below looked like tiny weeds. The rock formations and colors were absolutely breathtaking, and the magnificent views in every direction were so incredible that we couldn't express ourselves with enough exclamation marks! And were the boys impressed? As usual they were unpredictable. They were sitting in the back seat playing airplane! After waiting for some expressions of awe, or even an opinion from the rear gallery, we would ask, "Did you see that frightening drop?" or "Just look at those colorful cliffs!" All we got in return was, "Ohhhhh yeah" ... all in unison! We heard that same answer so many times, expressing their apparent lack of interest, that we just turned our backs on the whole tribe and completely ignored them.

Our travel for that day had been so hectic that we decided to find a motel early, cook our supper, and just relax outdoors. We traveled for some distance further before we found a place that didn't look too bad. There was some type of a roadhouse or tavern on the premises that didn't particularly thrill us, but we stopped. They had boats for rent, a pathetic little puddle of water they called a lake, and some picnic tables. Herman went into the dilapidated looking bar with some hesitation. He returned with a swarthy looking man who reminded me of some sort of underworld character. My spirits were not lifted when another man of similar appearance joined them, evidently a partner. They said they would give us a cabin for a very reasonable rate, seeing as they were not too busy just then. We marched off with the questionable characters, while the boys romped around the small park like little colts just released from a confining corral. As we approached the cabin they wanted to show us, a veritable cloud of mosquitoes arose from their daytime hiding place in the tall grass. We all ran into the little cabin, slamming the door behind us. That was a futile gesture, because the screen in the bottom half of the door just wasn't there! The cobwebs, the ancient dust and the musty odors were just too much for me, and I hurried back outside. Herman was close on my heels, telling the man over his shoulder that he would think it over and let him know. The "reasonable price" they quoted was ten dollars! Also, after 1:30 A.M., all toilet accommodations would be locked up and we would be "on our own" for the rest of the night. We hustled the bewildered little boys into the car and made a hasty departure without even "thinking it over" any further. I am certain the boys felt they were deprived of a very wonderful outing in an ideal location!

Fortunately, we didn't have to drive too much farther to find more suitable lodging, and by this time we were perfectly willing to settle for a restaurant dinner. I always tried to get the family to eat one hot meal a day, but it was money wasted that night. No one finished their dinner. Perhaps someday I would understand how they could eat hamburgers and grilled cheese sandwiches two or three times a day with no hesitation. But good nourishing food? Forget it.

After a night of unusually sound sleep, we were anxious to start the last lap of our journey. As was our custom, we started on the road very early and drove for an hour or two before stopping for breakfast. That morning, we had the heartiest, most enjoyable meal of the entire trip. We made up our minds that we would settle for nothing less than ham and eggs with all the trimmings. Ordinarily, we were satisfied with little more than fruit and toast and plenty of good coffee, but we broke all the diet rules on that trip. On this particular morning, we came to a little western town which boasted a water tower, a freight depot, not more than a handful of old buildings and a very old but neat hotel. I'm sure few easterners would have recognized it as such. It was a small white frame building with only the word "HOTEL" that identified it. Out front, it displayed a sign that read "Meals Served".

According to our standard procedure, Herman walked in to investigate before we all went in. If the place was good, he would return and escort his family in. If it was questionable, he would buy cigarettes or a pack of gum, and we would drive on. This time, he was only gone but a few minutes and returned with a big smile on his face. His verdict was "neat, clean and the smell of good coffee". With that, the family piled out of the car in a hurry. The dining room was rustic, with an Old West decor, but the wholesomeness of the place won us over completely. The smell of coffee and frying ham permeating the air was almost more than our impatient appetites could bear. As yet, nobody had appeared, and Herman was just about to start looking for someone when a big blond young man appeared. He towered well over six feet, with a smile as broad as he was big. Apparently, he was the owner, chef and waiter, and it was the first time in my experience that we were served without even ordering!

He didn't ask what we wanted to eat. All he said was, "Good morning! Hi boys! Are you hungry? Yes? All right! Coming right up!" With eyes twinkling, he turned around and disappeared as quietly as he had entered. Herman and I looked at each other with an unspoken "Now what?" To our appreciative delight, he sang at the top of his voice as he cooked our breakfast. Not a bad voice either. Evidently, his breakfast menu was the same all year around, and what a meal that was! He brought in tall glasses of fresh orange juice, stacks of buttered toast, flapjacks and platters of the most appetizing ham and eggs I've ever seen. The dishes were crazed and very old, but shiny and clean. I'm sure we've never eaten a better breakfast before or since. The pleasure was further enhanced with deliciously brewed coffee served in heavy, old-fashioned mugs, the best coffee we'd tasted on the entire trip. The only item shown on the crude menu for dinner was steak. Herman remarked that he bet that was one heck of a steak! Our young blond host replied, "Man, it hangs over the edge of the platter, and it's so tender it cuts like melted butter!" By noon of that day, we were sorely tempted to turn around and come back for another meal at that little hotel. If we weren't on the last leg of our journey to our new home town, we might well have done just that.

CHAPTER SIX
Home, Sweet Home???

Several weeks before we arrived in our new town, we had made reservation at a motel so it would be one less worry to deal with when we arrived. This cabin would be our temporary home while we searched for a house to rent. Considering the high cost of building and our unfamiliarity with suitable building sites in that area, we decided we would just rent for a couple of years and enjoy having some money in a bank account for a change. We also planned to buy a new car, which would have been the first new one we had ever purchased. That would be a real thrill because we had always owned second-hand cars. It's true that every time we bought one, it was a better car than the previous one; but to own a brand new one was going to be absolutely wonderful! The faithful old buggy that had brought us out west was definitely on its last legs (or last wheels, I suppose), having already given us the best years of its life. We had reached the point that every time we went for a ride, we would wonder which part of its anatomy would rebel next. Was it any wonder that our hearts were so light with so much to anticipate and to be thankful for? We had an exciting new future that would begin at the next stop—the last stop on our trip, Sidney, Montana.

The reds and deep purples of the western sky were fading to prepare the heavenly scene for the first bright stars to shine as we crested the hill overlooking our future home in the Yellowstone Valley. The town looked so friendly and inviting with its sparkling lights offering a welcome, beckoning for us to enter. From the back seat came the small voice of my ten-year-old philosopher, Dickie, who said, "Our future is spread out before us!" It gave me goose bumps as the reality struck us all. With a prayer in my heart for courage to face this new, uncertain future, and with thankfulness for being delivered safely to our new land, we entered the little town. We all became a little subdued then, perhaps with a touch of the reality and uncertainty about what lay ahead. But, we were all together at journey's end, and that's all that really mattered then.

We drove up to our motel with sighs of relief. We made it! As Herman switched off the ignition, he patted the dashboard of the faithful old car as if to say, "Well done, noble steed." One tends to develop a very personal feeling for a possession that has given so much service. But I don't know what you do for a car to show your appreciation. In the old days, a man could give his horse a pail of oats, clean straw and a good rub down. And in the old, old days, imagine what our trip would have been like in a covered wagon! I guess we had it pretty easy after all.

Herman hopped out of the car and ran up the steps to the motel office to find out which unit we were in and to get the key. I was so relieved we had a place to land. After a long wait, Herman reappeared without a key and a discouraged look on his face. Right behind him was a harassed looking woman, the wife of the proprietor. She tried to explain that there was some sort of mix up in the reservation and our arrival date, and someone else was in our cabin. There were no other accommodations available. Even the old car seemed to echo the dispirited groans that came from all of us. We just couldn't believe it! We had been so confident that our lodging was taken care of for this night. The woman was embarrassed and apologetic over the mistake, but nothing could be done. She assured us that we would have our cabin the next day without fail.

It was true that my sister, Helen, still lived in town. But we hated to impose on her and her family of seven, plus a boarder. There was simply nothing else we could do. We had wanted to be so independent, and there we were ... heading for Helen's crowded little house our first night in town. In a few minutes, our travel weary family stood meekly at her front door. The uproarious welcome and the greetings among the eight cousins was no louder that their elders. And as usual in such cases, they claimed to have "plenty of room" for all of us. It never ceases to amaze me that a big family is always able to make room for a few more. Within a half hour, they made a place for all of us, and with Uncle Bill's help, the kids were all quickly tucked in. After a brief reunion over some hot coffee and a bite to eat, Herman and I too retired. Insomnia was not a problem that night, and we fell into a deep slumber devoid of either dreams or nightmares. The nightmares were soon to come.

The following day, we moved into our tiny cabin. We soon discovered that our car had accommodated our possessions much easier than the motel room. Our only closet was half the size of a telephone booth. The cabin included a tiny kitchen and a miniature shower. At least we had indoor plumbing! There was only one main room which served as our bedroom, living room and dining room combined. Beds were the predominant furniture. As you came in the door, there was a double bed immediately to your right, a double bed to the left, and a narrow aisle between them on your way to the fold-up cot in front of the uncurtained closet. This was to be our home for an undetermined period of time. Not too glamorous, but we resigned ourselves to making the best of it. We really didn't have any other alternatives at the moment. The place was clean and the beds were comfortable. That's all we could ask for at the time. The present was going to be very interesting, and the future would take care of itself.

Since there wasn't enough closet space, other arrangements had to be made. We had to have a system, and the system had to be maintained. If we didn't stay organized, we would be smothered by all the congestion in that tiny cabin. Fortunately, the bed frames were quite high. Cartons and suitcases were placed under the beds, and each had a specific use. The clothing went under our bed, while the cartons under the boys' bed held items like pajamas, boots and rubbers. As soon as the boys entered the cabin, they shed their rubbers or galoshes and put them in the handy carton close to the door, and slid it back under the bed again. The other carton held three sets of pajamas during the day and three little piles of clothes at night.

After all my years of baking, including most of the bread and doughnuts we ate, buying bakery goods was a real treat for me ... for a week! The kitchenette had an ancient, battered old two-burner gas plate, which limited our cuisine somewhat. Hot dogs and hamburgers eventually wore out their welcome, and eggs and pork and beans soon lost their popularity. It was up to me in the following days to get creative and imaginative, and investigate new ways of cooking on a two-burner gas plate that served as our range top. An oven? What's that? No such thing in those little cabins.

The day after our arrival, I enrolled the boys at their respective schools. That process wasn't enjoyed too much, but they would make new friends after a day or two, and that would break the ice for them. School had begun early that year, before Labor Day. First, we deposited the two younger boys at the elementary school, and then took Jack to the junior high. Their quiet, nervous anticipation struck a chord in my memory of similar experiences in my own childhood. I knew that their first day would be a little tough for them, starting almost a month late in a new school with new faces and a strange environment. At their level, it would take as much courage to adapt to their venture as it would for us in our grownup world. But we placed our faith in the legendary western hospitality and friendliness. An old "homesteader" later told me that these folks didn't care how much you had, but did demand honesty and sincerity. Then, as an example, he related how a man had recently been run out of town for cheating at cards!

After dropping the children off at school, our next destination was the local newspaper office, the *Sidney Herald*. We picked up a copy of their weekly edition and hastily scanned the ad section. It didn't take us long to discover that there was a housing shortage out here, too. It was interesting that this little rural town in the northeastern plains of Montana, with no apparent industry of any kind except for ranching and farming, had the same problems of any other city in the U.S. Our confidence suffered a little jolt when we learned that there wasn't one place available to rent! Not one! So, we set out with a list to search for the very few houses that were for sale. After looking at the first houses, which I would call "dumps", we were sick. We became sicker still when we heard the prices they were asking for them. The first one we looked at would have been expensive at fifteen hundred dollars. They wanted ten thousand! We stood in the tiny kitchen looking at the cheap construction of the so-called house. Whenever anyone walked across the kitchen floor, especially someone like me, being on the well-upholstered side, the whole house shook! The floor sank a little under each footstep when I walked, like crossing a river on a suspension bridge. After searching all over for the bathroom, we were informed there was a lovely one in the cellar! Who builds their bathroom in the cellar? After one glance at the steep stairs, I flatly refused to go down. A ladder would have been safer. I couldn't help but wonder what would happen to a person living in that house if he had a hurry-up call from nature in the middle of the night. Scary! One bedroom was in the basement, and one very small one was on the first floor just off the narrow living room. The sellers were very proud of the third bedroom out in the back yard, which was a remodeled chicken coop! The stock yards full of bawling cattle were right across the street. How handy! That, combined with the nearby switching yard for freight trains, made for a most fascinating location.

After a day of house hunting, the Ma and Pa of this little latter-day pioneer family rambled "home" in their tired old buggy with lagging spirits. One inescapable fact loomed before us that we could not ignore. We would have to *build* a house, and we would have to do it fast! This became even more evident when we learned that our landlord was raising our rent to twenty-eight dollars a week for that tiny, inadequate, one-room cabin! The original agreement was fifteen dollars per week. Can you imagine that? Over a hundred and twelve dollars a month for one little room in this day and age? In 1948? They knew we had nowhere else to go! We had no choice, so fairness and decency walked right out the door, and greed walked right in. We didn't have to hold a long discussion to decide what we must do. We needed housing as soon as possible; there was nothing to rent and nothing decent to buy. We had to build!

We contacted a nice little Frenchman my sister recommended, who was in the concrete business. He suggested that we start with a basement immediately, and finish it off as a home inside until we could build the upper part of the house later, considering that it was so late in the year and winter would be setting in very soon. In fact, he told us that it would take a *lot* of "hurrying" now to seal it up weather-tight before the bitter Montana winter put a hold on all construction work until spring. It was in that little two-by-four kitchenette in the cabin that our new home was planned. In fact, Herman had already prepared some drawings for our "someday" dream house when we were still back in Wisconsin, so he had at least something to work with for starters. It looked like the "someday" had arrived earlier than we anticipated, but not with the same conditions we had dreamed about. Under the forced, accelerated conditions with which we had to work, and literally lowering our first floor plan into the basement level, the "dream house" in no way resembled our original vision. But once we got started on the hastily planned basement home, we regained some of our old enthusiasm and determined that it would be as homey and comfortable and attractive as we could possibly make it. At least it would be ours, and we would have some space where we could all dare to breathe at the same time. In my wildest dreams, I had never envisioned moving out west to the wide open spaces, only to be squeezed into a one room cabin for midgets, and then to live "underground" like a family of prairie dogs! But there we were! We learned that basement homes were not at all uncommon in that area at that period in time, and we later made friends with several families who also lived in basements.

In a very short time, the ground-breaking day arrived for the excavating. How important Herman and I felt with all the men working for us, plus the big bulldozer. Evidently, our workmen had the same feeling, because I heard one of the men say, "Gee, these people must have a lot of money to build such a big place like this!" All of the people we hired for our project had the same idea ... that we were wealthy ... because they didn't realize that the basement was all we were going to build for now, and all we could *afford* to build. We discovered the legend about our having big bucks too late. And that cost us big bucks! Half a dozen big trucks lined up to take away all our nice black dirt from the excavation, at our expense. When I asked just why they were doing that, they looked at me as if to say, "Boy, that's a dumb woman for you!" They explained that that is what they always do; and when we were ready to put our lawn in and needed some fill, we would get someone else's dirt. I may be a naïve woman, but this didn't sound like good sense to me, and it was a little hard for me to digest. We both suffered acute indigestion months later when we had to hire someone else to bring in fill for the grading of our yard. We had no way of proving that the other men had promised to return the equivalent of our dirt, so we learned another of many hard lessons in the building of our first home.

In a few weeks, the shell of our basement materialized, along with some very shocking bills. After the first wave of invoices, we decided that we may have to live in our basement longer than this first winter. With thousands of families all over the country living in basement homes for the same reasons, we couldn't complain too much. We resolved that it had to be a very special basement, and look like a real home on the inside. The estimated cost of our basement had more than doubled and soon depleted our nice bank balance. I guess those builders saw us Eastern dudes coming from a long way off.

Herman once again became a plumber, electrician, carpenter and sheet metal worker (or "tin knocker" as he called it) just as he had at the Olde Homestead; but even so, the total cost was unbelievably colossal! Christmas was just around the corner, and we had just bought the most expensive present we could ever imagine. I have wondered many times what we would have done if my husband hadn't had so many skills to do the work we couldn't afford to hire out. Our subterranean dwelling would have been a pretty dismal, primitive cave, I dare say.

Our temporary heat was a small, uncontrollable coal heater. The dilapidated antique stove was donated by one of our sympathetic carpenters who understood our plight. It was far from efficient, but it kept us warm if we stood within a radius of six feet of it. After we discovered the exorbitant prices they were charging for oil furnaces in this little town, we pulled out our trusty Sears catalog and did some figuring. Herman sent copies of the basement plan and the future main floor plan to the company for some information, heating calculations and cost estimates. With subzero temperatures most of the winter, it was essential that we have an adequate heating system or the basement would be uninhabitable. My smart hubby explained to me that living in a basement and utilizing the surrounding earth for thermal insulation was an advantage and would save us money on the fuel oil bills during the long winters. The insulating earth would also help keep us cooler during the summer as well. Nevertheless, he had to plan the furnace size to have adequate capacity for heating the future house above the basement. I sure love the way my man thinks!

CHAPTER SEVEN
Winter Life in a Cracker Box

The strong winds, characteristic of the northern plains, grew cold and vicious. The few remaining leaves soon vanished, leaving the trees looking bleak and forlorn. Then the rains took over, day after day. It rained steadily for a week. I was continually sweeping and scrubbing. The floor of the little cabin was easily littered with dirt and spattered with mud tracked in by five pair of feet, bringing samples of the "great outdoors" into the undersized indoors. A miniature lake just outside the cabin door insured the regular intrusion of sloppy, muddy tracks just inside the door.

Our neighbors were few, owing to the decline of tourists staying at the motel with winter coming on. But there were a handful of non-migratory residents, like us, who had no where else to live for the time being, inhabiting the place on a semi-permanent basis. They provided a variety of musical interludes to share with their fellow inhabitants in adjacent cabins. One next door neighbor was a religious healer (he said) who chanted prayers in a sing-song voice all day, sometimes adding hymns from a radio station to break the monotony. If they raised his rent as much as they raised ours, I'm sure his welfare check was stretched pretty thin. Of course, he had "contributions" to his income, too. People were going into his place off and on all day, and seemed to have great faith in his help. Come to think of it, he was probably doing better financially than we were.

The neighbor on the other side of us was a lonely old widower, a retired ranch hand. His high heeled cowboy boots shook the whole row of attached cabins when he paced back and forth. Hank's specialty was an endless stream of cowboy ballads and country tunes which he droned in a mournful, nasal drawl late into the night. The tapping of his boots to keep time with the "music" and the strumming of his out-of-tune guitar contributed to our insomnia for a good many nights. We learned early on that the thin walls of the cabin were not insulated against either sound or the cold. The blend of entertainment from these two neighbors alone was anything but harmonious. Still, they were kind, gentle people, and it was difficult to be upset with them. Hank, the neat old ranch hand who had spent most of his life in the great outdoors, was a conscientious housekeeper. One morning, he came to our door for the first time, introduced himself, and presented us with a jar of his home made pickles, much to our delight, especially the children's.

One dreary, overcast afternoon, I felt a sense of claustrophobia and depression creeping up on me, coupled with a nagging headache that just would not go away. I decided to lie down for the short time remaining before the boys returned from school. It was difficult to relax, with the prevailing problems troubling me, planting little seeds of doubt and misgivings in my mind. Had we done the right thing by coming out west with no carefully thought out plans, and no backup options? Had we relied on too many assumptions and believed that our faith would carry us through any calamities we might face? Should we have started to build the house, exhausting our bank account and putting all of our eggs into one basket? Would a heavy winter and unbearable cold set in before the basement was completed, bringing the project to a standstill? We didn't even have enough money right then to return to Wisconsin. And even if we did, what would we do when we got there? How many bridges had we burned behind us? Perhaps our friends and relatives back in Wisconsin were right. We must have been "teched" to take such a big, drastic bite. It seemed like I had just drifted off into a restless sleep when my family came home from school. With a twinge of guilt, I kissed each of the boys, thinking of the worries and new problems they also shared with us. Yes, we had all voted unanimously to move out west. But, the children didn't have the benefit of age and experience to evaluate the challenges we might face. They relied on Herman and me, and our crystal ball was very cloudy.

It was late October when Lynn was paging through that good old standby we were to use often out on the "frontier", the Sears catalogue. He had already written up his Christmas list of gifts to wish for, "inexpensive" items such as a bicycle, an accordion and a movie projector. I was sure they had the impression that financial problems were of no consequence to this family. I hastened to set them straight! I may have overplayed my dramatic role, however, telling them that the gifts this year would have to be *very* modest, if indeed we would have any gifts at all. In fact, I explained in a quavering voice, I wasn't sure we could even afford a Christmas tree this year! Yes, I played my role very convincingly, but this was to be another one of those "boomerangs".

A couple of days later as I lay on the bed after supper that evening, Lynn came over to me with great concern written on his innocent little face. He kissed me on the forehead and said, "Don't worry, Mother. We'll have a Christmas!" A faint apprehension began to grow in the back of my brain. "Today in class," he continued, "our teacher announced that anyone not able to have a tree this year should leave his name on her desk, and not to be embarrassed. Along with the tree, the Boy Scouts will also bring a basket of food. I left our name, Mom. Now, don't you feel better?"

I can't remember clearly if my headache worsened or went numb entirely. I do know I sat bolt upright and said, "What? You didn't! Why on earth did you do that?" The little boy's face clouded up with confusion and hurt, and tears welled up in his eyes. He explained that he had only tried to help. After all, hadn't I told them that we didn't have any money? I hugged him appreciatively and calmed myself down. I carefully informed the boys that we did have a little money, enough to clothe and feed us and keep that tiny old, uninsulated roof over our head, and even enough for a nice Christmas... somehow. But we had to be careful about spending what money we had so that we could have a real home again. I hastened to assure them all that we would indeed have a Christmas tree. I made my apology to the boys, as well as a silent vow to be a little less dramatic in the future.

The next morning, I wrote a nice note for Lynn to take to his teacher to get him off the hook and avoid embarrassment. Some weeks later, his teacher and I discussed this little episode. She laughed and told me how she had removed our name from the list with some misgivings, thinking my note was a demonstration of false pride. It continued to bother her until she talked with my sister, whom she knew well. Helen convinced her that we were struggling a bit, but not in dire need. I don't think any of us realize to what extent our children really share our worries, happiness and love, even if they don't fully understand what's going on. They may seem distant, oblivious and uninvolved at times, but they are an integral part of our lives. They develop the intelligence and some understanding of us and our problems at a very early age, much more than we ever give them credit for. I need to remind myself at times that my boys really are quite intelligent and perceptive.

Christmas was fast approaching—too fast! We were trying desperately to make our basement home habitable so we could have our own possessions around us at this most important time of year. Every day, the boys would check with me to ask if we were still planning to have a tree—and Christmas cookies. I assured them that we would definitely have a tree no matter what, but I couldn't see how I was going to bake cookies on that two-burner hot plate. I had noticed an old pie oven way back in the lower kitchen cabinet, so one day I pulled it out to examine it. I cleaned off as much of the rust as I could, and noticed it had a temperature gauge on it, hopefully still working. Once it was cleaned up, I was almost as thrilled as if I had just found a ten dollar bill. I could picture the surprise and excitement of the family when they came home and found me baking Christmas cookies. That would sure be a big boost for our morale. I dug further into the cupboard and found a big bowl with a crack in it, but still usable.

I was soon stirring up the recipe for one of our favorite cookies. Placing the old box oven on the two burners and guessing at the amount of gas flame needed, I waited for it to heat up. I glanced nervously at the thermometer's pointer for movement, for some sign that it still functioned.

My first surprise came when my little cookie sheets didn't fit into the oven. I transferred about four of the little mounds of dough to a small pie tin, somewhat shaken and quite doubtful about the efficiency of working with such a little pan for such a big batch of cookie dough. At this rate, I would be baking for a day and a night just for one batch. I needn't have been concerned about that, however, because in less than five minutes, smoke began pouring out through a crack in the isinglass door. In a second, I removed the pan containing the most hideous looking cookies I had ever seen, unbaked dough on the top and charcoal on the bottom. This was the last straw! I sat down and cried like my heart would break in two. It's funny how one can go along, handling one disappointment after another, until some inconsequential episode like this will knock you for a loop! In the last couple of months, I had gone through terrifying thunderstorms that shattered my nerves, a car that enjoyed breaking down at the most inconvenient times, discovered we could not find a home, had lived a very compressed life in a one-room cabin so small that nobody dared to gain weight or we all wouldn't fit, and I still managed to cope. But looking at this little pie tin with four small mounds of yucky dough and cinders was too much! It took me apart at the seams. Fortunately, I had ample time to recover from my crying spell before my family came home for dinner. They never heard about the cookies, and the primitive oven was back where it belonged, out of sight for the archeologists to discover some day in the future.

That night, we had beans and bacon for dinner. The two-burner hot plate didn't allow for multiple entrees. The next night would be beans and wieners, then eggs and pancakes, then stew and so on. Somehow, supper always tasted good and I had no complaints. Lynn never leaves the table to this day without coming over and giving me a kiss, saying "That was delicious, Mother," whether it was potato soup or chicken. That old standby, macaroni and cheese, was always a winner!

Homework had to be finished before supper. If the table was covered with food and dishes, a suitcase on the bed served as a desk. After supper, our customary routine became settling the boys down for the night, and then driving out to work in our basement on the northwest edge of town. The concrete work was finished and the "roof" (future first floor) was in place. It was a strange looking dwelling compared to what we were used to. A long, rectangular black and gray platform rose about two-and-a-half feet above the surrounding lot, with the entrance and stairway enclosure protruding above the "platform" roof on the middle of the north side, facing Highway 16. There would be days ahead when that entrance cupola was all you could see sticking out of the snowdrifts. Regularly spaced black stripes crossed the roof where the tarpaper was lapped and sealed with tar. Herman told me the contractor's term was "dried in", meaning that the basement was now sealed or weatherproofed. Now it was up to us to make a home out of what we had to work with, which was a large concrete box sunk into the ground, with a wood framed lid on it.

After wading through the mud surrounding this house cut into the ground, aided by the weak beam of a flashlight, we descended into our future residence. Herman was working on the wiring at this point. I never ceased to be amazed at his ability to work with this mysterious marvel, electricity. With great admiration, I watched him line up the different colored wires, and install them exactly where they needed to be according to his precisely drawn diagrams. It looked very complicated to me, but he obviously knew what he was doing. He put in heavy wiring for my electric stove, intricate wiring for the water heater and furnace and thermostat ... very busy and puzzling stuff. But when he got to the little three-way switches for the kitchen, he was perplexed! I couldn't believe it, but after blowing a couple of fuses and hearing some loud, ominous pops, I realized all was not as it should be. He wouldn't admit that he was confused, certainly not stumped. And I was certainly in no position to pass judgment, but I wasn't the least bit surprised when I heard him say, "Well, I'll be damned!" Being a woman, I could only sit and silently fret, and pray he didn't electrocute himself … and try to keep my mouth shut! It *can* be done! I wanted so badly to help, but all I could do was calmly sit and watch the puzzled expression on my husband's face, hoping for some ray of light.

As I absent-mindedly gazed around the room, I spotted a small box on the floor in one corner. My main responsibility on the project was to follow my husband around to hand him tools and "things", and to keep some pathways clear of sawdust and debris. My tools were the broom and dustpan. In the line of duty, I picked up the little discarded carton and was amused to see that it was the container for one of the three-way switches that had so badly confounded my husband. On the side of the box was a detailed diagram and instructions for the installation of a three-way switch!

"Honey, would this help you out any?" I asked hopefully. Herman was very grateful, to put it mildly, and I was overjoyed to be able to contribute some help for my perplexed man. Feeling slightly foolish, he proceeded to finish the job without further difficulty.

The weather was growing noticeably colder and continued to be soggy and rainy to the point of monotony. The little antiquated coal heater in the basement ate the fuel we fed it with a ravenous appetite that was never satisfied. It had no draft control or damper, so it just gave out a concentrated heat at close range as long as it was supplied with anything that burned, wood, coal or shavings. At the end of the evening's work (daytime on Saturdays and Sunday afternoons), we would drive back to the dreary little cabin and try to relax with a cup of steaming hot coffee. The old car's heater would just start to warm up by the time we arrived "home". The tiny kitchenette in our cabin was cold and drafty, so relaxation was almost impossible. If it was night time when we returned, the boys would be sound asleep, and we would sit at the little table bundled up in sweaters and bathrobes, with blankets wrapped around our legs and a shared heating pad under our cold feet. Imagine trying to unwind when you're sitting erectly on hard old straight-backed chairs, wrapped up like mummies! On really cold nights, we would crank up the inadequate little gas space heater to full blast, and try in vain to imagine that we were warm and comfortable.

After about an hour of such "relaxation", we transferred the heating pad to the bed, turned down the air-consuming heater, and wearily turned in.

We would sit at the little table wrapped up like mummies.

At first, the beds were the predominant feature of our temporary living quarters, but now it was the cold. Unlike Wisconsin's bone chilling dampness, Montana's winter chill is a dry cold that you don't feel too much at first. It sneaks up on you before you realize it, and it penetrated the cabin's thin walls as an unwelcome guest, refusing to leave. It was difficult to fall asleep quickly, even as tired as we were on most nights. Contrasting radio programs from neighboring cabins filtered through the paper thin walls. And then there was the cowboy singer on one side and the hymn singer on the other, mixed with the groans, snores and otherwise heavy breathing of an entire family in one small room. The sounds were not what one would call a harmonious blend, and certainly a far cry from a lullaby! But in the warm comfort of each others' arms, and with the love that has always been steady and deep, we would eventually drift into temporary oblivion long enough to rest us for the next day's trials..

At five in the morning, Herman would bravely jump out of bed, slam shut the window and turn up the space heater to warm up the room before we all had to get up. The window needed to be open a crack at night so we wouldn't be asphyxiated while we slept, due to the oxygen-consuming gas heater. He would then quickly dive back under the covers and try to warm up again, teeth chattering and ice cubes for toes. As the winter days grew colder, I noticed that he was performing this little exercise with greater and greater speed, until he was practically just a blur in motion. I believe he eventually perfected this daily ritual to the point where he could pull it off in less than five seconds! He is an amazing man, my husband! So we survived liked Eskimos under the mountain of quilts and blankets piled onto each bed. Before the heater was turned up again in the morning, the *inside* of the walls were actually covered with frost! Herman would tell us to be careful about folding our blankets back when we got out of bed. We might crack them. I remember trying to remove my coat one morning from the hanger rack on the door, only to discover that it was frozen solidly to the door! The coat had gotten wet in the previous evening's rain, and now it was as stiff as a board. I had to wait until the room warmed up enough for my coat to thaw so I could pry it from the door! A silly thought occurred to me. I wondered if I could warm the room up faster by leaving the refrigerator door open.

If the night hadn't been too cold, and one of us turned up the heater by 5:00 AM, we could dress in relative comfort by 6:30. Taking a shower in the two-by-two bathroom was the most disruptive activity in the whole cabin. Shower time was an event that upset everything and everyone in the place on a daily basis. First, the clothes basket with its heavy load of soiled laundry had to be removed from its hiding place behind the shower curtain, covering the corner floor drain. It was placed somewhere in the cabin, as was every other removable object sitting on the floor. There was no curb around the shower "area", so the water merrily wandered without restraint all over the floor, wherever it had a mind to go. The steam, confined to the small area of the kitchenette and the shower space, dampened any remaining dry space above the floor. Naturally, all other occupants of the cabin had to restrict themselves down to one spot and stay put until the showering individual had completed his turn. This temporary disruption and displacement of possessions left no free space for roaming about. If anyone was unfortunate enough to come to the door during our shower hour, they would have to wait outside in the cold, or just go away and come back another time. There wasn't even room enough to open the door at that point!

When we originally headed west full of hope and optimistic dreams, we could not have predicted in our wildest imagination that the five Foells would be squeezed into the smallest possible un-insulated space for almost four months during arctic weather conditions. We had no choice but to learn what winter life might be like in a cracker box—an unforgettable experience everyone should try at least once.

CHAPTER EIGHT
Home for Christmas

The spirit of the approaching Christmas season was trying its best to enter into this makeshift little one-room domicile. With three little boys, who could be unaffected by that joyous holiday? A hundred times a day, I heard, "Will we still have a tree?" "Will we be in our basement by Christmas?" "Are we gonna have our old furniture and our toys and stuff that we used to have by Christmas?" They seemed to be wishing more for their familiar old belongings than thinking about new gifts from Santa Claus. Only two weeks until Christmas, and we were still working desperately to have our new home ready in time for the holidays. We could only hope and pray that we could keep up our strength to make enough progress so we would be settled in time.

Right in the home stretch, so to speak, Herman developed a terrific head cold. This wasn't surprising, considering our daily trip to the cold basement every night and back to the chilly cabin, day after day on top of his regular job at the tractor company. The poor man was worn out and a ripe target for the cold germs to attack. Simultaneously, Lynn came down with the sniffles, and both he and his daddy went to bed feeling sick and miserable. With its wall to wall beds, the cabin seemed quite appropriate as an infirmary. I was genuinely homesick for our dear Wisconsin doctor who had nursed us through many trials. I called Dr. Harper, the local doctor my sister recommended. He wasn't available that day, but his associate, Dr. Pennypacker, would be over shortly. Jotting down his name, I wondered if his forbears had been extremely thrifty people. I didn't ask. When he dropped by later, I was comforted to see that he was very personable and efficient, thoroughly understanding our predicament. After a brief examination and the inevitable penicillin shot, he wrote out a prescription and left, assuring us that there was nothing to worry about. My patients would be up and about in a couple of days, he said. The patients did survive and were up and about in a short time as the doctor promised.

Finally, the big day we had been working so hard for arrived. Although not all the work was completed, the immediate essentials were finally in place and functioning in the basement, including indoor plumbing and a temporary coal-burning heater. A new, efficient oil burning furnace was already on order. It was actually time to MOVE IN! On moving day, I hurried the boys off to school and started rounding up our belongings. It wasn't too difficult because, out of necessity, our simple life had been very regimented and orderly. Also, for the past few months, we had been literally living out of our boxes and suitcases. After a few trips to the basement with carloads from the cabin, we were moved into our new home... such as it was. Granted, it wasn't the new home we once dreamed of, but it was still home, and it was ours! None of us shed any tears upon moving out of the cracker box at the motel that had given me a good case of claustrophobia for some time. We went from one extreme to the other. The basement looked huge by comparison with its six big rooms.

The living room looked like a warehouse, packed with uncrated furniture that had arrived a few days earlier. Everything appeared to be in excellent condition as far as I could see, and for that I was thankful. The invoice from the moving company was exactly twice the estimate we had received some months before—of course—just like all the other bills we were receiving. Storage fees for the furniture had run the tab up considerably. When added to the monthly rent for our tiny motel room, the cost of our thrilling sojourn thus far was depressingly pricey—all for the privilege of being squeezed into that tiny space for four months. But then, our family had never been closer.

We spent the first few hours in our new home just wandering around aimlessly, a little dazed, poking into this box and that one with stupid expressions on our faces. Where to begin? Building materials were stacked in every corner. We needed to get organized and develop some semblance of order. I made a special effort to settle our kitchen and the bedrooms so that we could all feel like we were really home again. Fortunately, the kitchen was large enough for our small kitchen table that easily accommodated the five of us. Herman would have made a good architect. Having the large kitchen was important at that time because the dining room wouldn't be ready for awhile yet. I found the boxes with my pots and pans, and I unpacked dishes and put them away in the beautiful cupboards Herman and Dad Wilson had installed. The refrigerator was now plugged in, but the stove wasn't hooked up yet. I would have to rely on an electric hot plate for the time being. But we would manage just fine. After those long months in that one-room cabin, I was in paradise now, and anything and everything was now much easier to deal with.

Modern living is complicated by confusion and routine struggles in spite of all the modern conveniences, time-saving gadgets and inventions to make life "easier". But life is still what you make it. Fate has a way of stepping in once in awhile and dealing out "surprises", but so much depends on what the individual does with what he or she is dealt. We all watch for the latest improvements in radios, appliances, cars and modern homes with new trends in design; and so many of us get so preoccupied with this that we overlook the happiness around us, just waiting to be recognized and taken. Simple, uncomplicated happiness is always there for the taking if you bother to notice it. You don't even have to hunt for it. It will find *you*.

The thing that impressed Herman and me the most about Montana was that huge expanse of western sky. We loved it! We drew much needed encouragement and a strong sense of freedom from the endless, uninterrupted reach of the sky that seemed to tell our spirits that we could go on as far as we dared. And God was always there, standing by with a clear view of His entire kingdom. I have often thought about the fact that this same sky, the same sun and moon, had seen many ages come and go, many generations of people, each with their own particular problems, struggles, calamities and joys, and each with their own miracles whether or not they were witnessed. These notions often pass through my mind when I take my walks through the countryside at the end of a day. I've always received great comfort and peace walking or riding along some little side road in the country, talking with God, away from the confusion and bustling routine of daily living, alone with my quiet thoughts as the day's pace settles down.

In spite of all the chaos and the novelty of living "down under", our first night in our own home was a happy one. We felt very secure and content with our familiar worldly possessions around us once more, and in such spacious quarters. This was to be the first phase of our new home in that big state that held so much promise for us, Montana, the treasure state. We honestly felt that it was not only the foundation of a future house, but the foundation of a new, exciting future for all of us. That first night in our underground haven brought to all of us a sound, peaceful night of sleep.

Morning came with its invigorating clear, cold air. With revitalized energy, we rolled up our sleeves and made good use of that last precious week before Christmas. There was so much to be done that we hardly knew what to do first. Bravely, we tackled the "front end" of the house which was to be our living and dining rooms. It had no ceiling at this point. Innumerable obstacles blocked our path. The balance of our furniture, carpets, lamps, and stacks of crates and barrels were all crowded right in the center of our "working zone". In order to install insulation plus the large 4' x 8' sheets of Celotex, we had to stand on improvised platforms made by placing heavy planks on sawhorses. No one can imagine the irksome chore of moving our heavy, bulky furniture and boxes from one spot to another as our work area changed. In spite of my "generous" figure, I became very adept at crawling up and down from floor to platform while balancing an awkward, pliant sheet of Celotex above my head. I felt like a circus performer.

Dad Wilson came to our rescue once again with his saw and hammer. He was just as determined as we were to have some semblance of order out of all this disarray by Christmas. He walked in with his tools in hand and shouted, "Let's get going!" His experience in carpentry gave us many timely ideas and suggestions for badly needed shortcuts. Herman and Dad were installing a beautiful knotty pine wainscot on the walls of the living-dining area. The wall above the wainscot would be painted Celotex. The irony here was that I had wanted a recreation room all my life. We had owned nice homes with basements, but never got around to finishing the play room I had dreamed about. This time we would have the recreation room already built in the basement, but no house upstairs just yet! Now I could dream about the house instead of the rec room. I think change is good.

The interior construction continued at a hectic pace during the week. The day before Christmas, I demanded that Herman connect my electric stove. This had become a necessity. With a great deal of reluctance, he put his hammer down, interrupted what he was working on, and tackled *my* priority. Christmas cookies are such a tradition in our home, that to be without them would be a terrible disappointment for the children—and their mother. The electrical installation was completed in short order and done well, as usual for Herman. I said I was going to make "a few" cookies, but when I listed all the old favorites before beginning, I realized there would be *more* than a few batches. I love to bake, and when it's something special like Christmas cookies, I really have fun! Christmas Eve day, I baked from morning 'til night, filling the air with tantalizing odors that distracted the busy men in the front of the house. "Snitched samples" disappeared regularly as each new batch was taken from the oven. Herman said, "Now I *know* I'm home again," departing from the kitchen whistling... with a handful of cookies.

Pandemonium mixed with anxiety continued to reign as we all hurried to finish jobs we felt we couldn't complete in time, but we kept trying anyway. I wanted to put the tree up by late afternoon of Christmas Eve. All of a sudden, I thought "What tree?" In all the chaos and haste to be ready for Christmas, we had overlooked that particular errand... buying a Christmas tree! I sat down heavily in the nearest chair. What now? Coincidence or miracle, something happened in the next moment that was unforgettable! I heard someone coming down the stairs, someone big with heavy boots tromping down on the wooden treads. It was Uncle Bill (my sister's husband). With his timely arrival, our problem was solved. He was carrying a tree… yes, a tree, and the cutest little tree you ever did see!

"Can you folks use this? We used it at our lodge party last night and I hate to throw it away! Thought maybe you've been too busy to go out shopping for one, so I'd just check with you and…"

Could we use it? Our exuberant shouts of unbridled joy and my spontaneous hug were all the thanks he needed. Our temporary anxiety, relieved by Bill's very thoughtful gesture, made this the most beautiful Christmas tree we ever had.

At about 4:30 on Christmas Eve, Herman and Dad were still hammering feverishly on the homestretch of the knotty pine wainscot when I shouted, "That's enough! We are going to lay the rugs, place the furniture and decorate the tree whether you are finished or not, or there will be no Christmas!"

The hammering sounds fell silent. It didn't take much persuading for the family to fall into line with my ultimatum. The boys had patiently hovered and waited in the background, of which there was plenty, all day. I realized then how good they had been, playing quietly in their room most of the time, thoughtfully staying out from underfoot with all the work in progress in my kitchen and the front area of the house. Now, hammers, boxes of nails and boards were stacked neatly on one side of the dining area, and Grandpa helped Herman unroll our big living room rug and pad. The "unrolling" unveiled at least a half bushel of moth crystals that had been placed there by the warehouse where our furniture had been stored. Their generous precaution against moth damage was verified by the overpowering odor that invaded the entire basement. It was so strong that everyone began coughing and gasping. Oddly enough, Dad decided it was time to leave, and he seemed very much in a hurry. With the promise that he would be right back, Herman got the car out and took my carpenter-father home.

No sooner had the door closed when I called the boys together. "Okay, it's six o'clock, boys. Let's see what we can do before your dad gets back." That was all I had to say. With a shout of unified approval, they pitched in. They lifted, shoved, carried and worked like little men. We settled the living room in a matter of minutes, and then started on the dining room. We unrolled that rug, and again went through the odiferous job of disposing of the moth crystals. We set the table and chairs in place, shoved the heavy buffet against one wall, and even put the lace tablecloth and candles on just as Herman walked in. Soft lights, rugs and quickly arranged furniture had transformed the front room of this basement into a home in less than an hour. Why, this looked positively elegant as the lamplight reflected warmly off the knotty pine paneling and cast a golden glow throughout the room. Herman sank into his favorite old upholstered rocker with tears in his eyes. We were all quiet as we sat in our favorite chairs and sofa for a few minutes, feeling very humble and very grateful.

With all the cookie sampling, no one was very hungry, but I prepared a light supper while the rest of the family unpacked books and placed them in the new built-in bookshelves. It was a real effort to force the food down at that meal, something I can't say very often. But it was wasted effort for me to prepare even that light meal, with Herman and I nearly exhausted, and the boys' patience suddenly supplanted by excitement to "get going" on decorating the tree. While Herman stabilized the tree in a stand, I hunted for the ornaments, which was like looking for the proverbial needle in the haystack. After looking in vain through all the boxes in the utility room yet to be unpacked, I became a little panicky. I began to wander on an aimless search with a silent prayer on my lips when I accidentally noticed a collection of boxes marked "fragile", odds and ends neatly stacked in the shower stall, of all places. The ornaments were at the very bottom of the stacks... of course!

With amazing coordination and efficiency, and a little supervision, my three elves finished the tree in record time. The boys had not forgotten the thrill and excitement of decorating the Christmas tree. For some time, we had allowed them to take part in this ritual, and the great moment had arrived. Then finally, the table lamps were turned off and Lynn was given the honor of flipping the switch to light the tree.

With the tree lights glowing and reflecting off the colorful ornaments, the happy little faces staring at the spectacle that never loses its fascination, and the sweet harmony of hallowed Christmas carols filling the room, Christmas had finally arrived... and it arrived beautifully! All the tribulations of the laborious week and the hectic day simply dissolved. Peace, love and joy for Him whose birthday we celebrated permeated our spacious, new home.

Christmas had finally arrived!

I carefully placed the holiday table decorations and lit the tall, red candles. With great pride, I was arranging the traditional festive cookies on huge glass torte plates when I was startled to hear voices in the entrance landing at the top of the stairs. It was my sister, Helen, and her husband, Bill. They had come to see what they could do, feeling sorry for what they expected to be the complete disarray and construction clutter that Bill had seen when he'd brought the tree to us earlier in the afternoon. What they discovered was a very happy family enjoying Christmas Eve in a lovely home setting. They stood looking into the room in obvious amazement, their mouths literally agape. Bill kept saying, "It can't be! It just cannot be! This is miraculous! You people are incredible! Well... well, Merry Christmas, everybody!"

CHAPTER NINE
Montana Blizzard Season

After the relaxing holiday break that was richly deserved, we all felt revitalized and ready to get back to business. Many jobs still remained to be done. That of course turned out to be an understatement! As I sit before my typewriter in our basement remembering that period, I know there was a lot more to accomplish than we ever bargained for. Like most people, we had typically underestimated the amount of time and work required for tasks we had not done before. I just glanced over at the electric desk clock and noticed a little ant that had somehow found its way under the glass face of the clock. It is madly scurrying around the dial of the clock, seemingly looking for a way out, lost and disoriented. The second hand goes around and around, sweeping the little ant out of its way as it passes. How true to life that is! We are all in such a hurry to reach the goals we have set, but if we take a wrong turn somewhere, time just pushes us out of its way as it goes by. Time waits for no one.

Speaking of time, it didn't matter what time of day or night we passed the greedy little coal burner, we had to feed it. It always needed coal. It had an insatiable appetite! With the arrival of the very cold weather, it was almost a twenty-four hour job to keep the little heater fired up. When the wooden forms used for the basement's concrete walls were removed, Herman cleverly used them to construct a temporary shelter for our car and for extra storage space. We kept our coal supply at the back of this shed. It was located only a short distance from the house, but on cold, windy days when the mercury dipped to twenty below zero and even lower, it seemed like five times the distance to go and fill the coal bucket. We were never completely warm and cozy until our oil burner was installed a couple of months after we moved down in. But, more about that episode later.

Another convenience we often take for granted is hot water. I kept an old boiler on the stove filled with water all the time. I remembered this practice from that summer cottage back in Wisconsin. This was used for dishes, baths and daily cleaning chores. We had to revert to the old fashioned style of bathing… once a week, wash tub style. One advantage of enduring a very cold winter was that nobody got very sweaty. The bad news was that we needed more hot water in cold weather. It took all day to heat enough water for one bath, so it took all week for the family to take baths, one turn at a time. This long, drawn out ritual had a definite influence on our budget-juggling decision to install an eighty gallon electric water heater, the one essential we hadn't been able to take care of initially.

One by one, the water heater and remaining plumbing fixtures on back order arrived, awaiting installation by Herman the Plumber to save a few dollars. I don't recall how many dollars we saved, but that was our intent, and I'm sure it was a considerable amount. Herman's fine work was so superior to any of the locally available talent that he would have done the work himself even if money wasn't a factor. It always took him a lot longer, what with his day job and his compulsion for perfection, but it was almost always flawless when the job was done. When all the indoor plumbing was completed, including the large shower stall, we felt very rich indeed, considering the way we were living only a couple of months earlier.

I was even happier when our water softener arrived and was finally added to the water system. The water was so hard in this locality that it turned some of the best soaps on the market into scum. With the cold weather, the low humidity and the hard water, my hands were so cracked and grimy by this time that they didn't look like they belonged to me anymore. They were more like those of an aging scrub woman. Even my feet would be more aptly described as hoofs. I wondered what it must have been like for the pioneer women in these parts. My first loads of laundry took forever in the washing machine before the plumbing system was improved, due to the lack of hot water and soft water. I had to wash and rinse, wash and rinse constantly. It seemed like I was doing the wash all day long almost every day. The tub had to be emptied and rinsed and emptied again after each load. This left me with a back shaped like a question mark, and a questionable disposition to match it.

In February of 1949, about a month after the holidays, the oil burning furnace that had been back-ordered finally arrived. The freight men delivering it agreed reluctantly to bring the crates down the stairs, but they sure did plenty of heaving and shoving and scraping and cursing in the process. After going a short distance down the stairway, they suddenly realized that the crated burner unit was too large to get through the lower doorway. They couldn't continue down, and they couldn't ease it back up. Terrific! They had to uncrate the unwieldy thing right where it was. It was so cumbersome and tightly jammed that they couldn't budge it. After a lot of tugging and pulling, heavily laced with colorful commentary (the air was blue), they finally removed enough crating material to coax the beast down to the foot of the stairs, where it promptly wedged itself between the bottom step and the top of the door jamb. They pushed and pulled, cussed and pleaded, sweat trickling from their faces in streams. Just when I decided we would have to dismantle the entire doorway, the stubborn burner unit slid through with a lurch like a cork popping out of a wine bottle, cracking off half of the bottom stair tread as it went. And this was only the first container of the delivery! Box after box of piping, ductwork, registers, cold air returns and the furnace housing followed. The heavy furnace parts and burner unit were left in the central utility room, which thankfully was just inside the bottom entrance. But there wasn't enough room for the rest of the materials there, so we pushed the dining room table to one side and stacked everything else in my dining room where it was destined to stay for some weeks as the laborious installation dragged on.

The blueprints and diagrams for the furnace installation had preceded the delivery by several days, so Herman had already studied and was well versed on the art of installing an oil burner and associated ductwork, etc. Day after day, night after night in his spare time, the parts were meticulously assembled. That's the way Herman always works: meticulously. I have already mentioned his cheese sandwich assembly operation—meticulous. There was enough piping for both the basement and the future upstairs. We were still very optimistic then. After the assembly work came the tough part. Herman patiently hacked and sawed through partitions, and bored holes through 2 x 4s and 4 x 10s. He had been very emphatic that all the supporting beams were sturdily engineered for the big home we were planning to build above the basement, and he was satisfied to discover that his orders and plans were carried out to the letter. With no standard sheet metal tools to work with, but using his experience, ingenuity and a lot of old fashioned grunt and groan, the job was finally completed. I was convinced that he had installed the best looking set of pipes, ducts and registers a person could find anywhere!

The last part of the job, but not the least part, was installing the combination timer clock and thermostat. Another major milestone had been reached. The little overworked coal heater was disconnected, and a shiny, new flue elbow was connected between the new furnace and the main chimney. The shutoff valve on the big fuel oil tank was turned on. That tank had previously been set in place and filled before the roof was built because of its size and weight. Now the big moment had arrived, and I was granted the thrilling privilege of switching on this big, modern oil furnace. There was no drum roll, no trumpet fanfare, just an anxious silence of anticipation. Frankly, I admit to being a little apprehensive and a bit fearful of the outcome. Would it work smoothly, or would the darned thing blow up in our faces? We had quite an audience for the big event, as the entire family including Grandpa and Grandma looked on from a safe distance, waiting tensely. I took a deep breath, squeezed my eyes shut tightly and flicked the switch. There was a slight "fooomp" sound, a low, spontaneous rumble, and the soft whine of a fan starting up as this heating marvel began to do its job. From the very beginning, it functioned exactly as it was supposed to. Why would I ever think it wouldn't? It not only dispersed heat evenly around our entire home, but it radiated hope and security. It was another big step in the continuing slow process of building our own home. Herman was rewarded by many compliments and hugs for his fine job, as well as the satisfying pride that his own work was operating with perfection. As always, I was so proud of him, and I continue to marvel at his endless skills and abilities.

The new furnace couldn't have been installed any too soon. No sooner had we switched it on than the big snow arrived, as if holding back until we were warm, snug and ready. When I say "the big snow" arrived, I don't mean the light dusting of white powder we had already seen, but the *big snow*! The first snowfall is always the prettiest. We woke up the morning after the grand furnace ceremony to see every one of our twelve big window wells filled with snow, "the pretty stuff". We might have slept the clock around had it not been for our faithful little alarm clock. Since our windows were all completely covered with snow, it was as dark as pitch in the basement. We all dressed warmly and turned out with shovels. After two hours of hard work, clearing out all the window wells and shoveling a clear path on the long driveway, we didn't appreciate the pristine snowfall quite as much as we did before we started our shovel brigade. Still, we congratulated ourselves on a job well done as we put away the shovels and prepared to "go to town" to stock up on much needed groceries and supplies. Herman climbed into the car, stepped on the starter and got nothing more than a sluggish growl in response. This was to be one of the first of many "sit down strikes" performed by our faithful old car. Our local garage mechanic made a pretty penny on towing us this particular winter, until we learned about a marvelous device called a head bolt heater. I don't understand how it works, but it sure seemed to help.

The boys had a mile or two to walk to school, so I packed three hearty lunches every morning. The thermometer hugged twenty below and lower on a regular basis. A good stretch of open country between us and the town had no buildings or trees affording protection from the ever-present, biting winds. As I waved goodbye to my three little sons as they trudged down the highway, I felt a twinge of pity. But I soon dismissed that feeling, realizing that they were strong and healthy and would soon get used to it, just like their school mates. They were bundled up like small mummies, breathing out clouds of frosty vapor. Dickie's worn out joke was, "Look Mom! I'm dusty inside!" Back in Wisconsin, a few blocks of zero weather would bring my youngest home in tears. But not here in Montana! That surprised me. Outside of an occasional "Gee, but it's really cold outside", I heard few complaints.

During one of our very cold nights in the early part of winter, I was awakened suddenly and rudely with a start and sat straight up in bed. I heard a loud report, almost like the sound of a heavy gun. Then I heard it again, and again. After almost fifteen years of married life, I learned that it is nearly impossible to awaken my hubby at night once he has slipped into a deep slumber, especially when he had been working so hard. But this night, I gave out one loud bellow, "HERMAN!" There was enough distress in my voice to rouse him from his dormant state. As I was about to explain my reason for alarm, he heard the same loud *crack*! Somehow, he knows most of the answers to even the strangest of questions. His powers of observation, plus a memory like an elephant, enable him to talk about anything and everything knowledgeably, a trait I'm not blessed with. He explained that it was the green lumber in the roof joists and floor planking overhead that were contracting with the extreme cold. He said that noise would diminish when the lumber became better seasoned. I didn't know what kind of seasoning I needed to sprinkle on that wood, but I would have given worlds to know. I never quite got used to the sound of those sharp gunshot-like cracks that were to continue on and off through much of that first winter, mostly in the late night hours when everything was so quiet and still. They unnerved me and disturbed my sleep. In no time at all, Herman was sound asleep again, but it takes some time for me to relax after being awakened so abruptly. So, I lay there, musing about the happenings of the past few months and enjoying foolish thoughts.

We had given ourselves little time for recreation, going out to dinner or a movie, or even visiting. There was always too much work to be done. However, when Dad's birthday came around, we were invited to dinner at the folks' tiny apartment, along with Bill and Helen. Our combined offspring, Helen's five and the three of ours, were too many for the small apartment; so they were excluded from the birthday celebration. But, to appease the grandchildren, Grandma had wisely invited them to a pancake supper later in the week. Grandpa's pancakes were legendary among his grandchildren. Helen's youngsters referred to them as "the best in the West"!

I had fun looking forward to the dinner. It will always be a treat for me to go out for a meal I haven't cooked, whether it is a four course dinner or just a hamburger. The date arrived along with new snow, building huge drifts around the house mounting to several feet in height, practically burying the basement and towering above it like small mountains in several places. Our car was isolated in the buried makeshift garage, so Bill called for us in his big reliable Suburban that he claimed could plow through anywhere. Luckily, we live on the highway, so we were always sure of remaining in contact with the town and civilization, unlike a few of our neighbors. It was the first time in quite awhile that we'd had any reason to spruce up our appearances, so we dressed in our very best for the occasion. After all, this was February already and we had arrived in this little town in September, so it was high time that we indulged ourselves a little bit. It's remarkable what putting on "your best duds" will do for your self-esteem. We strutted around our underground "mansion" as we waited for our "chauffeur". The flattery showered on us by our boys would have elated Mr. and Mrs. America themselves. What a real pleasure it is to have a family that bolsters your ego once in awhile!

A horn on the highway honked. It was time to go. With last minute instructions to the boys, and hurried farewells, we went up the stairs and out into the great white open spaces. After sizing up the great white drift I would have to bridge without benefit of snowshoes, I lost a little of my self-confidence. Herman read my mind.

"Oh, it's okay, honey. Just walk slow. Don't be afraid. You can make it just fine!" he encouraged.

Reassured, I started out. Then I felt the snow give a little under my weight. I got panicky and started to run. Big mistake! That was just what I should *not* have done! I partially disappeared... straight down... up to my waist! After much effort, and very unladylike sprawling, I managed to free myself with Herman's assistance, who couldn't have kept a straight face if his life depended on it. That plus the hysterical laughter from the waiting Suburban on the highway, was enough to give me a grouchy disposition for several minutes. I was angry and humiliated, to put it mildly. As I sat in the vehicle, hat askew, shoes full of melting snow, wet from top to bottom, I was in no mood for friendly chatter. But all was soon forgotten as we greeted Mother and Dad, and soon basked in their warm hospitality. The good food, companionship and conversation were a tonic for me after the struggles of the past few months. The sun came out as the clouds dissipated, and the snow looked beautiful, even to me. Helen and Bill had to leave early, so with Dad's promise to drive us home later, we stayed.

Later, when it was time to leave, the evening was so clear and beautiful that we decided to walk home, a distance equivalent to only about eight city blocks. Realizing that it was quite cold, we insisted that Herman tie his scarf around his head and ears, which he did only after much persuasion. We started out with enthusiasm and light hearts. The air was clear and fresh, only we didn't realize how "fresh"! The first block we enjoyed immensely. It was invigorating. By the end of the second block, I found myself very short of breath and breathing through my mouth, or should I say "gasping"! This was the sneakiest cold I had ever experienced. At first, you aren't cold at all. You can barely feel it. Then, the next thing you know, you can't feel *anything*! Herman kept telling me to breathe through my nose. I couldn't breathe, period! Block by block, it kept getting colder and colder. This was ridiculous! We only lived a little more than half a mile from the folks' apartment; not like it was a huge distance. By this time, it was pitch dark. We lived on the very edge of town, as I mentioned before, and that night it might have been on the edge of nowhere. We couldn't see but a few feet ahead of us. There were no streetlights to guide us or illuminate our stumbling footsteps. The slippery snow underfoot made it difficult to get any traction, and made walking treacherous and painfully slow. I was practically convinced that night that even the stars had been turned off, for we hadn't noticed the overcast that had crept in, making the night even darker. It seemed like the longest hike in my memory.

Somehow in the dark, we found our way to the highway that passed by our underground hideaway, now hidden under mounds of snow. That meant we had only one or two more blocks to walk. Encouraging each other, we stumbled on, trying to keep each other upright with the precarious, slippery footing. I definitely have sizable legs, but that night, I felt neither legs nor feet. Finally, even my hands and face seemed to drift away from my body. After what seemed an eternity, we saw the dim outline of our car shelter. That left only one more snowdrift to surmount. Wonder of wonders, I scaled that small mountain with little or no effort, perhaps because I had no feet or legs!

Our modest "dugout" home never looked so beautiful to me, nor felt so warm! As we opened the door at the bottom of the stairs, we faced a huge banner the boys had made and tacked up in the utility room that read, "HOME SWEET HOME". Similar signs and messages were posted all over the house, a custom of long standing when any of us was away for any length of time. In that somewhat isolated, underground haven on the outskirts of civilization, the boys must have felt we were absent for quite awhile. I was very glad they were all asleep, because they had gone to bed picturing us having a wonderful time (which we did have... before our Antarctic adventure), and probably envisioned us returning home full of laughter and light banter as we usually did after a rare night out.

Herman was literally blue with the cold, and he paced back and forth the full length of our home, trying to stir up some circulation in his limbs that had practically ceased. I staggered into the bedroom with one thought in mind. I just *had* to get something warm on my legs and feet. With great effort, I peeled off my nylons. Yes, I mean "peeled off", because they were actually frozen to my legs! They came off like large strips of adhesive tape! When we were beginning to feel a little warmth in our extremities, Herman checked the thermometer just outside the entrance door. It registered thirty degrees below zero! No wonder we felt like we'd been on an arctic trek! Since that memorable night, we have learned when to take long walks and how to dress appropriately for that winter weather in Montana. We gulped down some hot coffee and went to bed under a pile of woolen blankets.

After a short period of deep sleep, I was awakened by the continuous blaring of a horn. My subconscious mind was trying to figure out why anyone would sit out in the country in the middle of a bitter cold night and blow their horn. With a start, my mind cleared and I realized it was *our* car's horn. It must be an electrical short or something. With great effort, I shook Herman awake. I didn't have to say a word. He said, "Oh, good grief! That's my car! There must be a short!"

He grabbed his boots and donned his heavy "sheep liner" and dashed out of the house. He must have been a comical sight as he practically flew over the top of the basement roof like Dasher and Dancer, mounting a huge snow drift, his heavy coat clutched tightly around the lightweight pajamas. I don't know when I've known him to cover so much territory so fast. It was only a matter of seconds before the horn stopped. We both laughed heartily, visualizing the sight of Herman surfing the high snowdrifts to the garage at two in the morning in his odd costume, barely touching the snow.

It wasn't easy to get to town during the winter months. The sudden, vicious blizzards would strike without warning. Along with the weather warnings, the local radio station would also broadcast special messages to remote ranches, telling them to pick up their school children on a designated highway or road at a specified location within an hour or half hour's time. That was a new wrinkle for me. When the storms were particularly severe, it could be days or even weeks before these ranchers were able to plow their way through the huge drifts to a main road. Often, the winds would cause their private roads to drift shut as fast as they tried to plow them open, and they would remain isolated.

One night during one of these blizzards, I was scheduled to attend a meeting of the local Women's Club in town. When I saw the severity of the storm, I immediately called to tell them that I wouldn't be in. The lady I called simply laughed and told me that no one stays home in Sidney because of a blizzard. She arranged to have a local mechanic friend pick me up on the highway. I was to listen for three short beeps of his horn, and then get out to the road. In a short while, I heard the horn's signal, and Herman led me out to the highway, with me hanging on to the end of a broom handle while he grasped the other end. It sounds silly, I know, and it was only a short distance. But the wind was so strong and the blowing snow was so heavy, that it was the only way I could reach the highway without stumbling and falling with the treacherous footing. After I reached the car safely, we waited while Herman struggled back to the basement. When he turned the porch light off and on, we knew he was back safely, and we headed for town. The same routine was repeated much later in the evening when I came back. The obliging mechanic was a native Montanan and didn't even talk about the weather. This stuff was just normal, "old hat" to him! The little plow on his sturdy truck did a very efficient job of getting us through the drifting snow. Since then, I no longer use weather as an excuse to stay away from a previously made engagement.

CHAPTER TEN
Herman Leaves Home

When Herman first applied for his new job, they told him that it would be necessary to go to Minneapolis as part of his job training. The company Herman worked for was a dealership for the largest manufacturer in the world of tractors and earth moving equipment. All of the dealer's technical employees had to be factory trained, so Herman was scheduled to spend two weeks at the Minnesota factory, learning to be more expert in diesel mechanics. I have always said my hubby was amazing. He can fix anything from the biggest bulldozer to the tiniest lady's watch and make either one hum like new! I was very proud of him, but I dreaded his leaving. We had never been separated more then 24 hours since the day we were married. That probably sounds silly in this age of frequent separations. Nevertheless, neither of us was too enthused about this trip, even though Herman is always excited about opportunities to learn something new. I read in some dumb magazine once that it's a good idea for couples to take separate vacations. But my husband and I are so happy when we're together that we could never accept that philosophy.

The night he told me he was leaving in a few days, my heart skipped a couple beats. Together, this life had been challenging enough. But alone, buried in the ground under this immense blanket of snow at the farthest edge of town in mid-winter, I felt that I just couldn't take it. But that's life. Sometimes we just have to do what needs to be done, like it or not. The day of his departure, Herman had to leave at four o'clock in the morning. What an hour to leave! We telephoned the local cab driver. A woman answered. Herman asked if he could have a cab to catch the early morning bus that would take him to Glendive, which was the nearest train station. She said, "No! Well, just a minute." Then he overheard her say to someone on her end, "Some damn fool wants a cab at four in the morning!" Herman hung up the phone without waiting for a further answer, muttering that he hoped he would never meet that woman.

In desperation, he called Bill very apologetically, explaining his encounter with the little cab company. Bill, bless his heart, agreed to give Herman a lift. How quiet the house became after he was gone! In spite of the early hour, Herman had kissed each of the boys as he had promised. The big lump in my throat was just about to give way to tears when I heard a muffled sound in the boys' room. Opening the door, I discovered they were all doing what I wanted to do, sobbing as though their hearts would break. I suddenly realized that they had never been without their daddy either. As is so often the case, I could have sat down and had a good cry with them. But under the circumstances, I cleared my throat and scolded, "I thought you big boys told Dad you would take care of me while he was gone, and you are letting him down the minute his back is turned!" The effect was immediate. The water works shut down and there were no more tears. That sure snapped me out of my pity party, too. I actually went back to bed and right to sleep… for a whole hour. After that hour, I lay awake listening to all sorts of imagined noises, and I was happy to just get up a couple hours early.

Before Herman left, he made sure the car was winterized and in running order. He even set the car out on the front street, so glamorously named "Sunset Boulevard". But this was Sidney, Montana, not Hollywood; so at this stage of development, Sunset Boulevard was either frozen solid, or a rutted, muddy or dusty road, depending on the season. And our fine coach parked along this glamorous boulevard was a '39 Dodge. You get the picture. Herman had left the car on that particular street because it connected to the highway and it was the only one in the neighborhood that wasn't drifted over. The other streets were impassable. The day after he left, being Sunday, I decided to take the boys for a ride. We bundled up, got into the car… and then got right out of the car again. It refused to start or show any sign of life. This turned out to be a daily ritual for a time, and then we gave up. The car just sat there for the whole two weeks Herman was gone. I almost wept to see our faithful old car sitting out there, lifeless on the deserted, wind swept "boulevard". It's peculiar how sentimental a person can get over an old car, and yet simultaneously look forward to the day when you can have a new one.

… our faithful old car sitting lifeless on the wind-swept "boulevard"

My first Sunday alone started out in a hectic manner. About nine-thirty in the morning, Bill telephoned and asked if I had the radio on. I replied that I didn't, and he said he'd just heard something about the train Herman was on. I sat down abruptly with a queasy feeling in the pit of my stomach and turned on the radio for some news. After a long, anxious period of time, I finally learned that the train he was supposed to board Saturday at a station more than fifty miles south of our little town was twelve hours overdue. My first reaction was being irked that we had to get up in the middle of a cold winter night just so Herman could wait for twelve hours until his train arrived. Then, I pictured the poor man sitting in a depot all day, or wandering aimlessly up and down the streets of the huge metropolis of Glendive. The actual picture was quite different, however. Herman was sitting in a window seat of a slow "milk train" on his way to Minneapolis that whole time. His train took twice as long to get there as the fast "streamliner" would have, but it was still better than the picture I had in mind. So you see, woman-like, I was fussing and fuming while, man-like, he was enjoying an easy, comfortable trip, getting to his destination slow but sure.

A few days later, after watching the boys walk down the cold, wind-swept highway to school, I dived into my daily routine, trying to overcome waves of loneliness that threatened to engulf me. It was always so quiet after the children's departure. There were times when I welcomed the quiet, but not this day. The sky looked heavy and foreboding and it grew darker by the minute. The wind rose to a terrifying velocity. Wind has always frightened me, especially when accompanied by a storm. My terror grew with the mounting strength of the wind. Had I been able to look out a window, perhaps I wouldn't have been as frightened. As it was, alone in the basement with no view but what I could see looking upward, the sounds plus my very active imagination produced near hysteria! I didn't have to be a native of this country to know that there was a rip-roaring blizzard on its way.

Shortly after noon, Mother called to tell me that Dad had tried to get to me, but there wasn't a car on the road brave enough to drive out on the highway, so he turned back. The boys were instructed to stop off at Grandpa and Grandma's place after school if the weather was bad, so they were safe. "Never mind; not to worry" Mother said, a little too nonchalant I thought. "You are nice and warm where you are, so just stay put. We'll keep the boys here in town with us overnight, so everything is fine." I didn't mean to appear ungrateful, but I couldn't appreciate being in a state of isolation, even if I were nice and warm. I made an immediate decision to get into town somehow. I was so determined not to be alone that my mind completely blocked out that fearsome thirty-below-zero night that Herman and I walked home after Dad's birthday celebration. Somehow, my brain malfunctioned and I didn't connect that earlier experience with the howling blizzard outside on this day, maybe because it was daytime. There are times when it is all right for a person to be impulsive and strong-willed. This wasn't one of those times.

The following disclosure may come as startling to some of my closest friends, but I *do* own a pair of slacks that are buried in the darkest recesses of my closet… for emergency only! Hardly anyone in the world has ever seen me in anything but a dress. I'm definitely not the pants type, but this was clearly an emergency! So, I cast my pride to the winter wind and donned the slacks. I pulled on an extra pair of my husband's woolen hunting socks, two sweaters, an old coat, two pair of mittens and two scarves around my head. That, along with my little overnight bag, comprised my traveling gear. I knew if I called the folks, they would only worry themselves sick until I got there. So, I took one final look at my warm, snug home, and was on my way.

It was quite a struggle to open and close the outside door. It was no easy task to even reach the highway; but this time I didn't sink in. The snow was too hard packed and frozen solid. Facing the wind's icy blast for even a few yards was bitter punishment. All I needed now was a dog sled to complete the picture. It wasn't funny then, but I can laugh now as I envision myself trundling down the highway through that ugly blizzard, bundled up to twice my size. Starting out, my main fear was tipping over. Getting vertical again might prove to be very difficult, and I might rock myself to sleep in the process. Visibility was almost zero. I couldn't turn back and I could hardly make much headway moving forward against the heavy wind. The usually busy highway was completely deserted. It seemed like I was in an eerie, white world with me as its sole inhabitant. I finally reached a residential neighborhood where I received some respite from the full fury of the storm, with the houses and a few trees breaking up the ferocity of the wind. I did run across our milk lady. There was no "milk man" in this town. This dedicated woman made her daily deliveries conscientiously in every kind of weather… except for those rare times when our house couldn't be reached. You see, we were at "the end of the line". I asked her for a couple quarts of milk. She tried to pretend she was not looking at a strange apparition and that I appeared to be normal to her. After staring at me for a few moments, she was shocked when she recognized who I was.

"Well where do you hail from?" she asked. When I told her I was a little frightened by the storm, she laughed and said, "You ain't seen nothin' yet!" That's getting to be a real cliché around this town. I didn't want to think about what that remark could mean, so I just forgot about the milk and staggered on in the general direction of my folks' apartment.

I finally reached my destination and gratefully stumbled down the steps. The folk's place was a half level down, but not *way* down like our place. They had normal windows they could look out of, although it was kind of like looking at the world when you were kneeling way low. Not wishing to startle my family too much by just walking in as I usually did, I rapped softly on the door. My own mother opened the door with nary a sign of recognition, and politely asked what I wanted. After a closer look, she gave a loud shriek. "RUTH!" Dad, sitting nearby, almost choked on the cigar that was practically a permanent accessory to his face. They were just as happy to see me as I was to see them. There was a great deal of chatter and rejoicing as if it were a great reunion with the theme being "the wayfaring daughter returns". The cheery welcome I received and the lazy, happy afternoon visiting with my folks gave me the lift I needed. By the time the boys arrived from school, the storm had let up to some extent, so I decided to go back home again. The roads had been plowed and Dad drove us back with little difficulty, but he protested all the way. He thought I was crazy to crawl back under the snow again, all alone on such a bad night. But home is home to me, no matter where it is, and it was beckoning to me right then because I had my boys with me. It felt as good to be home as I imagined it would, and I was perfectly content to stay there after exercising my little spirit of adventure, and having a nice visit with my folks. I was no longer afraid of the storm I had just weathered face to face.

My evenings were long with Herman away, especially after the boys went to bed. I was prone to writing long, sentimental letters every night, with a daily report thrown in. Our minds ran in the same channel, because I got just as many such letters, some silly and some serious reports on his daily sessions. I dreaded the nightly ritual of locking the doors and turning the lights out with him not being there. By reading until I reached a state of semi-consciousness, I would finally go to sleep. The empty half of the bed was a silent reminder that I was the sole "master" of the house at the time. There are times when a woman feels she could do pretty well without the male of the household. But give a woman sole charge of the household for a few weeks, and most will invariably find that the other half is quite necessary. It works both ways, though. Put a man in charge for a few days while mother takes an emergency trip, or is away visiting family, and he's more than willing to swallow all those nasty little words he uttered about how lucky the little woman is to stay at home all day.

I was cold all night, every night, and couldn't warm up until I had the extra pillow at my back, added extra layers of covers, and rested my feet on the heating pad. What a sissy, huh? One night, after fighting a headache for several hours, I got up in the dark and went to the medicine cabinet for some aspirin. Without turning the light on, against my better judgment, I fumbled around in the dark feeling for the familiar shape of the bottle. It had its own particular shape, so it was easy to find... I thought. I removed the cap and poured the tablets into my hand—except they weren't tablets—and "poured" was the appropriate word. Instead of aspirin tablets in my hand, I had the most repulsive, slimy mess one could imagine. I turned the light on, as I should have done in the first place, and discovered after a glance and a whiff that I had a nice dose of castor oil drizzling off the edge of my palm into the sink. I spent some time trying to remove the goo, but the horrible odor remained... and so did my headache. After that incident, I made sure to turn the light on first and read the label as I had been taught since childhood, never mind my nurse's training.

It was always a consolation to hear the rhythmical breathing of my sons in repose during these long winter nights. There were no immediate neighbors, and I may as well have been "out in the country', especially at night in the dead of a Montana winter. This sweet, angelic sleep of my offspring didn't always come easy, as any mother knows.

For instance, one evening, after repeated warnings to stop the giggling and whispering, I was determined to discover the source of their amusement. Such rash disobedience was fairly unusual and warranted investigation. This nighttime escapade was not raucous or loud, just a quiet undertone that went on indefinitely for several nights, regardless of my warnings of dire consequences. This night in particular, I decided to eavesdrop. Okay, so it was actually "spying". That was certainly a drastic action on my part, because spying would not be setting a very good example for my sons. Like a veteran undercover agent, I had tuned the radio in the next room to some peppy music to mask any small sounds I might make, and to help the illusion that I was really "out there". Yes, the stage was all set. I heard their prayers, kissed them all good night, and gave them the oft repeated warning, "No talking! Go to sleep!" I snapped the light switch off and closed the door. I had made sure the hall light was out so when I turned their bedroom light off, all would be dark and they couldn't see that I didn't actually leave the room when I closed the door. Very clever, I thought, congratulating myself on my covert operation.

At first, it was so quiet that I was positive that they could hear me breathing. I thought, now I've sure gotten myself into an awkward spot. Tonight, they will probably go right to sleep, and then how will I feel? Ridiculous, that's how! The silence went on and on, and I grew more despairing by the minute. I began to feel very small and ashamed of myself, and very much on the sleazy side. Finally, I heard what I'd been waiting for, the reason I had put myself in great jeopardy.

"Psssst!" came from one of them. That started the ball rolling. Jackie said, "What are you going to be tonight?"

"A Chevy pickup," Dickie answered in the darkness.

Little Lynn piped up, "I'm going to be an old 'flivver'!"

All of this illicit whispering was very quiet. Jack's Buick started with a stubborn starter, followed by an old fashioned hand crank on Lynn's flivver. Dickie got off to a smooth start. Why, these boys were experts at imitations! It must have taken quite a few rehearsals, because they sounded just like a parking lot in action. There were backfires, noisy tappets and missing spark plugs. I could hardly contain myself, I was so choked with restrained laughter. But I knew they were being disobedient, so with all the stoicism I could muster, I assumed my best poker face and turned on the light. The positions held by the offenders were frozen in suspended animation, petrified by my sudden, shocking intrusion. Their poses and facial expressions would have been enough to throw any audience into peals of hysterical laughter. The "flivver" on the upper bunk was somehow hanging by his feet, trying to discover mechanical trouble in the bedsprings. The "Chevy" was cruising with all the mastery of a seasoned driver, using one of my embroidery hoops for a steering wheel. And the "Buick" was flat on his back beneath his bed, apparently changing the oil.

There have been many times when I have had difficulty controlling my facial expression when disciplining the children. But I had never been so challenged as I was that night! It was my supreme test. I immediately shifted to my offended parent attitude, at a complete loss for any other ideas. The bewildered expressions on the faces of the culprits showed utter amazement at my magical ability to pass through a closed door. The eldest eyed me suspiciously, causing me to blush furiously. His eyes said, "You cheated!" I left the room without saying a word, and when I was beyond their hearing range, I laughed until I cried. I couldn't recall when I had ever seen anything so hilarious! It was very quiet in that room for many nights to come.

A few nights before Herman's return, I had just gone to bed and was drifting off to sleep when I heard a disturbance in the hush of the night. At first, I thought it was the oil burner kicking on. I never quite got used to the sudden rumble it made when it fired up. Until I grew more accustomed to the peculiar sound this big heating hulk gave out, especially late at night, I felt as though it was going to lumber right on into my bedroom. However, the commotion that initially startled me this night was a deep rumbling of large engines followed by the sound of men's voices, unusual in our somewhat remote location. It sounded like I was next door to a railroad switching yard. I heard one man shouting some kind of orders that reverberated across our flat roof. I may usually be a sissy, but I believe in investigating strange noises, day or night. I donned my robe and slippers and stumbled up the stairway in the dark, so as not to be conspicuous. I opened the door a crack and peered out, shivering at the icy night air that knifed through the opening. Two huge highway department trucks sat idling out on the highway, with large plows mounted to the front of each. I heard the sound of heavy chains rattling, and men shouting back and forth, but I couldn't make out what they were saying. I thought perhaps another blizzard was on the way and they were preparing for battle on the roadways. Finally, they drove off in a flurry of frosty vapors and exhaust clouds. I looked up at the sky and saw a beautiful, clear, starlit night. No storm clouds were in sight. Probably they were just comparing work orders and were on their way to clearing the roads to some snowbound ranches. Sometimes that effort took weeks before they could break through to the more remote spreads. The incident didn't represent any problem for me, but it was just one more thing that spooked me because my hubby was far away.

The next day, our section of the country experienced a Chinook, a sudden warm, dry wind that would cause unseasonable thaws. We'd had some unusually heavy snow storms, so the accumulation of snow was very deep. We have a flat roof on our basement, naturally, because it is intended to be the future first floor of the house. This provides an ideal place for water to collect and pond. Before the end of the day, practically every part of every ceiling in every room was leaking steadily. I had pails, pans, pots, mixing bowls and anything that would hold water placed on the floors of every room, as well as on the beds in both bedrooms. Just when I thought I had every leak covered, I would hear another "blop... bleep... blip..." that I had overlooked. It was endless, reminiscent of the story about the little Dutch boy and the leaking dike. Toward late afternoon, the nerve-wracking musical dripping began to let up with the lowering of the temperature. Finally by nightfall, the symphony of melodious leaks came to a halt, and I wondered if I was going to have to deal with this for the rest of the week. Where was Herman when I needed him so badly? He was almost a thousand miles away, playing with huge machines named after a crawling multi-legged worm.

I had everything that could hold water sitting on the floor of every room.

The following morning, I received my last letter from my hubby, saying that he would be home Saturday… at 2:45 AM! That was just great! He very definitely asked me not to meet him, as he might be delayed. I got to worrying about how he would get home from the bus station, knowing from experience that there were no taxis at that hour of the night for "damn fools". I called our friendly auto mechanic and had him tow the car down to his garage and have it conditioned for driving. Its "rejuvenation" cost me twelve dollars. I was told that "short trips in the cold weather" was causing the problem, and that I should drive it for longer distances once in awhile to build up the battery. I said that was just fine, but assuming I am able to get the car started in the first place, what long trip would he recommend as a good "battery builder"? He couldn't advise me on that, but he did suggest that I keep the engine running for a few hours before I went to pick up Herman… just in case. Consequently, I took my young family for a ride that evening, a rare treat after all the enforced isolation and hibernation in our underground cave. We drove up and down every street in that little town, which didn't take very long; so we did it several times. When we got home, I left the motor running for an hour.

I was very excited with the anticipation of surprising my darling. Wouldn't he be pleased to see the car from the bus window in the wee hours of the morning? I knew that would be a tremendously welcome sight for him. I kept the boys up way past their bedtime to pass the hours more quickly. When I called the depot down in Glendive, I was informed that the train would be on time. That meant that the bus connecting with the train would be on schedule and bring my sweetheart home to me as planned. I baked Herman's favorite cinnamon pecan buns, put the coffee pot on and set the table for two. How cozy that looked after seeing just one coffee cup for so long! I finally tucked the boys in bed and waited patiently for the time to leave. I intended to leave before 2:00 so I could drive the car around town for awhile to warm it up and get it in smooth running order, like the man said. While I waited, I played the radio and heard the national anthem over several stations as they signed off for the night. Then I read and dozed until it was finally time to leave. It seemed like an eternity; waiting always does.

It was a beautiful night, clear and decorated with a billion stars, but crisp and cold. I knew that the car just had to start after all the preliminary conditioning we'd gone through. Still, I held my breath as I stepped on the starter. It didn't fail me. It started right up without hesitation. With a last look at the little porch light radiating its welcome, I drove towards town. For nearly an hour I drove up and down each street until I had covered the entire town several times. I cruised back and forth on Main Street so many times that a few tipsy drunks began to eye me suspiciously, so I shifted to the darker side streets. How quiet and deserted everything looked at that hour. The whole town took on a totally different character late at night compared to its bustling, dusty appearance during the day. Five minutes before the bus was scheduled to arrive, I headed for the little hotel which served also as the bus terminal. The car was warm in spite of the bitter cold outside. I had a nice pot of hot coffee waiting on the stove at home. What a welcome this would be for a travel weary husband! The bus arrived on time, to the minute. This was almost unheard of. I could see a surprising number of people standing up in the bus, preparing to get off. I slid over and left the driver's seat free, heaving a great sigh of relief. Now someone else could share the responsibilities I had been shouldering alone. One by one, the tired passengers left the bus until the last man, not Herman, entered the hotel.

I had been so sure I would see him immediately! Maybe I missed him. How could I? I jumped out of the car and ran into the hotel. Still, no Herman! By this time there were several curious glances thrown my way. As I turned to leave, I heard a man say, "Ruth, what in the world are you doing down here this time of night?"

It was our nearest neighbor, Mr. Lilly, who lived a block down from us closer to town. He was just returning from a business trip. I couldn't keep the tears back. With a lump in my throat, I told him about my big disappointment. He quickly informed me that the train Herman took was six hours late, contrary to the information I had received from the ticket agent. But my trip was not without a purpose. This poor man had no way of getting home, and being lame, he couldn't have walked the mile even if he had to. His extreme gratitude took the sting out of my heart, though I could scarcely speak all the way home. My disappointment was almost overwhelming to me, after all the planning and waiting and setting up the surprise welcome ... almost the last straw! After dropping off my grateful passenger and parking the car, I walked cheerlessly back into the house. Turning off the porch light, I went sadly down the stairs and walked quietly into the cozy kitchen with its coffee setting for two. Tears welled up in my eyes again, and I just turned off the coffee, turned off the light and went to bed in tears.

I slept restlessly until about seven a.m., dozing off and on. I heard a lot of subdued whispering and talking just outside my bedroom door shortly after seven, and after a few timid knocks, the boys burst into the room. Suddenly they stopped in their tracks and stared in disbelief at the empty side of the bed. A hush fell over the room, and their puzzled expressions turned to me for an answer to their unspoken question, "Where is Daddy?" They all crawled into bed with me while I told them about my disappointing, futile trip in the middle of the night. My story was interrupted by the ringing of the telephone. This time, it was the voice I wanted to hear. He was at the hotel bus station.

I told Herman the car was working just fine and I would be right down to pick him up. Wouldn't you know it? The jalopy refused to start! I couldn't believe it. I guess it too was being temperamental after last night's wasted trip. After waiting for a cab for over an hour,

Herman finally arrived home. He was really beat, and he felt pretty grungy after riding in a train coach for the better part of two days. He told me they were right on schedule for most of the way until they reached the western part of North Dakota. There, the train avoided a nasty derailment by a close call, screeching to a stop only a few yards from a broken rail that was spotted just in time. They had to back up to the last little town they had passed through and waited almost six hours until the track was repaired so they could continue.

All the loneliness and troubles of the last two weeks melted away as my darling man held me close and kissed my tears of joy; and the three boys surrounded us with an enthusiastic, noisy group hug. Our family was complete again, and I felt secure and confident once more.

CHAPTER ELEVEN
The First Flood

Herman returned to work at the tractor dealership and I remained at home with my new duties as chief "drip watcher" during the mild weather days. As spring approached, the heavily packed snowfall gradually dissipated into puddles and little trickling streams, then fast running washes and even vicious flash floods here and there. The Montana spring thaw is typically a series of alternating periods of warm and cold days, so the results were not normally as disastrous as they were this particular spring. That year, 1949, the snow and ice thawed steadily, with no intermittent freezing weather to slow the growing streams.

Looking out across the great expanses of snow on every side of our sunken home, we had a growing premonition of trouble. Sometimes I heard the town people talking about the two big dams in the hills a short distance west of town. They said the dams had a pretty large capacity in their reservoirs to retain melting snow for summer irrigation; but they were built primarily of compacted earth... just plain old dirt! That worried a lot of folks, afraid the earthen walls might some day give way under the massive pressure of the water if the winter snows had been too heavy and the thaws too rapid. We had become aware that a pending disaster hovered ominously and literally above our heads, although we knew more hearsay than facts about the damns. But right now, our concerns were more immediate. The scanty "fill" placed around our house in the fall had settled and compacted with the thawing temperatures, forming a moat around the entire basement, filled to the brim with icy water. We worried about that water right next to the basement walls, but hoped it would gradually be absorbed into the ground below. Little did we realize how deep the earth froze during these long, cold Montana winters, and how long it took to thaw this deep, thick barrier that prevented the soils below from soaking up all that trapped, excess water.

Trickles of melted snow gathered into little tributaries which collected more rapidly into larger creeks that fed frigid ponds and formed new temporary lakes in the low lying areas. There were bodies of water collecting and growing larger everywhere, but with no apparent means for it to drain off. The street on the west side of our lot was not graded favorably for water to flow away from us. The drainage ditch along the highway on the north side of our property was so densely packed with ice and snow that would take many weeks of mild weather to melt. In fact, the elevated grade of the highway acted more like a dike to keep water within our land rather than away from it. I watched each day as the "moat" around our house widened to become a lake, and our house literally became a flat, charcoal-colored, tar-paper-covered island. The small, solitary structure that projected noticeably above the rising waters was the sloped stairway enclosure, our main entrance—our *only* entrance—or more critically, our *only exit!* It began to look more and more to me like the conning tower on a submarine! That metaphor was very unsettling to me because I like to open a window now and then.

One quiet, peaceful afternoon, I heard water running. I looked everywhere, but failed to find anything that even resembled the fast running water I thought I was hearing. That evening, as Herman sat in the living room reading, he also noticed the same unmistakable sound of running water. He got up and searched everywhere that running water could possibly be. But he, too, failed to find the source of the unnerving sound.

The next morning, my sister, Helen, brought her clothes over to wash, as she often did. With the large laundry-utility room at the center of the basement, I had a lot more drying space to use than she had at her house during the cold months. Helen also had more laundry to do, with a husband who worked out in the fields and five active children. Her loads were hung from every inch of available clothes line strung back and forth across the drying area, creating a heavy, humid atmosphere in the middle of the house until the clothes dried. But I didn't mind. Her laundry day gave us a good excuse to visit and keep each other up to date on our lives and our families. When she finished all the washing, she would take a little time off to relax and visit with me over a cup of coffee in our big, comfortable living room. As we sat talking, Helen remarked that she still couldn't get over how lovely and cozy it was down here, and that she often found it hard to believe that she was actually sitting in a basement. Little did we know that our lovely basement house was about to become the center of a disaster!

A few hours after Helen had left and I was alone, I noticed some water seeping onto the living room floor at the bottom of one area of an outside wall. On closer inspection, I noticed a few other small puddles forming along the edge of the floor in both the living room and the dining room. Trying to quiet the fears and panic quickly rising within me, I tried to remain calm and wipe up the offending water. About that time, I was greatly relieved to see my dad walk in. I explained my fright, which he noticed on my face as soon as he came in. If he were worried, he didn't show it, and that helped. So far, I had only noticed seepage in the "front part" of the basement, where the living and dining rooms were located.

"Don't get excited, dear. There's nothing to worry about," Dad said as he picked up a shovel and went outdoors. A few minutes later, I followed him upstairs and noticed that he was digging some drainage trenches, trying to divert the water away from the basement. When I went back downstairs, I was shocked to see water seeping into our bedroom now, which was at the opposite end of the basement from the living room. After a hasty inspection, I noticed that water was invading *every* room of the house all around its perimeter. Trying to suppress the rising panic in my voice, I called Herman at his work and explained what was happening. His aggravating attitude of indifference caught me off guard. "Well, what do you want me to do, honey? I can't just walk off the job every time I feel like it," he scolded. "It'll have to wait until I get home in a couple hours."

After he hung up, I felt a little foolish and inadequate... but for only a few moments. I heard someone rapidly running down the stairs and then the door opened. A strange little man asked if I was okay. More than a little startled, I replied that I was okay, and then asked why and who was he? A bit breathless, he explained that he was an insurance man, but he wasn't trying to sell insurance on this trip. He was called to assess damage in our area. He said our neighbor to the east of us, the Lillys, had just suffered a serious problem. His basement floor had heaved upward like a huge blister last night from the terrific pressure of the saturated soil beneath, and then exploded violently, shaking the entire house off its foundation like an earthquake. The insurance agent continued with the story of our nearest neighbor to the south of us. This very afternoon, two of his concrete block basement walls had partially caved in from the force of the drenched, expansive soils, leaving the house teetering precariously on what remained of the basement walls. The basements of both houses were flooded and both homes had to be abandoned. I wondered how blasé Herman would be now if he really knew the whole story. At this stage of the game, I was ready to faint, or simply burst into hysterics. Before leaving, the insurance man warned, "If you hear any kind of cracking noise, just run and get the heck out of here!" Very reassuring!

I ran into each room, finding the same ugly situation. The water was no longer seeping in, it was *pouring* into our home at a frightening rate! As if that weren't enough, cascades of muddy water began to belch through all of the windows high on the walls. With this additional menace, I lost all semblance of rationality. I ran upstairs screaming for help. Upon hearing me, Dad dropped his shovel and headed for town as fast as his old car could take him to look for help. The "moat" around the house had risen up to the window wells, which poured into the wells as small waterfalls and then cascaded into the house itself. In mindless desperation, I tried to catch some of the water under one window with my pail. This hysterical attempt was as hopeless as bailing out a sinking ship with a bean can!

The next few hours were a veritable nightmare! Both Dad and Herman suddenly appeared on the scene after what seemed like only minutes since Dad raced into town. Right behind them were several men, good men who immediately volunteered to help upon hearing of our plight. To this day, I don't know how or where they heard of our situation and responded so quickly. There was a sheet metal man, a city worker, the baker, the banker, and even our wonderful minister who had hurriedly donned a pair of blue denims for the emergency. I didn't even notice he was there until Herman told me later as they were carrying things out. In fact, most of the men were strangers to me, but Herman remembered who they were. All I knew was that help had materialized out of nowhere, and I was no longer all alone.

After a quick survey of the situation, they decided to remove everything from the basement that could be moved, and stack it up on the flat roof. They reasoned that if the basement had structurally survived the soil pressures so far, when everything else around us was collapsing, it would probably hold together. Yes, it had paid to invest in a good foundation after all. Instead of concrete block basement walls, Herman designed 10 inch thick, steel-reinforced, poured concrete walls. He had even wisely insisted that the floor slab have steel reinforcement in it to resist the... let's see... the "hydrostatic forces from expansive clay soils". Impressed? Don't ask me what that means. I had to ask Herman why all this was happening and asked him to write it down for me so I could explain it correctly to someone else later. Anyway, the living room furniture went out first, followed by the dining room furniture. How all the dinnerware, glassware, hurricane lamps, electric lamps, delicate bric-a-brac and fragile what-nots went out intact, I shall never know.

As the men hauled out the heaviest furniture first, I was trying to stuff everything I could get my hands on into chiffonnier and dresser drawers. There was no time for planning or careful packing as one would do in an ordinary move. This was just a frantic effort to save as many of our possessions as we possibly could in the diminishing time allowed us. By that time, I was minus one water-logged "wedgie" which was floating around somewhere in my own private boudoir swimming pool. The "petticoat" on my bed was now submerged in dark, silty water, dragging like the soiled skirts of some weary, dirty woman of the streets. The water kept rising steadily, mercilessly, but I was no longer conscious of that. I was just trying to focus on finding important things and putting stuff together in any kind of container I could find.

Suddenly, I heard the nerve-wracking sound of crashing glass from the direction of the stairway. Four straining, perspiring men were trying to get my huge, modern birch buffet up the stairs. Naturally, there was no time to remove or individually wrap the delicate contents. As the workers tilted the unwieldy buffet to carry it up the stairs, everything inside slammed to the lower end... my lovely stem-ware, an imported coffee set, old cut glass and crystal pieces, fine china and porcelain... all crashing noisily to one side. For a brief second, one of the struggling men, our minister, hesitated and glanced at me with deep regret and understanding sympathy. "It's all right," I yelled. "No time to worry about that now! Don't stop; just keep going!"

For a moment, I pictured that precious little coffee set my husband's mother had brought with her from Germany when she came to live in America, and she later wanted me to have it. Herman came to the U.S. at the age of nineteen. He had sent the money for his mother to buy that coffee set out of the first wages he ever earned. A few years later, Herman and a brother living in Milwaukee saved enough money between them to bring their mother over to live in America as well. My sentimental thoughts were rudely interrupted as the men came into the bedroom and grabbed the first thing they could lay their hands on while the floodwaters continued to rise. I watched one man dump a lampshade, books, shoes and a mirror into my prized, crocheted bedspread, roll it up and carry the whole thing up to the roof, where it would be thrown in a pile with the rest of the growing disarray on the roof. After toiling so hard to create some semblance of a civilized lifestyle in an underground concrete box, we had come to this state of affairs in a matter of a few hours... piles of furniture, clothing and miscellaneous possessions dumped unceremoniously on a tarpaper-covered roof top, exposed to the elements of the weather, and with no possible means of security against theft.

My feet were ice cold and numb, but even that failed to concern me. Everything had happened so fast that it hadn't fully registered on my brain. It was all like some horrible nightmare, but in a blurry, unreal kind of way. I was subconsciously trying to help, to contribute to my own family's rescue, but really doing nothing important. For years, I had very conscientiously kept our valuable papers in a special place, within easy reach so I could grab them quickly in case of an emergency exit because of a fire. I had mentally rehearsed what I would do should a dire event actually occur. But this wasn't a fire. I had never even thought about a flood. So, did I keep cool and remember what I had schooled myself to do? Did I grab that little metal lockbox and run to safety with it? No, instead I was trotting around with one old bedroom slipper in a shopping bag, looking frantically for its mate! Psychologists would probably say that it was my subconscious response telling me that my feet were cold… or, more likely, they would just look at each other and sadly shake their heads. One of the helpers, a very kind man, came over and tapped me on the shoulder, saying, "You're all wet, ma'am. Please get out of this cold water. Nothing more you can do here. We'll get the rest of it for you."

As I walked out into the utility room, I was startled to see a big husky westerner walking up the stairs with my tall "what-not" cabinet. All of the fragile contents were still in place. The shelves were filled with Hummel figures, blown glass, fragile little figurines and statuettes, antique plates, and one of my real treasures… an ancient sugar bowl that had belonged to my great, great grandmother more than a century ago. This entire assortment of unique and treasured collections were poised very delicately on the many shelves of one big cabinet, and I held my breath as it began its journey upward in the huge arms of only one man. This big, gentle man carried that big cabinet of treasures single-handedly up to the roof and set it down without disturbing or displacing one article! I, personally, have never been able to gently dust this fragile array without knocking over at least one item. Even though the situation was very grim and the afternoon was extremely hectic, miraculous things did happen, and they did not escape my attention or my gratitude.

This big, gentle man carried my big cabinet of treasures up to the roof.

Wading back to the front of the house, I watched five hefty men trying in vain to lift the water-logged, rolled up rugs and pads in the living and dining rooms. After several fruitless attempts, they had to give up and walk away from them. Except for those rugs, everything else had been apparently rescued and removed to the roof before they were submerged in the murky waters, even the motor from our pride and joy, the big oil burner!

"Well, we're all through," groaned the tired men in a chorus as they started to trudge wearily up the stairs. The door at the bottom of the stairway shut behind them, revealing the doorway to the boys' bedroom... still completely furnished and knee-deep in water. The lower stairway door had been open all this time, blocking the entrance to that bedroom, so no one even took notice. Small bedroom slippers were floating around the water-filled room, in the company of small items of apparel and a few lightweight toys. At my frantic call, the men returned to see the room full of furniture. They began hurriedly moving once again, but with considerably less enthusiasm. I heard one man say, "Why do people have to have so much furniture?"

There were three maple beds, three small dressers, in fact three of almost everything. Herman had laboriously hand-crafted all the wood furniture himself. The room was full of goods. I tried to help, and thoughtlessly grabbed the electric clock off the wall. It was still plugged in. I heard a loud pop, saw a blue-white flash, and received an instant jolt to signal me that it was still connected to enough volts to knock me clear across the room and against a desk. It was like water skiing backwards. By another unexplainable miracle among a growing list of miracles, I escaped with nothing more than a good case of the jitters, a condition I had grown quite familiar with. Two men in the room who witnessed what had happened were frightened into frozen positions, just staring at me in disbelief. They didn't move a muscle until I regained my composure, smiled sheepishly at them, and waded back across the room which I had just traveled in reverse. They were astounded that I could even walk, much less actually remain conscious.

Finally, the very last of the bedroom's contents was up the stairs and on the roof. Yes, it was a pathetic picture, but I was in such a daze and so stunned by the unexpected deluge that I felt no emotions whatsoever. I was told later that I had behaved very bravely, with no display of hysterics whatsoever, even though that would have been forgivable given the circumstances. Oh yes, that was a very calm piece of humanity that went galloping around, calf-deep in icy water, with the shopping bag and one old soggy bedroom slipper! I never did find that other slipper.

After several concerned people pleaded with me to leave the scene and find a warm, dry place to rest, Herman emphatically but gently commanded me to leave immediately and go to my mother's. I dragged my cold, aching, weary body into the front seat of Dad's car, which was piled high with essential clothing we had recovered. I rode in a sort of stunned stupor during the whole short trip. I just couldn't comprehend this sudden, unwelcome turn of events that had so strongly and unpredictably disrupted our lives! To us at the time, it was a real tragedy, a true calamity. But thinking about it and discussing it after a short while, the event was almost insignificant in comparison to the real misfortunes that occur every day to people like us... except that those people sometimes lose everything they own, and many have nowhere to turn for help or shelter. In the overall scheme of things, we had suffered a major annoyance and what would become a lengthy inconvenience… but no more. We had far more to be grateful for than to grumble about.

I tried to convey my sincere thanks to all the kind people who helped us that day, and in the days that followed. But words are so inadequate when a person is as thankful as I was that afternoon. The Western hospitality and charity I had heard about so often was certainly very much in evidence on that memorable day. People were genuinely concerned about our troublesome predicament. So many people extended a helping hand in one way or another. Several families offered to take the boys until we could restore our home again, but my sister said, "We wouldn't let them go anywhere but right here with us! We want them!" When we reminded her that she already had five of her own, she replied, "So what's three more? We have enough room!"

My three boys were thrilled to death with the prospect of living on a farm. It was a small place only a mile north of town. Owned by the State of Montana and run by Uncle Bill, it was an experimental farm for the Department of Agriculture, primarily to study crop variations and new farming techniques. But they had chickens and ducks, an outdoor pump and outdoor plumbing, so to my boys this was a real farm even if they didn't have cattle, pigs or horses. The cousins all got along amazingly well together, and Helen's three girls were more like the sisters my boys never had. Herman and I stayed in my folk's tiny apartment, in spite of the many invitations from all of our friends. Mother wouldn't hear of us going to any other place, even though we were quite crowded there, because "family takes care of family". And that was that!

I became terribly depressed, running very short of courage and patience. My family was physically split apart, and our furniture and possessions were on the roof of the house, covered by huge tarpaulins, but otherwise unsecured. Even the tarps had lots of gaps in the covering, allowing the snow and weather to blow in. This worried me plenty, as all of our earthly possessions were in that huddled collection that was so vulnerable to weather and theft, basically exposed to the elements except for that thin, drafty covering of canvas. Finally, Herman's employer offered a clean corner in the new shop he had recently built, for temporary storage. Moving the furniture off the roof and over to the highway was no small undertaking. The movers had to carry everything from the roof and "walk the plank" over the big drainage ditch alongside the highway to reach the truck. The heavy articles plus the weight of the men really caused the thick plank to bend downward to its stress limits. Finally the last piece of furniture was loaded on the big truck, and as it rode down the highway to its temporary shelter, I couldn't help but wonder how long it would be before I saw it again. I began to feel like a displaced person all over again. Once again, we were without a home.

The County loaned us three huge planks to use as a type of footbridge from the highway to our small entry enclosure. Water filled the "moat" around our basement and stayed at the same level for many days. It sure wasn't a castle, with or without the moat. It was just a messy, flooded, deserted basement, with no sign of the happy home atmosphere that had reigned only days earlier. A good many of our dreams get a little messed up sometimes, or run off the track. That's life. But somehow, in some way, we go on with our lives without too much hesitation. What other choices do we have?

After the waters finally receded, I ventured down into the basement. The flood water left a hopeless looking, silt covered mess in its wake. The walls were stained and the linoleum in the kitchen had started to develop an evil smelling mold. For the first few days, I just wandered around listlessly, poking at this and that, and turning things over with the toe of my boot. Then, I would just close the door and leave, feeling greater despair than when I entered the smelly, underground cistern that had once been our cheerful home.

My regular Saturday morning ritual became picking up the boys out at the farm, and palling around with them all day. I looked forward to this all week, and I dearly missed seeing them every day. On one particular Saturday morning, I decided to take them down in our basement to take showers, a luxury they didn't have out at the farm because they had no indoor plumbing. As they bathed, I sat on an old box feeling dejected, totally defeated, staring at all the muddy havoc around me. I had no desire to return. I felt that I just couldn't come back and start all over again. Little Dickie had been watching me as he stood near me, drying himself off. He quickly dressed, came over and put his arms around me. This gesture alone was almost unheard of from Dick. He had never been very demonstrative as far as emotions go. His nature was more stoic, like his father.

"Don't cry, Mom," he said softly. "We'll get by okay. Remember before we left Wisconsin, when Daddy got us all together and told us the going would be rough? He told us that if we loved one another, had faith in God, and all stuck together, we would have a home again some day!" All this from little scatter-brained Dickie! It was just the jolt I needed to jar me out of my doldrums and start planning a clean-up campaign. What sound wisdom and inspiring motivation can come from a child at times when you least expect it… and need it the most!

Early Monday morning, I was back at the basement to declare war against the filthy muck that had taken our home from us. I was well armed for the attack with plenty of ammunition in the form of soap and brushes; but more important, I was armed with renewed courage and ambition. Starting with the bedrooms, I intended to work methodically from one end of the house to the other. Silt is about the most stubborn kind of dirt there is to remove, and I made very slow headway. But I had plenty of time, and as long as I could see some visible progress, I was okay. The moldy linoleum was the nastiest job, but I soon discovered that I could remove the mold and stains with a lot of extra "elbow grease" and a strong cleaner, without damaging the surface.

Dad walked in that first day, ready to help as always. He was very evidently surprised to find me in such good spirits, and suggested that we try to get the pathetic looking rugs up on the roof in the sun. With a lot of tugging and pulling, we were able to drag them up the stairs and onto the roof. There was no way on earth the two of us could have carried them. As far as I was concerned, they were completely ruined, covered with a musty smelling mold and infused with slimy silt. I couldn't imagine ever being able to restore them to an acceptable appearance. Dad took over the job of brushing them thoroughly, then left them to the sun and fresh air. After I took a second look, they didn't appear quite as bad; but they were as limp as a pile of dead fish, and just as stinky.

Surprisingly, we accomplished a lot during the first few days. Most of all, we had finally begun the back-breaking job of cleaning up the silty mess and restoring our lives. I cannot find words that begin to describe what an ugly, discouraging, time consuming chore that is. About this time, the song "Cool Water" was quite popular. We heard it often on the radio and juke boxes wherever we went. I would laugh when I heard it, but perhaps didn't enjoy the song quite as much as others. The sound of gurgling water is not music to my ears any longer. I get very squeamish whenever I hear running water, particularly if I don't know the source of that sound. I think I'm developing a phobia to water in almost any form.

Several times during the day, I would take a break from the scrubbing work and the odor of detergents in the basement and go upstairs to the fresh air outside. I put those "breaks" to good use, too. I would pull on my boots and grab a shovel that was always handy in the entry shelter at the top of the stairs. Stepping out into the sunshine, I proceeded to expand the series of small dams, dikes and trenches Dad had started in the muddy yard to divert some of the stationary water away from the house. This slow, tedious process gradually began draining some of the little "lakes" that populated every area of our lot. Meanwhile, the drainage ditches along the highway had also been cleared, so the rapidly thawing snow was now able to flow away freely. People might laugh if I told them, but my ears had become so attuned to running water that, even when I was downstairs in the basement, I could tell which direction the water was flowing.

The dredging of these intricate waterways was no easy task. I soon discovered that the gooey, slimy mud behaved somewhat like quicksand. If I pushed my shovel in too far, I could hardly pull it out. The first time I became aware of this, I came very near to sitting down in the slippery muck. After a strenuous pull on the embedded shovel which refused to come out, I nearly went sprawling, but regained my balance in the nick of time. I have seen Herman mired in this mud so deep that he literally had to crawl out of his hip boots and then retrieve them from the sucking, brown slime with great effort, one at a time. It gave me great satisfaction to see the crude little canal system I had built mostly by myself actually carrying the water away from the basement. Little by little, I even drained our submerged driveway in this manner. Then, a stream of rapidly flowing water suddenly began coming across lovely, muddy Sunset Boulevard and threatened to refill the "moat" next to the house. I quickly built a low dike and dug a trench to divert that water to the highway drainage ditch where it belonged. And so the battle continued; but we seemed to be winning at last, and could look forward to some dry land next to our dwelling.

After days and days of cleaning and repairing, our work was completed to a point where we could at least move back in. My floors were all clean again; the rugs were dried and cleaned; and the linoleum in the kitchen sparkled with a fresh coat of wax. Everything showed a little wear and tear, and it wasn't hard to find evidence of the waterline that showed just how deep the water level had gotten. But it still looked beautiful to me once more, and new paint would soon hide those water marks on every wall that were ugly reminders of a horrible experience. Remember those "rose-colored glasses" I like to wear? I had put them on again.

Herman hired a couple of men to help move our furniture back into the house one Saturday. I couldn't bring myself to look inside the big buffet, remembering that resounding crash of glass when those four men were struggling to carry it up the stairs. My Dad was here, helping out as we moved back in. I was glad he was retired, although he did enjoy working part-time at the cabinet shop not far from our house. Dad had witnessed those men carrying that big buffet out of the house, and he also remembered the sound of the crashing glass. He told the helpers who were moving us back in to just set the buffet down outside so he could clean out the broken dishes and glassware before they carried it into the house. Dad looked at me for a moment and told me to go inside the house while he took care of it. He said I shouldn't need to look at the heartbreaking mess inside the cabinet. I went downstairs, turned around, and came right back up again. My curiosity got the best of me and I just had to see the "casualties" for myself, or better yet, see what I had left to work with that had survived. Resigned to having lost most of the contents, I took a deep breath and stepped out the door, stopping short in amazement. Dad was bent over, carefully examining the contents inside the buffet and laughing his fool head off. He was saying over and over, "I can't believe it! I just can't believe it!" He held up a cheap little glass ashtray that was broken into three pieces, and announced, "This is the extent of your damage! I can't find anything else that is even cracked!" Talk about miracles! With all the glass stem ware, fragile china and fancy plates, this cheap ashtray was the only casualty? This just added one more item to all the other unexplainable miracles that arose from that calamity!

After several more trips with the hired workers and their pickup truck, the moving job was completed. Herman helped me to make up the beds, and I began to prepare a light supper while he drove over to the farm to pick up the boys. Our personal belongings were all in a very bedraggled state. For example, shoes, lamps, bedding and pajamas were all mixed and rolled up together in our haste to save what we could from being claimed by the rising waters. One rusty wastebasket sat in the corner of our bedroom, containing a few of my choice novels, a quart of dark green, moldy milk, and a roll of mildew-covered toilet paper. That was typical of many such colorful sights around the house, particularly the central utility room. Nevertheless, the warm lights were glowing brightly once again down below and the basement was inhabited by a reunited family. Gratefully, I sighed with relief and we all joined in a prayer of thanks. We were together again. It was a home again.

Several nights passed before I finally overcame a chronic case of insomnia. My state of mind wasn't helped much by the sound of lapping water that still returned at times to the moat surrounding our basement. It would be awhile before we could get more dirt hauled in close enough to fill up that troublesome trough. Yet, that water also gradually flowed away or was finally absorbed into the slowly thawing ground. The moisture inside the house appeared off and on all during the summer, particularly on very hot days due to the super saturated earth under the floor. The end of summer brought this annoyance to a halt. One by one, we believed we had finally eliminated the flood hazards, with the cooperation of the city and county public works people. It puzzled me that everyone but us seemed to know that our corner lot always flooded every spring. Now we know it, too, for sure! The only thing we heard when we were looking it over to buy was that it was a beautiful location and a very good price for such a corner lot… and that it was.

The flood experience was followed by one more little episode, brief but very nasty, just to top things off. Actually, it was an aftermath that was caused by the flood. Our drains and sewer refused to function. After Herman's efforts with a plumber's snake refused to unclog anything, we called in the city for help. Their maps showed that we were at the very end of our branch of the sewer line. So, they began to apply a powerful back flush to clean out the silt that had built up like a cork in a bottle and was plugging up the end section of the sewer. That action also nearly put an end to my sanity, which I had been carefully trying to reconstruct after the flood. Almost immediately, the back-flushing broke through, but on *our* end! The toilet, the floor drains, the shower drain and every sink drain began to spew geysers of the most offensive, putrid sewage imaginable all over the place. Before too much damage was caused, the men shut down the operation and started cleaning up the mess, in a half-hearted sort of way. My ability to absorb any more shocking surprises had been eroded to its lowest level at this point, so I immediately went to pieces. The water and sewer commissioner, who was on hand to supervise the solving of our problem, put his arm around me and tried to console me, saying, "I am so sorry, Mrs. Foell. This is just too much after all you've been through. It's a damned shame! Just don't you worry. My men will clean it all up and everything will be good as new. You'll see."

After gallons of soapy water and disinfectants, and a thorough fumigating of the living quarters to make it smell a little less like the stock yards, we were able to settle down again, and wait for the next chapter in our lives. Perhaps for us, it would be yet another new frontier.

CHAPTER TWELVE
Home Improvements

"Have faith! Have courage! You will win! You will win!" That was what I wanted to believe the meadowlark's sweet song was saying to me as it awakened me one beautiful spring morning. The meadowlarks sang from dawn to dusk all through the spring and late into the fall. Helen told me the Western Meadowlark is the Montana state bird. They were so pretty, dressed in their yellow "vests" and black "bow ties". At least, that's how they appeared to me… cheerful little messengers in sporty outfits. But since we had no trees, we seldom saw many birds except on the wing or perching on the electrical wires across the highway. I was very conscious of the fact that we didn't have any trees on our lot. With only the barren hills to look at, and the rolling plains that stretched for miles and miles across eastern Montana, I think I missed the lush, green forests of Wisconsin more than anything else. No wonder they call Montana the "big sky country"—no trees to block the view! Trees. Yes, we needed to plant some trees of our own!

Inspired by the arrival of spring, the disappearance of all that standing water, and with that horrible flood catastrophe behind us, we went to work, picking up where we left off before the flood. There was a lot of unfinished carpentry work to do, and shelves and closets to build. The first job Herman tackled was the kitchen ceiling. It had been left partially unfinished, so that the heating ducts could be installed, and he just never got the chance to get back to it after the ductwork was finished. I was keeping myself busy at some menial task in the corner of the kitchen, trying to stay out of Herman's way. He was carefully fitting the missing sections of Celotex board, and as he proceeded to nail the last piece to the joists, I heckled him about being sure to nail it to the water pipe. He remarked snidely that he wasn't *that* much of an amateur! The ceiling was finally acquiring a finished look as the plumbing, wiring, ducts and insulation were covered over by the new ceiling board. My wall cupboard was about a foot from the panel Herman had just nailed into place. As my cupboard space was limited, it was jam packed with dishes and glasses. My ears, having been very well trained to detect water sounds, heard a single drip land in a glass on the top shelf. I had become such a drip expert by this time that I could zero in on the exact location of a drip in a matter of seconds.

The first drip was rapidly succeeded by many more. I heard Herman mutter, "Damn! Another fast thaw and another leak under the roof!" Patches of accumulated frost beneath the roof and above the insulation thawed gradually all spring, so that it was frequently dripping somewhere around the house. I emptied the filled glass, thinking this wouldn't last very long. But after emptying the glass several times, I gave my husband a suspicious glance.

"Well, Herman? I'm beginning to suspect that we *do* have an amateur carpenter around here. Do your skeptical wife a favor and pull out that last nail you hammered in... the one near the water pipe." He did. The telltale result was immediate. A stream of water shot out with such force that it knocked a small saucepan out of my hand when I tried to catch the water with it. As the pan clattered across the floor, Herman shot out of the kitchen like a bolt of lightning, heading for the main shutoff valve. As the squirting ceiling slowed to a few drips, Herman returned with a very sheepish look on his face. "Well, we sure do have good water pressure" was all he could think of to say. Silently, he began to remove the sheet of Celotex. As he tilted one end of the board downward, he executed mistake number two. A sheet of trapped water sprayed down onto the table and splashed over practically everything in the kitchen, much to my added annoyance and Herman's dismay.

It took quite awhile to solder the copper pipe. After several failures, the patch finally held fast, and the water stained Celotex was nailed back into place again. The tattletale water spot remained as a sore reminder to Herman of another lesson learned. In the days to come, many more lessons would be learned, and Herman wasn't the only student.

The basement had cost us far more than we had expected, and the flood had set us well behind in our planned schedule, both time and money-wise, so we necessarily postponed "going up" with the rest of the house for the time being. Maybe 1951 would see us moving up in the world. Meanwhile, improving the grading and drainage away from the house was the most important priority to prevent any recurrence of that flood that had dealt us such a wicked blow just a short while ago. Besides, we didn't want to confine our home improvements just to the indoors. We wanted to take advantage of the summer weather outdoors as well. After canvassing the contractors and dirt haulers in town for fill dirt, we finally tied down a promise for the delivery of thirty truckloads of soil. The best deal we could make was not cheap. For quite awhile after the new topsoil arrived, the huge, odd-shaped mounds of dirt in our yard more nearly resembled the Dakota Bad Lands across the river from Sidney than the yard of a private residence. By July, we were still shoveling and grading and pushing that dirt around, with a lot of work still remaining. It was back-breaking work, shoveling dirt into a wheelbarrow, wheeling the heavy load over soft ground to some distant point on our big lot, then dumping and spreading the soil where it was needed. Herman even rented a motorized mini-grader one weekend to try to expedite the heaviest part of the rough grading. We would get up at four in the morning, put on old clothes and work until it was time for Herman to eat breakfast and go to his job. I never realized so many people are up that early in the day. We made quite a few friends with the early risers who drove past our property and waved a cheery good morning. Some even stopped to comment on our progress and hard work, and a few offered helpful tips about things they had learned when they were doing their own landscaping.

I have already commented about the sudden and often unexpected appearance of strong winds coming across the Great Plains. I'll never forget how a few of those severe dust storms affected our earth moving project that summer. We were working about a hundred feet from the basement one clear Sunday afternoon when I paused and leaned on my shovel to rest for a moment. As I casually glanced over my shoulder, I saw an ominous looking black cloud appear very suddenly to the southwest. It seemed to expand and swell even as I stared at it. I pointed it out to Herman who immediately dropped his shovel and yelled, "Run for the house! Run!"

I've never seen anything travel so fast! Before we reached the basement door, the dust storm struck with an incredible ferocity. The dust stuck to our faces and bodies, delivering an unbelievable stinging, abrasive lashing, blinding us and causing us to gasp and choke as we desperately struggled to reach the door. We were no longer running, but staggering erratically against the sudden whipping forces of the wind. Our hair, eyes and clothing were covered with the suffocating, blinding dust. It invaded our mouths with grit between our teeth. Once we reached the shelter, it took all of our combined strength to open the door and close it again tightly behind us, fighting the strong, buffeting forces of the gale. The boys were in an uproar, racing around the house trying to close all the windows. After shaking off some of the dust that coated our bodies, and running to help close the remaining open windows, we were shocked to see what the dust storm had done to our home in only a few short moments. My lovely home, which I had cleaned thoroughly just that morning, was transformed into what looked like a neglected house that hadn't been cleaned for years. The air was filled with finely powdered dust that hung in suspension like a yellowish talcum, looking denser where shafts of light came through the windows and illuminated the haze. Drapes, furniture, clothes, walls, floors... everything was coated and permeated with the dirty stuff.

We could hear the frightening bellowing of the wind as it roared across the flat roof and whipped at the entrance shelter that dared to thrust itself above the roof so defiantly. As we cowered down below in the safety of our earth-sheltered stronghold, the storm reached down and ripped the entire roof from our garage, hurling it nearly fifty yards across the alley and into a neighbor's back lawn, barely missing his house. Of course, we were not aware of this little mischief of nature until later. After only ten or fifteen minutes, the raging winds subsided and the angry storm vanished as quickly as it appeared. In contrast, the sudden silence was almost scary. Cautiously, we climbed the stairs and peered outside, with Herman in the lead. He gave us the all clear, so we all piled outdoors to survey the damage. Jackie yelled, "Look", and pointed over to our neighbor's house. That's when we discovered that our garage roof had gone traveling.

Our nice neighbor, Mr. Lilly, was just venturing out into his yard himself. He walked toward us, shaking his head and grinning. "Whew! Wasn't that something, huh?" he chattered excitedly. "I was looking out the window at all the blowing dirt and stuff sailing through the air, and then I saw the wind pick up your whole garage roof and send it my way! Man, I just dove into my basement for my own self-preservation! Are you gonna need a little help moving that roof back over to your place, Herman?"

As we rolled up our sleeves and started cleaning up the mess, I kept one consoling thought in mind. It could have been a lot worse! I know that's a time-worn cliché, but still a good thought that makes a lot of sense to heed. The whole family joined in on the clean-up campaign, and the top layers of dirt were removed quickly. But it took days of detail work before everything was free of dust and completely clean again. And, of course, there were a few places that got overlooked at first. When we pulled the drapes in the bedroom that night, we were showered with more dust that had accumulated behind the curtains at the windows. Immediately after I got hit with my dust shower, I tried to warn Herman, who was about to draw the drapes on the other window. Too late! What else can you do but laugh at yourselves?

Herman spent the next two weeks of his spare time dismantling our garage roof that rested in Mr. Lilly's back yard, and putting it back on top of the garage, piece by piece. Without the aid of a crane, the roof was too big to move in one section, even though it had remained amazingly intact with little damage or splintering. Obviously, it was strongly built, and the same powerful winds that yanked that roof right off the garage walls in one piece miraculously set it down gently on our neighbor's lawn. This time, Herman was careful to nail down the framing members with steel straps and small "spikes" to make sure it stayed connected in the future… we hoped. He finished the job by adding a layer of tarpaper to keep out the weather. This part of the job was no easy task because it was a very windy day, naturally, when he found the time to apply the protective paper. Finally using his head, and using our three little sons as "paper weights", he was able to complete the work.

After the grass seed was sown, the first thing I planted in our newly graded yard was petunias… my old landscape standby for floral borders. My family was dubious about the success of this venture, because we had all learned about skepticism from the beatings we had already taken by the elements in this location. Undaunted, I set out several tomato plants along the back wall of the basement as well. After weeks of hot sun, dust storms and unrelenting wind, my little petunias bloomed in lush profusion. They were gorgeous. It's called "faith"! No one will ever appreciate how much inspiration I received from those brave, colorful little petunias. Even my tomato plants prospered and were heavily loaded with a bountiful harvest, believe it or not! Alas, no one warned me about the sneaky, early frosts that occur in this climate, so I learned another lesson. I went outside one morning in August to pick a few tomatoes, only to find the huge, sturdy plants sprawled all over the ground, black as pitch. The rich soil in Richland County grows some very healthy crops, but the growing season is very short. Timing and good luck is everything in the agricultural business, and now I am a little wiser in that area.

We planted two apple trees and three elms for starters in our landscaping program, but they didn't survive their first winter. Perhaps we started them a little too late in the season, because the following spring we found five, six feet tall, unadorned, unresponsive dead sticks in our new yard. We left them in place as "markers" to locate their replacements when we were ready to plant the new ones.

Everyone who was seeding new lawns seemed to have tons of fertilizer delivered, so I set out in a quest to locate the "fertilizer man". A kind neighbor gave me the man's telephone number, and I lost no time in calling him. When I asked if I was talking to the right person, he replied, "Oh sure! I'm your man all right, and I deliver really good stuff!" I asked when he could deliver it, and he was very accommodating. He said he could bring it out whenever I needed it. How many loads did I want? I hastened to inform him that one load should be plenty. Then, as an afterthought, I asked him how much it cost. When he glibly replied that it would be only twenty dollars a load, I was floored. I choked and said I would have to call him back to arrange a time for delivery. Oh yeah. You bet. My first impulse after hanging up was to call Herman and tell him to quit his job immediately. He could probably make more money selling manure than machinery! I refrained, however, and waited until he came home for lunch to discuss it. We decided that the man was too mercenary for his own good (and ours), so we would find another supplier somehow. That night at the supper table, we were still talking about the fertilizer thing… well, actually *after* we finished eating. Dickie told us that the fertilizer man's son, Aubrey, was a schoolmate of his. He said all the kids were always teasing the boy and making fun what his father did for a living, but the kid didn't seem to mind. The boy's mother always drove Aubrey to school in her new '49 Cadillac! I pointed out to Herman that we drove a '39 Dodge, not that my point was lost in the first place.

That same man, Mr. Manure, came to my door a few days later. He was trying to sell dirt for only two dollars a load, stuff he was trying to get rid of from a hilly property he owned. At that rate, we figured that the man who excavated our basement, carted away all of our nice dirt, sold it to someone else and charged us for "cartage" as well, probably had retired on the money he made from our project. Maybe that was the reason we couldn't find him when it was time to get "our dirt" back for only the cost of hauling, as he had agreed. He had no doubt retired to a more suitable climate.

CHAPTER THIRTEEN
Western Culture

There is something mesmerizing about this part of our great United States. It mystifies me why I love this tough, somewhat barren, sometimes unforgiving land. It's an erratic, fickle love, however. One day, it's an accepting, all-embracing kind of love; and the next day, I'm ready to pack up and move back to the lush, green land we came from not too long ago. Perhaps in the years to come, I will become as fiercely loyal to this "God's country" as are the good people all around me that I have met here.

I believe the unpretentious people themselves are a major part of the hypnotic nature of the West, their generous hospitality, their sympathetic friendliness, their open sincerity. Whether you live in a trailer, a shack, a basement or a grand house, you are treated with the same respect and thoughtfulness. From the first day of our arrival, we've had no lack of friends in this community. Until we became used to the friendly smiles and "howdys", we would turn to each other and say, "Who was that?" We soon learned it was just a friendly custom, and that you didn't have to know someone to greet them graciously. It didn't take us long before we were doing the same thing and loving it. I've noticed also that people are more reliant on each other out here, and more relaxed and trusting in the "wide open spaces" than they are in the more populous areas of our country. Smiles and open arms have a higher level of importance and seem to be valued more here than in the crowded cities. And folks here more readily look out for each other, instead of places where the predominant attitude is "me first, and the heck with the other guy". We saw ample evidence here of how people care about each other when we went through that awful flood episode; and there were countless smaller incidents where I was totally charmed by the goodness in people that just bubbles out naturally when the opportunity presents itself. Yes, there are always exceptions. Rude, pompous people and dishonest scoundrels emerge in any part of the world; but we seemed to encounter very few of them in this part of the world for some reason. Perhaps it is because they stick out like a sore thumb in this environment, and are simply not tolerated.

On Saturdays, after finishing my morning chores, I often gathered the boys together, got out the car and headed for town on my weekly shopping spree. They loved to go downtown and wander through their favorite stores and shops, too. On one such Saturday when I parked the car on Main Street, the boys all piled out in their excitement and started down the sidewalk, leaving the car door open. Now, this thoughtless behavior is contrary to all rules and regulations of our household, so I very noisily and disdainfully demanded, "Will you please come here and shut the car door!" At that moment, a very nice looking rancher was passing by, looking very smart in his broad-brimmed Stetson and high heeled cowboy boots. He paused, glanced in my direction looking a little puzzled and, without further hesitation or deliberation, stepped off the curb, shut my door and went on his way. Mortified with embarrassment, I jumped out of the car and called after him. "I was actually asking my boys to do that. I, I d-didn't mean for you to..."

Nevertheless, he looked back, smiled, tipped his hat and replied, "I figured as much, ma'am, but won't I do?" Then he hurried off, leaving me and the boys standing there with our mouths agape, staring after him. The man was the epitome of Western graciousness, but I still have the strange feeling that he probably thought I was just another bossy woman, sitting behind the wheel, running things and ordering people around.

In addition to the friendly people in the West, another captivating factor that accounts for our enchantment is the sky here that seems to dominate everything in a way I never felt back East. I'm constantly aware of the great expanse of sky overhead in an almost hypnotic sense. They call Montana the "Big Sky Country" for good reason. Most days, it is clear and blue, with tiny, puffy white clouds like cotton balls scattered across the otherwise deep azure field above me. Then again, it may brood oppressively overhead, heavy with darkening, sinister clouds that seem to suddenly crowd in from every direction. And sometimes, the more earthly dust clouds aggravated by the wind appear out of nowhere on a seemingly calm day, moving in as fast as lightening, wreaking havoc with powdery, choking dust at every turn.

A series of high hills rising just a few miles to the west of our basement home overshadow the little town of Sidney. I know it sounds goofy and it's not very scientific, but I would swear that those hills are the source of most of the vicious storm clouds. Perhaps it is just a coincidence that our worst storms come in with the prevailing westerly winds right over those hills. I suppose the storm clouds are formed far to the west and are screened from view by those hills until they pass above them and into sight of the valley. I know those are the logical explanations, but my mind believes those hills spawn the bad clouds because they create an atmospheric disturbance by sticking up so high from an otherwise flat terrain. I can't explain it. There is something about those hills that gives me a very uneasy feeling. I bet the Indians would agree with me, and they probably know a bunch of superstitions about those hills, too. Whatever the reason, I have noticed that the fiercest storms are always preceded by a huge fan-shaped cloud looking like an Indian war bonnet that appears to rise out of the highest hill. My childhood fear of storms still haunts me now and then, and the sudden, ferocious squalls do nothing to overcome those fears.

I must admit there is one other reason why those hills make me feel uneasy at times. I try not to think about it too much, but I am very much aware that tucked just behind the summit of those hills are the two dams that the town people talk about, the scary dams built only with dirt to hold back the millions of gallons of water behind them... perched for a disaster some day. I have developed a genuine phobia about large amounts of water from our recent experience, and I can't imagine what it would be like if those dams ever cut loose. I try not to even think about it.

I seldom start my day without going upstairs to stand on our little "porch", soaking up the peace and quiet of the early morning beauty, breathing deeply the fresh, clear air. Everything seems refreshed after the night's rest, and that great big sky just overwhelms the whole picture. As I look to the east of town, just across the Yellowstone River, I see the ever fascinating, changeable badlands. Each day they seem to present a different picture to me, depending on the position of the clouds and the sun, and the clarity of the air. One day they stand majestically resplendent, splashed with bright colors from God's infinite palette. The next day, they might appear somber, subdued and foreboding. On a cloudy day, the shadows work magic over these rough, deeply eroded hills and plateaus, emphasizing their weird shapes, sometimes cloaking them in flying mantles of wispy haze. In contrast to the otherwise barren landscape of the plains, the badlands stand out noticeably on a clear day when the visibility stretches for many miles.

Sidney is nestled in a shallow valley on the west bank of the Yellowstone River, a veritable oasis of green vegetation in contrast to the surrounding barren hills and plains that are painted with brown, pale yellow and tan most of the year. "Dry farming" methods are prevalent for wheat, except for the sugar beet fields, some corn and a few other crops that are irrigated. The drab scenery is so different from the green fields and forests I was so used to seeing most of my life. In town, however, the green lawns, shrubbery and trees are made possible by the local irrigation project, and the residents are encouraged to use generous amounts of water. The local water department even offers discount rates as an incentive for water bills that exceed the average monthly usage of water, certainly a new experience for us. This apparently was intended to insure Sidney's reputation for being the greenest town for miles around. Actually, Sidney was about the *only* town of any consequence for many miles around.

In the late spring, the Mexican migrant workers begin to arrive, and return again at harvest time. They come by various modes of transportation. Caravans of trucks, jalopies and very few late model cars find their way into our little town. Some of the local sugar companies imported their labor by plane. No matter by what means they arrived, they were happy to find work and were quite a noisy, festive bunch. As they streamed into town, it was hard to tell where one family left off and another began. It was apparent that there was no limit to the size of the family, or ages either, for that matter. I saw three generations represented in one Mexican family, possibly even four.

The evening that one of the first plane loads of farm labor arrived, we happened to be on hand at our primitive little airport to watch the scene. The night air was exceptionally cool as the transport touched down on the grass runway and taxied up to the small office building. As the first passenger stepped out of the plane and into the cold night air, his happy chatter stopped abruptly and so did he! For a moment, he just stood there, then turned around and tried to re-enter the plane. "Eet's too cold," he shouted in alarm. The pressing flow of other people behind him gave him no other choice but to continue down the steps against his desire. As was their custom, most of them carried their huge sombreros crowning high on their heads. Their dark skins, flashing white teeth as they smiled so readily, and their brightly colored clothing presented a very picturesque sight against the backdrop of a bright red, setting sun. The ranchers and farmers were on hand to pick up their human cargo with pick-up trucks, station wagons and Suburbans. As they received their allotment of labor, they loaded up and drove off into the violet dusk, one by one. The interesting scene was novel for us, because we didn't see this back in Wisconsin.

The majority of these people from south of the border are good, steady workers. Once in a great while, there is the inevitable, fiery tempered Mexican who drinks too much tequila, and loses his sense of humor, with gory results. I remember being horrified one Sunday morning (after a noisy Saturday night) when I saw a trail of blood from one of the local saloons to the door of a doctor's office down the street. I wondered if the victim had any blood left by the time he arrived at the doctor's place. I soon learned this was not a rare sight. My brother-in-law told me about one individual who was arrested for carving up "his woman". "She no good!" he explained to the judge. "All time nag! I find 'nother woman easy. I got seven already," he bragged. It is doubtful that he will find his next woman soon, because he became a "guest of the state" for a long period of time, after which he will probably be deported.

The small huts provided for these workers are part of every ranch. They are not what one would call glamorous accommodations, but there was a time last fall when I would have considered accepting one of those shacks or converted box cars out of sheer desperation. How those large families ever live together in these one room shelters, I'll never know. It's amazing what humans will accept out of necessity. What am I saying? Last fall, we were not living a whole lot better, as far as shelter is concerned. As you drive past some of these migrant workers' huts, you will always see a mother or oldest daughter outside washing in an old fashioned tub, using a sturdy washboard. Clothes of every color and description hang over the fences, or draped over weeds or anything that stands a foot or more above the ground.

The Mexican laborers work in the fields from the crack of dawn until dark, and summer days in Montana are long. It's not unusual for the temperature to climb to more than a hundred degrees in the sun, yet they show no sign of stopping or slowing down. They seem to thrive in the heat, for they all look healthy and they come right back again the next year for more. Across the highway from our home to the north, and right across Sunset Boulevard to the west, are many, many acres of irrigated sugar beet fields. Often, I can hear their lively chatter, spontaneous singing and happy laughter throughout the day. They must have backs of steel, because they keep moving right along, up and down the rows, bent at the waist, digging and swinging their knives to top off the beets with a methodical rhythm, hour after hour, day after day. At the end of toiling in such bent positions, they walk out of the fields straight upright, shoulders back, proud of their hard day's work. I would walk hunched over for weeks after only a few hours of such labor.

I love to watch these carefree people come to town on a Saturday. It is indeed a festive occasion. The week's work is done and they have money in their pockets, so all is right with the world. Family after family, they troop down the main streets, all decked out in recently acquired apparel. They love new hats and sport "loud" sweaters and jackets. The brighter the colors, the better. The more colors, the merrier. It seems like they are always eating something, candy, ice cream bars, or chewing gum fast and furious. It is their Saturday treat to enjoy the fruits of their labor. A person almost envies their very simple, carefree way of living. Live for today and let mañana take care of itself. The families, with few exceptions, walk in "step-ladder formation", from the tiniest toddler up front, to big brother or sister following with several steps in between. Grandpa and Grandma often bring up the rear. The little dark-eyed babies make a hit with everyone who sees them. They are so adorable!

One day, as I stood at my favorite meat counter in the market, I was eyeing some mouth-watering steaks. But, I bought the old standby instead... hamburger. The Mexican lady next to me bought the steaks. Yes, they eat well today and don't worry about tomorrow. Maybe I am doing something all wrong, I theeenk?

A few of the more impulsive, hot-tempered Mexicans tend to carry knives, which invariably gets them into trouble after too much whiskey or tequila. Consequently, most of their weekend is spent in jail. After one too many trips to the hoosegow, they are shipped back to their homeland. It's not uncommon to see the whole family having their picnic on the jailhouse lawn, carrying on a conversation with Papa through the window and making a gala occasion out of the whole post-brawling affair.

All of these ingredients blended together to make the recipe for Western culture, and that made our new life all the more enchanting. So much of this culture was so different from the life we were accustomed to in Wisconsin, and we embraced that as a bonus.

CHAPTER FOURTEEN
Adjusting to Life Underground

Since the very first day that we lived in the basement, the wind and unpredictable weather has frightened me, almost as much as my fear of flood waters. From down inside our home, I wasn't able to see a thing except for the churning clouds and those frightening flashes of lightning when it stormed. And I never quite got used to the weird whirring and whining sounds the wind made as it played across all those telephone and electrical lines that ran by our property along the highway. I can't quite describe those eerie sounds that changed in pitch and tone, depending on the winds direction and speed. The closest comparison I can think of is imagining several high pitched violins playing at the same time, but out of tune with each other. I'll tell you, it played on my nerves and was very spooky at times, even in the middle of the day when Herman was at work and the boys were at school—and I was alone. I decided that was why radios were invented, and I put mine to good use, drowning out the moaning and groaning of the wind on the wires.

The weather in this part of the country is more unpredictable than any woman I ever met. My brother-in-law, Bill, told me, "If you don't like the weather, just wait a minute." If the skies were threatening and cloudy, I learned to ignore it. Nine times out of ten, it won't rain anyway. On the other hand, when the weather seems beautiful and serene, beware, because it may change its mind in a matter of minutes. The next thing you know, you are high-tailing it for shelter, having spotted a dust storm heading your way. If you're lucky, you'll find a safe harbor in time. Another example is when you go outdoors just before you go to bed, and you gaze at the clear, star-studded sky. The air is calm and the big friendly moon shines so brightly, so soothingly, seducing you into a false state of euphoria. A couple hours later, you are likely to be awakened by the resounding crash of thunder and a rip-roaring electrical and wind storm. Sometimes hail is added to the nocturnal disturbance, drumming like an avalanche of rocks on our flat, tar paper roof. I could almost count down the seconds it took before three terrified boys were diving into our bed for protection. Herman isn't afflicted with the terrible phobia I have about storms, so he's the right one to settle the boys down. He can even get the boys laughing as they play games like counting the time between the flash and the crash; and he assures them that we are safer than most people in our strong, secure, underground fortress. Sometimes he almost convinced me, too.

After a good rainstorm, the boys and I had a standard routine to perform: sweeping the water off the flat roof before it started leaking through broken seals in the seams of the tar-paper and into the house below. No matter how many times Herman had resealed all suspected cracks in the tar-paper or joints, new rains always found new avenues to sneak inside and leak all over our basement. What really aggravated me were the gawkers on the highway, driving slowly by, gaping and smirking at a job they'd seen us do for months. They must have been really hard-pressed for entertainment.

One early summer night, when all was quiet and I was just on the verge of dropping off to sleep, I was conscious of a shadow passing across our bedroom window. That window was in a direct line of sight with the only street light on the block, just recently installed—a very welcome, civilized addition to the neighborhood, I might add. I sat up with a start when I suddenly heard a wild galloping across our roof! Even my usually sound-sleeping husband was awake and raised himself up on one elbow, a puzzled look on his face. A familiar rhyme was spinning through my head: "And then in a twinkling I heard on the roof, the prancing and pawing of each little hoof..." We lay there quietly for a moment, facing each other, listening intently and frowning. Then we heard it again, the scrambling and "galloping" of tiny feet racing all over the roof like the light tapping of a snare drum. This time, the rapid patter of little feet was followed by loud, squalling sounds associated with "back alleys". Herman and I both exclaimed the word at the same time... "Cats!" Relieved but peeved, we turned over and went to sleep. One of those rooftop Romeo's was to startle me again on another night, not too long after the first incident.

We had entertained friends one Saturday evening until the wee hours, and then went for a leisurely drive after they left. This ride, to nowhere in particular, had almost become a frequent ritual with us. If one of the boys should awaken and find us gone, they knew Mom and Dad were just away for our short ride and would be right back. We found it to be a simple pleasure, a good, relaxing nerve tonic to be moving around above ground for a short while before retiring in our underground burrow. It seemed even more enjoyable after the little town had gone to sleep. We seldom talked very much during these rides, just squeezed each other's hands three times every now and then, and enjoyed the peace of the night. The triple squeeze was our non-verbal message, meaning "I... love... you".

That particular night, we practically fell into bed after our ride. In reality, it was early morning, not late night. We had no sooner completely relaxed when the volunteer fire department's siren began to wail, followed in a short time by the wailing sirens of both fire trucks in the distance. I climbed out of bed and mounted a chair to look out the window, a necessary procedure when one lives in a basement—more so if you're only 5'-2". Even from an elevated position, standing on a chair, the view was still limited by the height of the window well's sidewall. I pulled aside the draw drape and peered out into the black night. Something was staring right back at me with eyes as red as glowing coals! I screamed "coyote" and nearly fell off the chair. Herman was instantly upright and joined me in one second flat, peering out the window to see how big the coyote was that caused me to scream. "Shucks," he chuckled. "That's just the big angora cat from down the street!" He laughed even harder the more he thought about it. I was still shaken, so I didn't share the humor of the situation.

Taking one more quick glance out the window to see if the prowler was still there, I was dismayed to see an ominous, shimmering red glow in the sky as I looked toward town. I could hear sirens again, indicating that additional fire trucks were probably called in from nearby Fairview and Lambert; and I shouted for Herman once more with alarm in my voice. "Now what?" the poor man mumbled as he climbed wearily out of bed to see what was disturbing his neurotic spouse this time. After one quick look, he gasped "Holy smokes!" (I'm sure no pun was intended.) "It looks like the whole town is on fire!"

We hurriedly got dressed and ran up the stairs, staring at the frightening reddish glare in town to the east of us. We thought briefly about jumping into the car and trying to get a closer look, but changed our minds as we looked across the fields to other roads leading into town. They were all clogged with scores of headlights as hundreds of curious people jammed into town. Whatever the source of the fire was, it sent flames and smoke for hundreds of feet into the air, a gigantic torch that could surely be seen more than fifty miles away in the moonless night sky… perhaps even a hundred miles! The raging inferno burned for more than two hours, undiminished and out of control, before showing any signs of dying down. We finally figured out that it had to be the town's grain elevators. Nothing else we could think of could create such a large blaze that sustained itself for so long. Later in the day, our guesswork would be confirmed when we witnessed the smoldering mountain of grain first-hand. Dawn was breaking when we finally crawled back into bed—just another exciting Saturday night in the metropolitan Sidney area.

It was only our first year of living "down under", and I was already looking forward with a touch of desperation to building the next level so we could live like normal folks do. Perhaps it was the horrible experience with the flood that drained so much from the stockpile of patience I usually hold in reserve. I found myself already becoming weary of climbing onto chairs or running up the stairs whenever I wanted to see what was going on outside. At night, my home usually didn't feel much different than an ordinary house, because I couldn't see outside in the dark anyway, and I would often forget that we were actually underground. In fact, it was even quite cozy most of the time and gave me a feeling of security, being surrounded by strong, protective concrete walls and embraced by Mother Earth. But in the daytime, it was a different story. To see outdoors, you were never looking "outward"; you could only look "upward"; and then, all you could see was the sky. It is natural to look up to the heavens when I am talking with God. But that is by choice when I am focusing on communicating with Him. Looking upward simply to see out into the world was a necessity, not a choice.

When you live in a basement, you may also develop a psychological complex that people are always looking down on you. We already knew that other creatures peered down at us through the window wells at night. It makes me shudder to think of it sometimes. Also, people who live in conventional homes aren't often shaken by the sounds of large and small members of the animal kingdom trampling across their roof at any hour of the day or night, like cats, dogs, sheep, and coyotes. Some "critters" apparently also tried to mark and claim their territory on this strange new tarpaper-covered platform that projected about two feet or so above the grade surrounding it. The boys didn't seem to mind at all. They pretended they were living in a cave, and that was a neat adventure to them. Besides, they were in school much of the time, or out playing with their friends, and Herman was away at his work during a good part of each week's daylight hours. I realized that I was really the only one who spent so much time down below grade, the only one who was significantly affected by our "lowly" living condition. But for now, we didn't have any alternative.

The first time they began irrigating the fields across the street, I prepared to evacuate at a moment's notice. The water source was those big reservoirs behind the earth dams. I had heard from so-called "reliable sources" that the water usually overflowed, and the irrigation ditches were a little too close for comfort where I was concerned. Helen's husband, Bill, knew the irrigation schedules because some of his farmland was irrigated, too. He tipped us off when the fields next to us would begin receiving their water supply. Before breakfast that particular morning, I had run upstairs to size up the situation, and found that the big ditch running along the highway past our basement was full to the brim and running fast. Every few moments all day long, I would run upstairs to check on the water. It wasn't until the end of a very uneasy day that I realized I had nothing to fear from that source. I felt even more at ease when Bill informed us that they had professional ditch-watchers who regularly monitored the water flow and runoff the entire time the irrigation was in progress. They operated the valves and gates that directed the amount of flow and direction of the water. We always get a thrill watching the rugged, tanned "ditch rider" galloping past on his beautiful horse. He never fails to wave, and the boys really admire him. In their estimation, he runs a close second to Roy Rogers and the Lone Ranger. To them, this was what living "out west" was all about.

Living underground, I have one up on the Indians. I don't have to bend an ear to the ground to listen for sounds of distant movement. I'm already *in* the ground, so I just stand or sit and listen. One day, as I stood at my kitchen sink doing the dishes, I heard a very unfamiliar noise. I had to go upstairs to investigate. Before we built up the grade around the basement and needed to install the window wells, I could get up on the nearest chair and get a pretty good view, but now that was impossible. When I reached the top of the stairs, I saw a huge herd of cattle approaching, with all the little doggies in tow. An old-timer was galloping back and forth, using profanity plus to keep the herd in line. Following this bellowing, dusty parade was a dilapidated old truck, driven by an unintelligent looking youth. In my estimation, there must have been over a hundred noisy, mooing "mama" cows and just as many bawling babies at their sides. The thundering roar of their hooves was deafening! But even with a homely, weather-beaten old cowboy and some unromantic cattle, I was getting a big thrill out of the whole procession… that is, until they reached our driveway. The leader of the herd decided to lead the rest of them right in my direction! When I saw all those big, bobbing heads aiming toward my general vicinity, I shrieked and made a bee-line for the door. I felt pretty foolish later as I recalled how I must have looked, making my hasty, panic-stricken dive for the porch. The elderly, weather-worn cowboy suddenly exhibited some surprisingly fancy riding and horsemanship, not to mention yelling and swearing a blue streak at the dumb cows, until he had them headed back up the highway. He laughed at me and called out, "They won't hurt you none, ma'am! They's jest a noisy bunch of dumb critters! I got 'em under control all right! They wasn't about to stampede or nothin' like that." I admit that little episode did liven up my morning routine a bit. All part of the charm of getting used to living out in the West… or should I say "living out *under* the West".

CHAPTER FIFTEEN
Summer Perils and Pleasures

Dick was scheduled to have his tonsils removed the summer of 1950. His entire young life had been plagued by countless ear aches and endless colds. We were fortunate to have a very good doctor with an excellent reputation for his competency. He recommended that an operation be performed as soon as possible while Dick was free from colds and congestion for the time being. My son had never experienced being in a hospital, so it was to be a totally new venture for him. Although his little mind must have been filled with unanswered questions, he never displayed any unusual anxiety or wonder. Bright and early one Monday morning, Dick and I set out for the small hospital. Plans were in the works to expand and modernize the facility, but at present it was quite crowded and somewhat antiquated, quite a contrast to the modern St. Joseph's hospital we were familiar with back in West Bend. Dick was assured that this was a simple, common procedure that doctors do all the time—nothing to be frightened about. He would just have a sore throat for a couple of days, but he could have all the ice cream and fruit slush he wanted. He liked that idea.

The nurse showed us to our little cubicle in the eleven-bed ward annexed to the main building. Men, women and children were all mixed together in the long, crowded, old infirmary-type room. Small, portable partitions or screens placed between patients afforded very little privacy. Dickie, much to my surprise, hesitated to undress with so little seclusion. Modesty in my young son was something entirely new to me. In a short while, the laboratory technician arrived with his tray of assorted tubes and vials, and proceeded to take a series of blood samples for testing. After he was finished, he disappeared down the corridor with his tray. Dick stared at the retreating vampire in the white coat and commented, "Gee! I could do with a blood transfusion now!" We had no idea at that moment just how prophetic his words would prove to be.

After waiting for half the morning for some kind of activity, for someone to appear and get the show on the road, I lost my patience and decided to investigate. I didn't go very far before confronting the nurse who had ushered us in a few hours earlier. She informed me that she had just gotten the test results back from the lab, and the report showed that he had some sort of "bleeding" tendency. His operation would have to be postponed for at least a week until the doctor was able to remedy the problem. After all this suspense and mental preparation, nothing would be done that day. With a sigh of relief, Dick got dressed again and grinned at me, the first sign that he had dreaded the ordeal in any way. As young as he was, he was already beginning to show the stoic traits that I knew so well in his father, who generally controlled his emotions so well it was difficult to read him sometimes.

We left the hospital with a prescription medicine to be administered for a week. It was supposed to add coagulating properties to his blood that he seemed to be lacking. They said he was suffering from a deficiency of vitamin K for some unexplained reason. No doubt about it, my little family including myself, never does *anything* the easy, normal way. The most simple, conventional activity or procedure always seems to turn into a major project for us. A "normal happening" for most people is an uncommon phenomenon for us.

After a series of tests a week later, Dick was pronounced ready and qualified for surgery. He went through the ordeal without too much discomfort, or at least without letting anyone know he was hurting very much. He was the proverbial "little soldier", never uttering a protest or whimper, although he commented that he hoped he would never have to have ether again. That nasty anesthetic made him terribly nauseous, and he seemed to be exhaling the odor of the gas for days! The operation was performed without any unusual incident, and we all heaved a sigh of relief. I spent the night in the hospital with him to make sure he was all right, and was allowed to take him home the following morning. We were all comforted that the unpleasant business was behind us ... or so we thought.

Two days later, after my pale little boy failed to show any appetite or pep, Dick began to hemorrhage. Frightened, we bundled him up and rushed to the hospital with him. After receiving medication for a day, the bleeding stopped and he was dismissed once more. I was a little skeptical about his condition when he remained listless. He had no energy whatsoever. Sure enough, he began to hemorrhage again and we made another rush trip to the hospital. This exercise in panic was repeated three times before the situation reached a near fatal climax a week later!

It was a Sunday morning and Herman and I were sleeping in after visiting and playing bridge with our friends, Don and Maxine Nutter. They were at our house until well after midnight. We were awakened at dawn very abruptly with screams from the boys' room. Grabbing robes, we rushed into the room to face Jack and Lynn screaming hysterically. Dickie lay on his back limply, with his head turned to one side, his pajamas and the bedding around him drenched in blood. It was one of the most horrible, gory sights I have ever seen before or since! His eyes were barely open and his breathing was very shallow. We learned later that he had been swallowing blood all night long, too weak to move or call out for help. At some point in the morning, his stomach rebelled and he threw it all up, awakening his brothers with the retching. All the poor little guy could do was to turn his head to one side to keep from drowning. Herman hurriedly dressed, then watched over Dick and tried to comfort him as I threw on some old clothes. He carried Dick to the car, wrapped in a blanket, and laid him in my lap to hold while he drove to the hospital at high speed. Fortunately, being early Sunday morning, there was hardly any traffic. My son was barely alive, barely breathing.

When we arrived at the hospital, our little boy was in shock and in very critical condition. The doctors and nurses were gravely concerned as they took Dick into the operating room to try to save him.

He seemed semi-conscious most of the time, and completely out part of the time. Herman was as tense as I have ever seen him; and I was left out in the corridor alone, so scared that I couldn't see or hear anyone or anything around me. One of the nurses had taken Herman downstairs after a hurriedly whispered powwow just outside the operating room. Someone found a chair for me to sit on... and to wait, and wait. So many hours of a mother's life are spent waiting, and her only consolation is prayer. I had a lump in my throat that would have choked a small horse, but I managed to keep a grip on myself somehow. I remembered someone saying that when you reach the end of your rope, tie a knot in it and hang on. I just couldn't let myself fall apart or I would be no good for anyone when I was needed.

I don't know how long I sat there in the hallway by myself, praying, wondering, and choking back the tears. It could have been an hour, or two ... or even longer. I don't remember. But suddenly, I was terribly thirsty. I couldn't swallow, and my mouth felt like it was filled with dry cotton. I walked around, desperately looking to find a drink of water. A nurse at the nurses' station asked me what I wanted, looking at me curiously. She asked if I was all right, and I finally gasped that I needed water. She coolly informed me that there were no clean glasses on the floor. I was sure that a cold glass of water would dissolve that big lump in my throat, but I was even being denied that relief.

More time passed and I still sat alone. Herman hadn't returned to tell me any news, and the suspense was driving me to the brink of hysteria. What if Dickie hadn't pulled through and they were afraid to come out and face me with the news? I just couldn't bear to sit there by myself any longer, not knowing anything. Overcome by mounting fear, I walked rapidly toward the operating room. As I drew near, I heard talking and laughter. Immediately, I became calmer, knowing that the situation must be under control. When I peeked into the room, I didn't see Herman, but a nurse spotted me and said, "Why don't you come in and keep your boy company?"

Tears rushed to my eyes and spilled over. It was such a relief to see Dick smile up at me. There he lay, small and white, with a big plasma tube inserted into his arm and a bottle of blood plasma hanging from the IV hook above him. Weakly, but with a twinkle in his eye, he murmured something about that "stuff" they were pouring into him looking like spoiled orange juice. Leave it to Dick to try to make a joke when he had been so close to death. For the next few hours, I bathed his hot face and fed him little pieces of crushed ice. During that time, Don Nutter, the good friend we had seen just the night before, appeared as if by magic and stretched out on a gurney alongside Dick's. They immediately tapped a vein in his arm and he proceeded to generously donate the life-giving "whole blood" that Dick needed so badly.

Right after Don showed up, Herman reappeared and explained that he had been given a list of blood donors with the type of blood that would match Dick's, and hopefully recognize a friend we could call on to help. The doctor told Herman that they could bring Dick out of shock and keep him stabilized for a short while with blood plasma, but the plasma was only buying them time. Without a transfusion of whole blood, he didn't stand a very good chance of surviving. He had lost too much blood and was very weak. Don's name was the first one Herman spotted that he recognized immediately, so he called them right away, apologizing for disturbing them so early on a Sunday morning. Don's precious wife, Maxine, answered the phone, telling my hubby that there was no need to apologize. Don was already up and out on the golf course. Herman was amazed, because they had been at our house that previous night, playing cards with us until the wee hours. When Herman told her what the situation was, she told him to just hang on and she would call out to the clubhouse and have somebody track him down right away. He would be at the hospital as soon as possible, even if she had to track him down herself. They are such sweet, genuine people! We are so very fortunate to have such special friends.

So here was this husky, energetic, former Air Corps bomber pilot stretched out next to our son, willingly giving up his rich blood to help save Dick's life. The doctor, who also knew Don personally, told Herman that now we would surely have an aviator in the family. And Don quipped good-naturedly, "I just don't know about you guys,

Herman. It's not enough that you beat Maxine and me at cards last night. Now you want my blood, too!"

Several hours later, we were informed that our son was out of danger. It had been a frightening, emotionally exhausting battle for us all, including the doctor. But, we had thankfully emerged victorious. The doctor said he had never experienced a case like this over a simple tonsillectomy in all his years of practice. Of course! It would have to be *our* family that would give him such a frightful novelty.

They kept Dickie in the hospital under observation for a couple more days until he regained some strength and they were reasonably sure he would not begin to hemorrhage again. It didn't take us very long to get back into the groove. Dick recovered rapidly, as most children normally do, and with an appetite now that equaled his friend Don's. We all consider Don as a blood relative now and to Dick, he was a more personal hero than his heroic war record. Dick told me he was a little sad to leave the hospital, though, because the little rascal had developed quite a crush on one of the young nurses there. I think she thought he was pretty cute, too, and spent quite a bit of time visiting with him. As we left, she commented to me that Dick was quite an interesting little man for the mature age of eleven! Yes, he was back to normal again, that was for sure.

As the summer moved right along, it was soon time for Jack to leave for Boy Scout camp. I suddenly realized that it would be the first time our oldest son would be away from home for more than just a couple of days. We all reviewed his long list of camp requirements, and studied all the camp regulations. Somehow, we managed to gather together the necessary supplies and equipment for what seemed more like preparations for a long military campaign. The day before Jack left, we bought him a much coveted sleeping bag, reducing our remaining bank balance to almost nothing after all the medical bills.

The local scout troop's camp cook, unofficial counselor and young man's confidante was "Ernie", a stocky, elderly English gentleman with a thick crop of snow white hair. He was an excellent chef who was equally competent at the kitchen stove or over a campfire. The boys all idolized him, and the grownups loved him. His many years of experience, as well as his legendary cooking skills and good nature, made him extraordinarily qualified for the strenuous summer camp sessions. I was comforted to know that Ernie would be at their camp. Early on a bright, hot Sunday morning, Jack left on his expedition to the western "wilds" on the Lame Deer Indian Reservation. This fascinating, beautiful campground was located in central Montana in the foothills of a very grand mountain. We would see it for ourselves when we drove over to pick him up a week later. The scout troop was comprised of quite a large group of boys of all shapes and sizes, each one feeling very important and excited in his uniform, anxious to "head out". Jack's little brothers clearly envied him as he waved goodbye.

The following Sunday, we all drove over to Lame Deer to pick up our son, bringing back a wiser, tanner, weary-but-happy boy. His lips resembled a Ubangi native, chapped and swollen to ugly proportions. This condition was aggravated by the long, hot ride home. Two unfortunate blow-outs in our aging tires turned a normally pleasant trip into a long, tedious journey. The highway leading to the camp was lined with neat, modern homes built for the Indians by the government. Adjacent to most of these modest little houses were teepees. Upon inquiring about these strange phenomena, we learned that the Indians still preferred their own traditional shelters, and many used their new houses for storage while they lived in the tents, at least during the summer. Yes, we all worry and fret about the welfare of the Indians, and try to "improve" their way of life, but heredity and tradition win out over imposed change. They ask for and need aid, but they want to use that help in their own way, which is not necessarily the "right" way as the white man sees it. I'm not sure who or when somebody decided that everyone else should live exactly the same way we live. I'm not even certain that we always know the "right way" either.

Shortly after Jack came home, we sent Dick out to the ranch owned by some very good friends we knew from our church. We all thought he would build up his physical condition and develop more pep by being out in the country. Jim and Abby Peterson were wonderful people and agreed wholeheartedly! They both taught Sunday school and attended church regularly. These folks had two young children, Bobby and Mary Lou, and lived out in the hills west of town in quite a remote area. Even though the distance to their ranch was only sixteen miles, it was a slow, rugged drive that usually took more than an hour, because there was no paved or graded road leading to their place. You really had to know the way, because the route cut across fields, pastures and ranges, and followed a pair of worn ruts that resembled a wagon trail more than a road. Frequent stops had to be made to open a gate, drive through it, and close it again behind, because it wasn't all open range. The bumpy, dusty pathway never allowed one to build up a very high rate of speed, so it took great patience and tolerance to undertake that rugged little journey. Except for neighbors who lived several miles apart, they didn't have a lot of visitors. But in spite of this semi-remoteness, their attendance at church on Sundays and special occasions was almost flawless, even in the winter. They set an excellent example for all of us who find excuses so readily for not going to church sometimes, even when we live only five or ten minutes away.

In spite of weeks of talking about Dick's outing at the ranch, his departure was very sudden. Bobby Peterson came home from Sunday school with the boys to read the funny papers and wait for his folks. About five minutes before Bobby was ready to leave, Dick informed us that he was leaving, too! Before I could approve or disapprove of his departure, Dick had thrown his pajamas, sweat shirts, extra jeans and tooth brush into a duffle bag and was heading out the door. Typical of this particular, impulsive, independent little boy, he was up the stairs and out the door before he remembered to kiss his mother goodbye. That's my boy! He's always good-natured and usually obedient, but off in a cloud of dust before his little brain starts to function. Mother-like, I was torn between two emotions: I was gratified by his opportunity to get a little taste of ranch life, but I lamented his apparent rejoicing upon leaving me, his family and his home, even for a short time.

I know it sounds like I'm always scheming to farm my boys out, especially during summer vacation from school. The truth is, I always hate to see them go, even for a few days, but I know it's important for them to develop some independence and self-reliance as they grow up, so they will be better prepared to leave the nest when that time comes. They also needed to spend some of their youth living *above* ground for a change. I sometimes worried about the psychological effect this basement living might have on the boys if we continued to do so for very long. A few evenings later, Dickie called me to tell me that he was all right. His voice sounded as small as he is, and I wanted him home very much. "Do you want to come home?" I asked.

"Heck no!" was the answer. "Mom, I'm having a swell time!"

A few days after that phone call, we paid a surprise visit to our son and his nice hosts. As I said, the unpaved "road" out to their place is very narrow, hilly, full of ruts, rocks and potholes, and is downright treacherous. For one of the rare times in my life of driving with Herman, who is truly an excellent driver, I hung on for dear life and silently prayed as my husband hurtled along the rutted trail at what I considered to be reckless speed. I tried tactfully to slow him down, but ohhhh no; he said he was anxious to get there. I replied that I did, too, but preferably in one piece. That remark was lost in the clamor of the tires hammering the gravel, and in the roar of the dusty wind rushing through the open windows. A frightened porcupine scurried across our path just in the nick of time, but I think there were a couple of prairie dogs that might not have made it. I didn't want to think about that.

We arrived in one piece at last, and I gave a silent prayer of thanks, adding our safe arrival to the growing list of miracles that have blessed us since we left Wisconsin. As we pulled up to the ranch house, I looked out the car window and was astonished to see our little "convalescent" galloping along on a huge chestnut mare… bareback! He looked like a typical little ranch boy, hair flying in the wind and perfectly at ease on his high, wide mount. I had a definite feeling that he would never come home of his own accord. He had found a world that suited him just fine! I instructed Mrs. Peterson to use her judgment as to when it was time to send him home.

This small ranch was located miles from any neighbors, and exuded happiness and contentment. It was the epitome of what one could call "the good life". The tranquility of their home was nurtured by the clean, uncluttered outdoor environment, income from their crops, food from a huge vegetable garden and the animals they raised, and graced by the love of God. They were fairly self-sufficient, and so far away from the noise and traffic of the cities, the smell of exhaust fumes, and the occasional strife and sounds of closely surrounding neighbors. I strolled through the yard filled with a beautiful array of flowers, past an abundant garden and an old-fashioned buggy, and on up to the corral. No wonder Dickie loved it so much here. It was an endless world of wonders and adventure compared to the confines of our basement. Was this the way life on earth was really meant to be? It certainly was for the Peterson family.

Bobby's little sister skipped along at my side as I walked, calling to her various pets. As we neared a beautiful gray horse, she called out, "Dusty!" He raised his large head and watched her as she drew near, then lowered it to nuzzle her with his soft, cool nose. Then, with a loud whinny, he galloped off and stood gazing at us from a distance. This horse had grown up with her since he was a colt, and he was hers alone. On the way back to the house, Mary Lou took me past a pond at the foot of the hill just beyond the house. Some young ducklings were noisily skimming back and forth across the water, while a large old gander waddled by with a small parade of docile geese, looking at the clattering young upstarts with disdain. I fondly remembered some of my childhood days spent on a farm, and how I had learned that even animals have personalities, sometimes quite entertaining.

After a sumptuous dinner that could only come from a country kitchen, and a blissful evening of delightful conversation, we reluctantly said good night. Before we could leave, however, Abby Peterson asked if we would like a couple of chickens. It didn't take long for both of us to say yes, as even chicken was still a luxury dish for us. Jim Peterson disappeared into the darkness, heading for the chicken coop not far from the house. After some scuffling sounds accompanied by a lot of cackling and squawking, he returned with a large cardboard carton. As he was placing the box into the trunk of our car, we heard the unmistakable clucking of chickens and realized with a start that our gifts were very much alive! This was further verified when our host said, "Just leave them in the box until you kill them in the morning. They'll be fine there."

Thanking them again for their gracious hospitality (perhaps with a little less enthusiasm after discovering that our dinners were still "on the hoof"), we headed home in the moonlight. On down the road a ways, Herman and I looked at each other and both began to speak at the same time. "Did you ever kill a chicken before?" And simultaneously, we both answered with a resounding "NO!" We both laughed heartily until the sobering reality struck us again. Herman sometimes hunted small game, but shooting down a pheasant or quail, or even a rabbit, was one thing. Slaughtering a farm animal was a different kind of activity—more personal—that we had no experience with. It seemed to me that we were still having a great many "first experiences" this second year in the West.

The next morning, Herman awakened early without even being called, a novelty itself. He was very aware of the gory chore he had to perform before he went to work. There was a conspicuous absence of enthusiasm as he prepared himself for the "beheadings". After stalling as long as he could over a cup of coffee, his *third* cup of coffee, he dragged himself up the stairs and outdoors with his little hatchet in hand, looking like the reluctant executioner. After a respectable lapse of time, I followed him and discovered that the deed was done. My brave chicken slayer was a trifle pale. It seems there had been quite a tussle. When he got out to our car, he had found the two chickens having a "free-for-all" in the trunk of the car, having escaped from the carton sometime during the night. Apparently, it is no small feat for the uninitiated to hold a squirming, thrashing chicken against a wooden chopping block with one hand and to deliver a swift, severing fatal blow with an ax in the other hand, and all this while trying not to close your eyes or accidentally amputate an important part of your own anatomy. I made sure Herman knew that I was very proud of his brave accomplishment and that he had triumphed over the uncooperative fowls in such a short time, too! He said that one of the creatures actually took off running for a short distance even after it was decapitated, which unnerved him considerably. It must have been awful for him, the poor, dear man.

... a conspicuous absence of enthusiasm for the beheadings.

I needed to use the car that day, so I drove Herman to work. On the way, I asked him when he was going to clean the chickens. His unenthusiastic answer was, "Sometime today I suppose." When I returned home and saw those two unfortunate victims, I decided that somehow, some way, I was going to dress those birds myself. I felt that Herman had certainly done his share, and furthermore, I remembered hearing somewhere that they should be drawn right away after they are killed. So, I resolved to carry on, no matter how I felt about the uninviting task. After circling my lifeless quarry several times, my memory recalled a hazy picture of my dad cleaning chickens when I was a little girl. I knew I had to have a pail of scalding water to plunge the chickens into, so I prepared that. It took me some time to get up the nerve to pick up that first chicken, but I finally managed to do it. Yechhhh! The gagging fumes rising from the hot, wet feathers just about bowled me over, but I was determined to suppress my sissy reactions and get on with the job. Without too many mishaps, I finished cleaning and dressing the two hens, and deposited them into the refrigerator with a great deal of pride. I just might make a good frontier woman after all. The spontaneous praise from the boys, not to mention the surprise and relief displayed on Herman's face later, was ample compensation for my efforts. Still, we all agreed that we would appreciate a chicken dinner much more in the future, so they were frozen and stored for a Sunday feast later on. It would have been more difficult if the boys had already named the birds.

A few days later as we were finishing our lunch and enjoying a relatively peaceful moment, we heard footsteps, many footsteps, hurriedly running down the stairs. The Petersons burst into the house with Dickie in tow. He was a decided mess! He had been sick all over their car and nearly everyone in it! It seems that they ate in a hurry before leaving for town, and didn't know about Dick's inclination to upchuck sometimes during a hot, bumpy car ride with his queasy tummy. Well, they sure knew about it now! Even the Peterson kids' grandma, all decked out in her summer finery, had been splattered by the putrid blast. Dick didn't play any favorites this time! I pushed him into the big shower stall and told him to strip, and then furnished the rest of the folks with plenty of soap, warm water and clean towels. They did the best they could and went on into town. It didn't take much to persuade them to leave Dick at home with me, but it took a lot more persuading with Dick to *keep* him with me! His disappointment was pathetic to behold. His heart had been set on returning to the wide open spaces to continue his wonderful vacation. I'm sure this was only one of the many times when he felt no one understood him, most of all, his mother. But that was the untimely end of Dickie's summer exile, and we were all together once more.

CHAPTER SIXTEEN
Seeking the Simple Life

I will admit to being just a simple girl. It takes very little to make me happy and content. When I smell a batch of fresh, homemade bread cooling on the racks and sending out tantalizing aromas, when I see my freshly washed, fluffy white sheets on the line billowing in the breeze against a deep blue sky, and when I have my family all together at the end of the day, I am so grateful to be alive and have so many things to be obliged for. It is always rewarding, too, to make a new friend, or to ease the pain of someone else's troubles by caring or just listening. I find joy in just helping another to realize that they truly have more blessings than they have sorrows, when they take the time to look at the whole picture.

One of our blessings is having such nice neighbors, what few neighbors we do have out on the fringe of town. Late in the summer of 1950, our newest neighbors left their pretty new home in our care when they left on a fishing trip to the clear, fresh mountain streams. I envied them for that trip. Upon their return, they presented us with two huge trout, much to our delight. They were very impressive trophies, stretched out on cold beds of dry ice. They reminded me of Herman's and my unfulfilled ambition to slip away and go fishing in the mountains. We often talked about it, and clearly visualized being surrounded by gorgeous snow-capped peaks, breathing in the spicy scent of the pine forests, and hearing the crisp, musical splashing of a tumbling mountain stream. Yes, one of these days we would invest in a couple of rods and reels and just do it! Alas, we didn't even own one single piece of fishing gear at all. Incredibly, only moments after those two trout rekindled our fishing dreams, an amazing coincidence happened to us—another little miracle I would call it. As Herman and I were admiring our neighbors' beautiful catch and talking about what it would be like to reel in one of those beauties, the doorbell rang. Herman went up to answer the door while I eavesdropped at the foot of the stairs. I heard my hubby say, "The Wilbur Malcom Show? No, I don't think so. I'm sure she didn't."

I caught a glimpse of E. E. Krebsbach, the owner of our local radio station KGCX, and heard the mention of the familiar network program. Suddenly I came to with a pop! Just for a lark, I had written a letter a few weeks earlier for a little competition they had on the radio show, and I must have won some sort of prize. I had only done it on the spur of the moment, and had forgotten all about it just as quickly. I hadn't even mentioned it to Herman, thinking it was just a silly, impulsive little thing to do that would never amount to anything. I ran up the stairs yelling, "I did too write a letter!"

"Well, it must have been pretty darned good to win a prize on a national show like that," Mr. Krebsbach remarked with a big smile. He picked up a couple of large boxes he had set on the porch and handed them to Herman. "By the way," he continued, "you not only won a famous brand automatic coffee percolator, but you also got an excellent fishing reel with a whole set of lures, flies and other fishing paraphernalia! The guys down at the station are just crazy about it! Well, congratulations, Mrs. Foell and enjoy your winnings!"

We both stared at him in stunned amazement as he walked back to his car. "Imagine that," I muttered in my stupor. "We live in a town so little that we even have to share our radio station with Williston, North Dakota, and yet I get picked to win a prize on a radio show that comes all the way from big ol' New York City! How about them apples?"

Herman grabbed me and held me tight, saying, "Honey, you are amazing! We are going fishing!" The boys were waiting at the foot of the stairs, catching snatches of the conversation and figuring out that their mother had just done something terrific on national radio. At the dinner table, they sat looking at me as though I were some kind of celebrity, while I explained what my prize-winning letter was all about. Lynn said, "Gee. Mom. You're good!" And at that moment, I really felt I was good!

Our simple life has not necessarily been just a string of miracles. I don't believe anyone's is... or should be. We all have our little humbling setbacks and hassles, and a good, jarring calamity thrown in for good measure now and then. The morning after the grand awards of trout and contest prizes, I awoke with high spirits. Who wouldn't? As soon as the family members left for school and work, I proceeded to enjoy a leisurely shower. The shower was blasting full force and it felt wonderful, but I suddenly realized that I had forgotten to take the big bottle of shampoo in with me. We kept the bottle on the floor outside the stall, so with my eyes closed against the water streaming down my face, I groped for the container and gave it a couple of generous shakes over my head. In a matter of seconds, I knew I had made a horrible mistake, just as I had done with the aspirin bottle caper. This time, it was bleach! I was panic stricken as I pictured myself with streaked white or yellow hair, a badly burned scalp, or even no hair at all! I dashed back under the shower immediately and turned it hotter, then icy cold. Don't ask me why... that just seemed like a scientific approach for some dingy reason. I didn't feel the water temperature too much because I was too busy trying to rinse the strong smelling stuff out of my hair. I squeezed my eyes shut as tight as I could, and made peculiar animal sounds like a mixture of squeals, sobs, grunts and whimpers. As I stood drying my hair, I pulled at it once in awhile to see if it was still attached to my scalp. So far anyway, I knew I was spared from being bald for the rest of my life. I postponed looking in the mirror as long as I could. I kept staring at the white spots on the bath mat where some of the bleach had drizzled, and it terrified me. My scalp burned with super sensitivity. Finally, I forced myself to look into the mirror. I just couldn't stand the suspense any longer. A sorry looking female with bloodshot eyes and a haunted look stared back at me. Outside of that, my hair was still dark brown and naturally curly. I've always been proud to have naturally curly hair, but at this point, I was just grateful to settle for HAIR! I have had several minor mishaps because I believed I knew what was in a container just by feeling the shape of the bottle. But this time, I had finally learned my lesson. Honestly! I swore an oath right then and there that I would study each label carefully, with my eyes open and the light turned on, from that day forth… forever after… for the rest of my life!

Last year was packed with about as much adventure as any normal family really needs in order to keep from getting bored for a long time. I had hoped that this year would run a little smoother, and even touch on boredom once in awhile, which I could have tolerated quite well. But, we seemed to be on a roll for new experiences and misadventures that weren't quite ready to end.

Our old car and I have always gotten along pretty well for the most part. I had come to know all of its little peculiarities and idiosyncrasies. But if there was ever to be any trouble, it would always occur when I had the car that day. I was driving down Main Street one afternoon, minding my own business, when I heard an odd noise. There was no one driving right behind me or ahead of me at that point, so I had to believe the unfamiliar sounds were coming from *my* machine. All of a sudden, it seemed as though there were hundreds of little gremlins with hammers under the hood, each pounding as hard and as loud as they could! We knew the motor was in need of overhauling, but had tried to stall the inevitable until a few urgent things around the house were taken care of first, like the new lawn for one thing.

I headed for Herman's shop, but didn't push it too hard because the noise was getting worse by the minute, and the clatter was making me quite conspicuous. I pulled into a parking space on the main street, unfortunately right in front of a group of Main Street loiterers who had nothing better to do than to discuss my situation, and not too quietly. My disposition wasn't improved a bit when I overheard the remark, "Yeah, it takes a woman to ruin a good car!" I slammed the car door, cast a few dirty looks toward my audience, and marched off with my nose in the air. Why is it that I always have the car whenever there's a flat tire, a radiator leak or a screeching fan belt on the car's agenda?

Two years ago, Herman took the car apart, piece by piece. After it was all together again, he swore it was the last time he would do a major overhaul on it. Well, he was at it again. The car resembled a mini junk yard after he tore it down. The fenders were in one corner, the pump or carburetor or whatever you call it was in another corner, the hood in another spot, and pans containing screws, nuts and bolts and odd shaped parts were all over the place in the garage. Herman resorted to riding Jack's bicycle to work, but I just had to hoof it if I needed to go anywhere. Ironically, the first day Herman rode the bike to work, the front axle broke. Fortunately, he didn't break anything on himself as he was thrown from his mount. It took him an entire evening without any supper to repair the bike at his workshop.

Day by day, little by little, the car's engine and all of its complicated parts were reassembled once again. Our fervent hope was that it would serve us just one more year. We said that for the last five years. Although the mainstream of our life seems to get a little turbulent at times, I feel like it's sort of a contest to see if we are worthy of living on this wonderful planet. It is not what the challenges are that we must face that is important; it is how we deal with them that matters. It is a glorious feeling to overcome one hurdle after another successfully. To me, that kind of satisfaction is what makes life worth living! Anyone can navigate a smooth, tedious road without any effort. But, maneuvering around the road blocks and tolerating the detours graciously makes you proud to know your skills at dealing with the rough spots in life's journey are working well for you. Thanks to Herman's skills, our chariot was riding smoothly once again.

All summer, I had watched a regular procession of children of all ages hiking along the highway past the basement. I had noticed that during the previous summer as well. Some walked in groups with knap sacks, and some rode bicycles; but I noticed that all of them carried their swimming suits and towels. When I grew curious enough to ask some of the passersby, I was informed that they were heading for "the dam". I had already heard about the dam from people in town, but I noticed there was a hint of fear when some talked about it. Actually, there were two dams in tandem, and both were built of nothing more than hard-packed dirt—at least that's what I've been told. They are located a few miles from us up in the hills. My brother-in-law, Bill, described them to us and said the dams created two large, man-made lakes with tree-lined shores providing a nice recreation area for fishing, swimming and picnicking. But the main purpose for the dams and reservoirs is irrigation, he told us.

"All these fields that receive water all summer, that's where it comes from," he explained, pointing to the hills just west of us, "the Vaux dams. With irrigation, we can grow crops we couldn't grow otherwise, because we don't get enough rain… crops like sugar beets. That's pretty important to our local economy." Bill said it was a mixed blessing for the town, adding, "Heaven help all the people in this town if those dams ever go out!"

We had lived in Montana almost two years, and we still hadn't seen those dams that everyone else seemed to know about. One Sunday afternoon in late summer, Bill volunteered to take us all out to this big attraction in his husky suburban van. After driving a short distance up the highway from our house and off into the hills, we turned off onto a side road. These "side roads" are a surprising revelation for newcomers to this part of the country. Most of the country roads here resemble the private farm lanes or rutted driveways that lead from a real, graded road to a group of farm buildings in Wisconsin. Bill was born and raised in this country, so he sees nothing unusual about the roads. As he drives, he casually looks around at the fields and surrounding countryside, pointing out interesting sights the average person wouldn't otherwise notice. The reason you don't notice many things is because you are so busy hanging on for dear life, and watching the road ahead for pot holes and big rocks. You don't dare look around! At least WE don't! The area had just experienced a brief but intense shower, not a very common occurrence here. Bill drove fast and furious, sliding from one side of the road to the other on the typically slimy Montana clay, so slippery when it is wet. We bounced over rocks, and rode up and down the roller coaster hills with eroded ruts from the recent rain, sometimes splashing through a newborn creek that would live for only a short while until the water all ran off to lower ground. Unexpectedly, Bill veered to the left without warning. My stomach tried to continue in the direction we had been going. Apparently he was taking a short cut through a field, scattering grouse and pheasants, plus a few skunk birds and magpies. He seemed to know what he was doing, but I didn't see any evidence of either road or trail that we were following. For all I knew, it was a short cut to hell. At length, after driving down a gentle slope, we reached the dam all in one piece, much to our relief. We were quite satisfied to stop for awhile after our bone-jarring ride.

The lower reservoir stretched out before us like quite a sizable lake, with a wide stream flowing away from it on the east end, tumbling down into a small, natural canyon nestled between the soft hills rising on both sides. Bill said that was "Lone Tree Creek" which flowed through the southerly part of town on its way to the Yellowstone River. It was an unexpected vision of loveliness in contrast to the barren, rolling landscape that surrounded it only a brief distance from its shores. Bushy green cottonwoods grew tall and flourished along with other lush vegetation flanking the dam, reservoir and stream for as far as one could see. I had no idea such a beautiful oasis existed so close to home. It was nothing at all like the ugly, dreaded dam I had pictured in my mind, but more like a huge, thick embankment that appeared quite solid. Bill pointed to a tall hill next to the dam. "That's called Staples Hill after the family that filed the first water rights on this creek back in the 1800s. They say Staples built little flimsy dams across the creek to store up water for irrigation, but they'd get washed out almost every spring when there was a heavy snow pack and an early thaw, and he'd have to start all over again. I'm told the graves of Staples and his wife are still clearly marked up on top of that hill, but I never climbed up there to see for myself."

"Hop in the van," Bill said, "and we'll drive up to the upper dam. It's larger than this one and of course has an even bigger reservoir behind it." A short distance upstream, we came upon Vaux dam #2.

I was quite impressed. This whole scene was so completely different from what I had assumed it would be. Herman asked Bill how old these earthen dams were and why they were called "Vaux dams", wondering if they were named after the man who had built them. Being a native of this area, Bill had a pretty good knowledge of its history.

"Yeah, Augie Vaux built them for irrigation like Staples did, only much bigger and stronger," Bill replied. "Augustus was his name. He was a pioneer settler and a merchant back in the early days of Sidney. I met the old guy once, some years back. He bought the land and water rights from Staples around 1915 or something like that. Actually, Vaux didn't build the dams himself. He hired Lalonde Construction Company to build the first one in the mid-30s. You know the outfit, Herman. They're still around and I think Lalonde is a big customer of yours, buying those big bulldozers and earthmovers that your company sells. Anyway, the first dam didn't hold enough water during the dry years, so Vaux had Lalonde build this second one across Lone Tree Creek during the war, about 1944 I think… and a bigger one, as you can see. Then the Amundsens bought him out a few years ago. We're on their land right now. They call it the Lone Tree Ranch."

After enjoying the beautiful view for awhile, and listening to my brother-in-law's interesting historical accounts, Bill said he had another place to show us that the tourists didn't know about. Even many of the locals didn't know of its existence. It was known as "Natural Corral", a small box canyon that was a popular picnic and camping spot. As we bounced along an even more rugged road than the one we took to the dam, we frightened innumerable jack rabbits and a variety of small game. Jack informed me that this was the trail the scouts had hiked a couple of times on their weekend bivouacs. It would be a long, hot, rigorous trek even for the infantry, I thought. Actually, they didn't hike the whole way, Jack admitted. That was 16 miles! They rode in a big stake truck part of the way. Dick said he had also camped at Natural Corral with the scouts once. How could I have forgotten that? I do remember the boys describing it, but I'd forgotten it was called "Natural Corral".

The fence posts along the way were a continuing source of amusement for Herman and me. They are all sizes and shapes, and range all the way from what would be a standard fence post in Wisconsin to odd shaped tree limbs and rusty old steel bars... whatever worked. Hundreds of grazing steers and horses dotted the landscape. Bill had to open one more gate before we reached our destination, and Herman hopped out to close it behind us. We actually proceeded cautiously after this point, unusual for Bill, because there was no road. There were plenty of treacherous rocks and some hills that were small, but abruptly steep and could cause you to roll over easily if you were careless.

Again, for the second time that afternoon, we found ourselves suddenly and unexpectedly in a beautiful piece of paradise hidden in the midst of drab, treeless hillsides. It was easy to see how this place got its name. It *was* a natural corral. Towering, multicolored rock formations formed sheer cliffs on three sides, encircling a Garden of Eden with lush, green trees and underbrush in a horseshoe-shaped strip of forest at the base of the cliffs. In the center of the area was a large clearing, rising gently to the flattened dome of meadow. Where the meadow sloped to the edge of the woodlands, a crystal clear creek formed a border, running through the little canyon in a wide arc and back out again. At the base of the highest cliff was a cold, clear pool fed by a natural spring from deep beneath the rocks. It drew us like a magnet, parched as we were from the exciting, dusty ride and the hot summer day. I don't think I have ever tasted more delicious, thirst quenching water than I drank from that spring in Natural Corral. I never dreamt such a beautiful place could exist out there in those dreary hills. The only drawback it had as a picnic site was the ample, odiferous evidence all over the lovely green meadow that the horses and cattle enjoyed this place as much as humans, perhaps even more. The meadow was spotted with considerable deposits of horse apples and meadow muffins. I asked Bill if there were also rattlesnakes around Natural Corral. He just smiled at me and nodded knowingly.

I had heard that there were plenty of rattlesnakes populating this part of the territory, but I was never fortunate or perhaps unfortunate enough to see one here, or on any of our summer trips. I suppose that was fortunate for me. Snakes petrify me, poisonous or not! There were a few occasions when we were out sightseeing in the Badlands, and we would step out of the car to see a spectacular sight a little better. We could hear a buzzing sound sometimes that I thought were locusts or something. Herman said it was the sound of rattlesnakes warning us not to come any closer. I usually climbed right back into the car at such times. I didn't need to see any further confirmation of Herman's wisdom. Helen told me that every once in a great while, mostly in the summer, you might hear a story about a rattlesnake crawling right down Main Street in town. It seems that they occasionally wind themselves around the axle of a horse trailer or hay wagon out on a ranch, and then drop off onto a street when the rancher drove to town for supplies or something. Usually they got run over and killed before they bothered anybody. Still, I never saw one, and that was fine with me. I asked the two older boys if they took any precautions about snakes when they were camping with the scouts. They both had lectures about dangerous snakes and first aid training for snake bites. They also carried snake bite kits in their first aid packs. Dickie told me that at night before they went to sleep in their pup tents, they would put a big thick hemp rope on the ground encircling their tent. They were told that snakes didn't like the feel of a hemp rope on their bellies and wouldn't crawl across it. That was another new one on me! So much to learn about this new world!

A family we knew from church told of a harrowing experience that certainly taught us to be ever on guard against rattlesnakes. The Boyds had some friends across the Yellowstone River, on the edge of the Badlands. They went over one morning to help brand some calves. Piling their three little children into the car, they drove across the long steel bridge and up the highway a short distance to their friends' corral. The branding was already in progress when they arrived, having started at dawn. They spotted an old wagon sitting next to one of the colorful, sandstone outcroppings, and placed the three little ones into the bed of the old relic. He turned to talk to a group of cowboys standing nearby, but suddenly had a strong impulse to turn back again and look into the wagon. Miraculously, at the *opposite* end of the wagon bed from where he'd placed the children was a veritable nest of rattlers, perhaps six or eight. Mr. Boyd said he didn't take time to count them. One was too many! They had evidently dropped down from the adjacent ledge. Needless to say, it took him only seconds to remove his terrified children from the wagon. He said he had nightmares for more than a week after that experience. That story was enough warning for me. Whenever we go out in the hills or the Badlands, we all use extreme caution, wearing sturdy boots and being careful never to put our hands in or on a place we can't see first.

With the approach of the annual Richland County Fair and Rodeo, we were all filled with excitement and anticipation. We lived right along the direct route to the fairgrounds, actually within walking distance, so we got a regular preview of what was going into the fair and rodeo grounds right from our front stoop. Farm equipment, livestock trucks and displays of all kinds rumbled past our basement all day and far into the night before the grand event was scheduled to begin. The pastures and corrals surrounding the fair grounds were well-stocked with Brahma bulls, steers, and horses. The boys worked hard at their summer jobs to save up enough spending money for the fair. The carnival and the rodeo were the main highlights, in their estimation. The exhibits weren't much of an attraction for boys. Even little Lynn had a job, taking care of a fifteen month old boy. Dick ran errands and pulled weeds, and Jack cut lawns and worked as a part-time chore boy at the radio station. The station paid him a silver dollar every week. They wound up with more spending money than Herman and I had!

The big day finally arrived. The first day is usually a record breaker for attendance, so we delayed until the last day, even though the boys were chomping at the bit. We had reserved seats in the grandstand, so we checked our picnic lunches and blankets with friends who were working one of the food booths, and visited the various exhibits until rodeo time. It is customary for many families to take a picnic lunch and a blanket for the cool evenings, and to spend most of the day in the grandstand because there were so many events that went on for hours.

In spite of the exceptionally dry summer, the harvest was beautiful and bountiful. There were golden grains and the biggest vegetables on display that I've ever seen, without exception. Most of the vegetables were grown by irrigation farming. The baked goods section is always the scene of stiff competition. Many of the same women compete year after year, so they become known for their favorite entries. It was amusing to listen to people's comments and criticisms, some good and some not too complimentary, as the local housewives (including myself) carefully inspected the blue ribbon winners. "Why, my pies look twice as good as those!" one cynic exclaimed. "Yep, wouldn't you know it? She got first prize again! I bet her husband is one of the judges," said another skeptic. I heard one husband whine, "You've got to learn to bake bread, Emma. Maw always used to bake our bread three times a week!" Even my own family was heard to say, "Gosh, Mom, they should see *your* stuff!" I was thinking the same thing. I'm usually a modest person, but I'm very confident when it comes to my cooking and baking. But talk is cheap, and it takes courage to deliver the goods and take your chances against some very good cooks who are also submitting their delicious entries. Delivering the goods, not just talking about it, is what wins the blue ribbons in this life. Maybe I would take a shot at it the next year.

After enjoying the exhibits and letting the kids go on some of the rides, we picked up our blankets and picnic basket and headed for our seats in the grandstand to watch the preliminary activities. The county was quite proud of their fair grounds and had a right to be. It was quite a layout covering quite a few acres and with some sizable buildings in the complex. It was good to sit down for a change after all the walking around the entire fair grounds. We now focused our attention on the arena. The clowns were amusing the crowd with their whacky and clever antics. I enjoyed hearing our boys laughing so hard. The cowboys were riding back and forth across the arena, resplendent in all their finery, with beautifully embossed leathers and the handcrafted silver trappings, mounted on carefully groomed, handsome steeds. They were quite conscious of the attention and admiration they were attracting. The band played the national anthem, finishing with an earsplitting salute of skyrockets, and the rodeo began.

None of us had ever been to a real rodeo before. We had seen them in the movies, and we understood a little bit about the different events, but actually being there was a very exciting experience for me. Herman watched the proceedings as if he were studying a whole new culture and the boys were out of their minds with the thrill of watching real cowboys and cowgirls in action. It was fascinating to watch the horsemanship, especially the young girls during the barrel races and trick riding events, but excitement filled the air even before the rugged bronco riding and bulldogging events when one of the cowgirls was thrown from her horse—and didn't get up. A chill ran down my spine as she was carried off in an ambulance, even though the announcer said she was not seriously injured and would be just fine.

The wild bucking broncos captivated me, trying to imagine what it might be like to be mounted atop a jarring, jerking, tornado-like crazy horse that obviously had some powerful objections to having a human on its back. I have had a little experience riding some tired old trail horses when I was younger, but these spinning, twisting, bucking horse-devils were beyond my comprehension. Why would anyone want to try to ride such ill-tempered animals in the first place? And on purpose? I soon learned there were even bigger, meaner animals to appear in the arena, the likes of which I had never seen before. Brahma bulls are enormous, have a killer instinct, do not particularly care for human beings, and have some of the most unpleasant, unfriendly attitudes I have ever witnessed in an animal. The bull riding event kept me absolutely spellbound. I had a lot of trouble keeping my mouth closed.

We were all quite exhausted when we finally got home. Fortunately, we didn't have far to travel since we lived almost next door to the fairgrounds. It had been a long, fun-filled, exciting day. My tummy wasn't too pleased with me, having assaulted it with sandwiches and hot dogs and cotton candy and pie and more things than I care to mention. Otherwise, I was quite happy for the new experiences and the time we had all shared together. We would be talking about the fair and rodeo for weeks, and the boys were already looking forward to the next one.

CHAPTER SEVENTEEN
Sweet Dreams Turn Sour

When we first started to build, we decided to plant all of our yard with grass. The summer of 1950 taught me numerous things, one of which was to set aside a large plot for a garden. I wanted two currant bushes and two baby apple trees for which I had already marked the spots. Next I wanted a strawberry patch, a melon patch, some tomato plants and lots of vegetables—cucumbers, carrots, onions, lettuce, beets, radishes, peas—the whole works! I had almost forgotten the thrill a person gets when she pulls that first carrot or onion out of her garden. The thought of a salad bowl from my own garden everyday, the vision of my own fresh veggies to cook with that stew or pot roast or homemade soup—ahhhh, now that's inspiration a plenty! Of course, we did have dry seasons to contend with, but we had plenty of water. We had hordes of grasshoppers too, but there was "pizen" for the asking at the county office. So, before the next spring, I was determined to send for those beautiful, appetizing garden seed catalogs, and then see what I could do with our yard for summer '51.

Some people say that dreams are just lazy folks' way of letting life slip by. Maybe for some, that might be true; but I heartily disagree with that in general. I've had many dreams, some possible and some impossible. The possible ones have not all been practical. In fact, a few have turned from ordinary dreams into nightmares. On the other hand, the dreams we have today are the inspiration we need for tomorrow and the days to follow, sort of like planning ahead so you have something to accomplish, a target to shoot at. If we stopped dreaming, for example, we would never get the main floor built and finish our home. I've always encouraged our boys to have dreams. It sparks the ambition to spur them on and feel the excitement when a dream turns into action. Many happy hours that we spent sharing our dreams will become lasting sweet memories.

As another winter approached, I had confidence that with the Grace of God we would not have to worry about another spring thaw and another flooded basement. We had put 30 truckloads of dirt on our lot and graded it for good drainage. It is vexatious when you consider that we had weathered the most severe winter that Montana had in years, the "floodiest" spring, the windiest summer, and record breaking heat. If the good Lord was putting us to the test, I fervently hope we passed with high honors. In spite of our trials, we still loved living in this big, beautiful state, and by golly we were going to stick it out no matter what! And yet in the back of my mind, I had this nagging feeling sometimes that maybe God was trying to tell us something… like, maybe we really shouldn't be here and we were not meant to stay.

There seems to be an almost paranormal effect one develops from living in a basement and always having to look up as you attempt to see out of the high windows. It's as if it caused me to communicate with God more often than in any other period of my life, because I had to look upward more often than ever before. I don't know if that's true, but I've thought of that often lately. If nothing else, I'm sure the whole family will have good posture from the habit of always walking around with their heads held high. My faith was strong, and I deeply believed that in the next year we would build. We would build the rest of our house together, with additional strength, faith and courage, because we would be building a blessed home on a good foundation for a happy, loving family. I couldn't fathom that we could possibly fail to accomplish that goal.

Winter arrived again, and by the end of February, 1951, all of our hopes and dreams were crumbling… and then they finally shattered. We woke up early one damp, eerie morning to find another "Chinook" upon us. Yes, our dream had turned into a nightmare. The unseasonably warm wind was causing a rapid thaw of the snow drifts, and water was again streaming past our house, too close for comfort. Our added fill and grading didn't mean a thing except that at least we didn't have a deep ditch or a moat directly adjacent to the basement walls. Otherwise it would have been full of water by now and pouring into the window wells as it had the preceding spring. That one was our second flood, but disaster was averted in the nick of time by a highway crew diverting most of the water away from our lot. Although it was notably less damaging than our first flood, the episode was extremely disheartening nevertheless.

This time, it was four o'clock in the morning when Herman wearily took his shovel out into the dark, sleety morning to try to divert the water away from our basement. About an hour later, he trudged heavily down the stairs, a picture of abject despair. He plunked down on a chair in the utility room and stared at nothing in particular. I looked at his pale face and started for the kitchen to get him some hot coffee, but I never got there. I heard a dull thud and looked around to see Herman sprawled on the floor. Lynn screamed, and after trying in vain to bring my husband to, I ran for the phone. Dickie was already there, trying to call the doctor. He was sure an unpredictable little boy that often bewildered us; yet he always showed a cool head and good sense in an emergency. Dr. Harper said he would be right out. The boys and I struggled to get Herman onto the bed. It was impossible to remove the mud covered hip boots from his limp legs, so we dumped him on the bed just as he was. He slowly began showing signs of life, much to our relief, and was fully conscious by the time the doctor came. Dr. Harper arrived in record time and performed a brief examination. He said it appeared to be mostly physical exhaustion, combined with his efforts out in the cold mud and water. Suddenly, we both lost all of that wonderful courage and faith we had always been blessed with when we needed it, that strength that had sustained us through one calamity after another. Our spirit seemed to be draining from us faster than we could drain the water away from our home, which seemed once again to be turning into an island.

As the doctor was leaving, help was arriving. I don't know who called them or where they came from, but thank God they were there, doing what Herman couldn't do by himself. We were spared from being completely flooded out this time, thanks to the many ditches the men quickly dug to divert water away from our house as they had the previous spring. The people of the town had been as confident as we were that the flooding problem would never occur again. But now, everyone was at a loss as to what to do next about the drainage. Somehow, we just didn't care. Out of total frustration, Herman said, "Enough is enough! We need to get out of here while the getting is good! God only knows what will happen next."

I had no will to argue with him. I felt defeated, resigned to taking our losses and pulling up stakes. Herman's job here in Sidney hadn't developed the way he thought it would, and there was clearly no chance that he would ever be part of the ownership or management as was intimated more than three years ago. We knew that job openings for Herman's skills would be plentiful now "back home" in the Midwest. With the Korean War in full swing, new defense contracts created many new jobs that were right up his alley.

I told the boys to go back to bed for awhile, and I snuggled up to my hubby to comfort him and to talk about our next move. "What do you think," he asked me softly, "about quitting and moving back to Wisconsin?"

The word "quitting" kind of startled me. I never liked the sound of that word. I told Herman I didn't think making new plans was the same as quitting. "Remember our dream of creating a restaurant called the Old Homestead," I reminded him, "not too many years ago? Well, we did it. We made that dream come true! We made it happen, and it was very successful. People loved the place! Its reputation spread like wildfire. But with the war, the food rationing and my getting sick, we were fighting an uphill battle we couldn't win. It was a wonderful idea, but it would have been more successful at another time. So we sold it and moved on. We didn't quit. It was an exciting, wonderful adventure that we'll never forget, and it was time to change our plans because it was the smart thing to do at that point."

I told him that our Montana adventure was the same kind of situation. It was a dream that we had to try on for size, and we had the courage to do it. It hadn't been all bad. It was quite an exciting adventure, going places, doing things and meeting people that many folks never experience. Some people only dream, but never do anything about their dreams. Well, we have lived our dreams, and we will have many more dreams and adventures in the future. I know that not long before this scary day happened, I had said we were going to stick it out no matter what. Well, when I said that, I hadn't carefully thought about all the "no-matter-whats" that might enter into the picture.

I reminded Herman that we had always placed our lives in God's hands, and tried to do what we believed He wanted us to do. Well, this was one of those times. I was having a very strong feeling that what happened that day was a warning, a message to take heed, an early alarm not to be ignored. That near flood, and Herman's collapse told me we had pushed our luck as far as we should dare and it was time to think seriously about what might happen next. There is a time to stand your ground because it is well worth the fight to hold your position. But there are other times when choosing not to budge is pure, stubborn foolishness. Herman agreed. Call it a premonition or whatever label you want to stick on it, we both had strong feelings of apprehension that we couldn't explain. We felt that if we didn't move back to Wisconsin soon, we might never be able to move at all.

Helen, my older sister in Sidney, was heartbroken by our decision to leave, but she understood. Florence, my younger sister in Wisconsin was overjoyed that we would be back together again. She even offered to find us a nice apartment where we could move in temporarily until our plans were more solidified. I told her I definitely wanted a second floor apartment so I could look *down* for a change, instead of just up. As for the boys, they *sort of* understood... but they didn't really. How could they grow up to be cowboys if we were living in Wisconsin? Two weeks later, we put our partially completed dream house, our basement home, up for sale and hoped for the best.

... our partially completed dream house up for sale.

[This was the last entry in Ruth Foell's journal, but not the end of the story.]

CHAPTER EIGHTEEN
Calamities and Miracles

Sunday afternoon, March 25, 1951: Sigvard Amundsen drove his pickup over to the Vaux Dam on Lone Tree Creek. "The dam" was actually two compacted earth dams built one behind the other about three-quarters of a mile apart. Their combined reservoirs extended for almost two miles. Amundsen was concerned about a leak that was spotted at the north end of the upper dam earlier in the week. It wasn't a major leak, just a steady trickle; but that was something one doesn't ignore in an earthen dam because it could quickly grow larger with erosion, particularly with alternating freeze-thaw cycles. He and his wife owned the Lone Tree Ranch where the dams were located. Both reservoirs were filled to capacity due to recent Chinooks that caused accelerated thawing of the snow pack in the hills, quickly adding to the reservoir depth and increasing the pressure behind the dams. Fortunately, cold weather returned to slow down the early thaw. In fact, the mercury plunged to 28 below zero just two weeks earlier, and the ice on the two reservoirs was about four feet thick. Still, they'd had several warm days above freezing since that cold spell, and that worried Amundsen. Eastern Montana had experienced heavier than usual snowfall this winter, which meant a large supply of ice and snow to melt and swell the size of the many small streams contributing to Lone Tree Creek.

As the sun lowered toward the horizon in the late afternoon, Amundsen inspected the lower dam carefully. It seemed to be in pretty good shape, even though it was the older of the two. Old man

Vaux had built it in 1936 for irrigation purposes. The furrows of his brow deepened as he approached the newer, upper dam about 4:00 P.M. Built in '44, it was enlarged just four years ago, shortly before Amundsen and his wife acquired the water rights. The leak on the north end of the fill appeared to be a bit worse, but he couldn't be sure. Hopefully, the nighttime temperature would drop far enough below freezing to slow down the leakage, and he could get a crew to repair and strengthen that section in the morning. He checked out the spillway that was built when the second dam was enlarged, and it was clear. The water hadn't risen quite high enough yet to run over into the spillway, but it was very close. Amundsen planned to look at it again early in the morning.

S.A. Amundsen wasn't the only man worried about the dam. Cort Olsen, his manager who ran the ranch operations for him, was on the dam at 9:00 P.M. that same Sunday night. Cort was startled to see so much water rushing through the spillway, although it was capable of carrying a tremendous flow of water if necessary. It was 32 feet wide at the base and 38 feet deep with sloping sides. But his concern was for the farmers downstream. The spillway was dry when Amundsen had checked it a few hours earlier. If the flow increased very much more, Lone Tree Creek would surely overflow its banks and endanger some of the livestock near the already swollen stream. Olsen returned to his house on the ranch and tried to call his boss on the phone. He was unable to locate Amundsen, and decided to call the Sheriff's office. After quickly explaining the situation to Deputy John Collins, Cort continued trying to locate Amundsen. Meanwhile, Deputy Collins notified all the farmers in the area, advising them to move any livestock or equipment away from the creek to higher ground.

About 10:30 P.M., Cort finally located Amundsen and brought him up to date. The men agreed to rendezvous at the upper dam. Cort Olsen was usually a laid back, easy-going man, but he was also very conscientious, and he had an uneasy feeling of apprehension tonight like he'd never felt before. Listening to the water gushing into the spillway, he turned up the collar on his heavy sheep-liner and pulled down the flaps of his Canadian Mountie-type winter hat to cover his ears. A dreadful feeling of foreboding was beginning to grip him, to overtake him with the fear that something evil was about to happen. He could feel the oncoming disaster in the pit of his stomach. Cort knew Amundsen would take this situation very seriously, but would anyone in town understand the gravity of the situation enough to take the necessary action to save lives? Could they even find anyone to heed their warning that a powerful, destructive force was about to be unleashed upon this vulnerable little town as it lay huddled in the night, sleeping peacefully? After all, it was late Sunday night and most folks were already in bed, resting up for the work week ahead. Sidney was totally defenseless and unaware that it lay directly in the path of a dark force crouching in the hills above the town, a growing, overpowering force that no man could stop or hold at bay any longer. Cort desperately wanted to share his terror, knowing how futile it would be to hold back a demon that would not be denied its night of fury and destruction. Who would believe that the Vaux Dams were about to collapse and the town might be wiped out before the night was over? Perhaps he was over-dramatizing the situation, he argued with himself. Maybe his fears were exaggerated and the danger wasn't as bad as he was imagining.

11:00 P.M., Sunday, March 25: Olsen moved his truck to higher ground, angled downward on the hillside so that it lined up with the heavy dirt embankment that formed the upper dam. The spotlight and headlights on his pickup were trained on the face of the dam where water was seeping at a faster rate through a small gap at the north end. More water was now gushing through the spillway at a tremendous volume. He just stood there feeling small and weak, transfixed by hundreds or perhaps thousands of gallons pouring into the spillway, bypassing the lower reservoir. The moon was high overhead, still nearly full, and bright enough in the cold, clear air to illuminate the snow and ice-covered scene with a luminescent glow.

11:20 P.M.: Olsen was relieved to see headlights moving toward him through the tense, lonely night. Standing vigil alone at this deteriorating situation was certainly not his idea of how to spend a Sunday evening. Amundsen jumped out of his pickup and asked Olsen for a status report as he ran a spotlight along the banks of the spillway. He could see that the unusually heavy flow was already gnawing away at the rock and gravel sides.

"Where the hell did all this water come from?" asked Amundsen of no one in particular. He already knew the answer… a heavy snow pack, early warm winds on too many days alternating with cold nights. The cycles of freeze, thaw, freeze, thaw steadily added to the watershed upstream until more water was pouring into his reservoirs than he had ever seen before. The huge spillway had always been a comforting safety factor for him, but now he wasn't so sure it would be able to handle such a heavy volume of rushing water. When his spotlight reached the bridge that the county had built across the spillway two years ago, he gasped and yelled "Holy Moses!" Cort's eyes followed the shaft of light from Amundsen's spotlight to see what had alarmed him. Not only was the unusually heavy overflow eroding the banks of the spillway, it was tearing out the roadway approaches on both sides of the bridge. The two men just stood there, unable to move, hypnotically watching the churning water's relentless attack on the bridge's abutments as they became more and more unstable.

"What are we gonna do, Sig?" yelled Olsen over the roaring sound of the spillway deluge.

"I don't know if there's anything we *can* do," Amundsen replied. "But if that bridge drops down and blocks the flow in the spillway, we're going to have one hellova problem here, I'll guarantee you!"

Sometime after midnight, one end of the bridge broke free of its withering foundation and splashed into the spillway with a resounding crash. The 50 foot span lay at an angle into the spillway for over half an hour, churning the raging water and valiantly defying it to overcome the injured structure. Amundsen shouted that if the other end of the bridge broke loose and dropped, they'd better pray that the force of the water would shift the structure the long-way in the direction of flow to offer the least resistance to the stream. Shortly before 1:00 A.M., the other end of the bridge tore loose from its crumbling abutment and the entire span plunged into the spillway. As the men watched anxiously, aiming their spotlights at the wreckage, they saw the bridge roll onto its side and lodge firmly into the sides of the spillway, stretching crosswise and forming a dam against the rushing waters.

Amundsen swore and headed for his truck, yelling to Olsen over his shoulder. "I'm going back to the ranch to round up some of the men. We've got to get some dynamite and try to blast that bridge out of the way before all hell breaks loose. I'll have my wife call the sheriff and let him know this whole dam could blow out at any time!"

Gravel, dirt and ice flew into the air from the spinning rear wheels of Amundsen's truck as he gunned the engine and tore off into the night at breakneck speed. Once again, Cort Olsen was alone in the chill of the night, and the situation was growing more dangerous every minute. He remembered that he still had a thermos of coffee in his truck, so he sought shelter in the warmth of the cab and found momentary solace in the cup of coffee that was still fairly hot. He may as well enjoy a brief respite while he could—before the inevitable nightmare shifted into full speed. Periodically, he checked both the clogged spillway and the weakening fill at the north end of the dam. He watched mud and debris building up behind the fallen bridge span stretched across the spillway. Even though water was gushing over the top of the wreckage, he knew it was causing a backup that only added more pressure to the upper dam, the bigger of the two dams with the largest reservoir, and the added flow might soon be topping the dam's crest. By nature, Olsen was a stable sort, stalwart and reliable, not easily rattled. But this night, he readily admitted to himself that he was flat out scared. This night, the devil himself was riding the wind and the water, and neither man nor beast could stop him.

2:05 A.M., Monday, March 26, 1951: Olsen was pacing back and forth alongside his truck, wondering what was keeping Amundsen away so long. Was he having trouble finding the dynamite? Did he slide into a ditch or sink hole and get stuck? Time was running out and even if there was no way to stop the inevitable, he sure didn't enjoy babysitting this time bomb all alone. Responding to a premonition that suddenly swept over him, Cort aimed his truck's spotlight at the north end of the fill. Unbelievably, right before his eyes, a fissure developed at the spot where the slow leak had been, quickly widening from the erosion as the breach moved downward from the crest of the dam to the base of the fill. In less than two minutes, the dam ruptured and opened wide like a giant gate, unleashing millions of gallons of frigid water to begin their terrible path of destruction.

The ground beneath Olsen shuddered and a deafening rumble awakened the sleeping night air as the torrent ripped through the dam, tearing out the entire embankment in a matter of seconds. So rapidly did the upper reservoir empty that the heavy crust of ice on top dropped to the bottom of the lake bed almost in one piece. The massive volume from the entire upper lake rolled toward the lower reservoir like a giant tidal wave. Olsen jumped into his truck and raced along the shoreline toward the lower dam, almost keeping abreast of the massive wall of water as if in a chase scene from some surreal Hollywood movie. Within three minutes, the full weight of the tsunami-like wave struck the lower body of water with such a powerful impact that the thick sheet of ice on the lower lake rotated upward like a huge translucent plate, forcing down the west end that was hit first, and lifting the far edge perhaps 20 feet or more above the top of the dam before it shattered with a thunderous roar and crashed back down onto the reservoir's surface. Cort's mouth was agape with awe and he covered his ears against the painful clamor of rushing waters and shattering ice, only to hear his own rapid heartbeat pounding in his ears. The entire terrifying drama played out as if in slow motion before his wide, disbelieving eyes—a horrifying, impossible scene illuminated by the bright moon and witnessed only by God and Cort Olsen.

Olsen drove closer to the older embankment. It still seemed to be intact for the moment, but how long would it hold? Water and major chunks of ice were already topping the dam, rapidly eroding the fill and rushing downstream, adding to the creek that was already overflowing its banks from the spillway of the upper dam... the dam that no longer existed. It wouldn't be long before the second barrier would give way from the tons of pressure behind it and the erosion of the additional water from the upper lake. The water that was already topping the dam would initially create a flash flood along Lone Tree Creek that would be insignificant compared to the horrifying scene to follow. The people in town would never believe the incredible events he had already witnessed this night. The people in town! Oh my God, he thought! What would happen to the inhabitants of the sleeping little town below him? He had no possible means to contact anyone in time. The anguish within him was unbearable.

It wasn't very long after 2:15 A.M. before the lower Vaux Dam also gave way and sent an unbelievable wall of water, boulders and icebergs cascading down into the valley. It roared past the golf course taking out some of the greens and fairways. Like a hundred powerful locomotives charging downhill side-by-side, the deadly wave loaded with enormous blocks of ice crashed into the County Fairgrounds. One frozen missile plowed into the main exposition building, tearing a ten foot wide hole through the wall and door. More hunks of ice followed the pathfinder into the large building, enough to leave two and three layers of ice blocks that completely surrounded and covered two new trucks and a station wagon stored there. The wall of water continued, leveling the other county buildings, and carrying splintered wood, twisted steel, tractors, bales of straw and other debris along with the tide as it rushed across the fields toward the unsuspecting town. As the wave crossed the main irrigation canal, some of the ice and water were captured and diverted by the canal, enough to save some of the homes on the north side of town from serious damage, but barely putting a dent in the ferocious energy of the flood's onslaught. The wave cut a swath several miles wide, tearing out two miles of fence and the laborers' bunkhouse on Jack Luna's farm. By the time the ice hit the valley, it had broken into countless smaller pieces, but many of the chunks still weighed between five and ten tons!

The icy wall of murky water continued its rapid, deadly pace as the first punishing wave raced toward the Yellowstone River, inundating 85 percent of the small city, striking and collapsing the middle 50 foot span of the bridge on Highway 16 just south of town, and choking the highway on both sides of the fallen bridge with ice chunks. That evacuation route was rendered completely impassable and useless. The relentless wave moved on east of the highway with a fury, striking the Northern Pacific railroad bridge, wiping out a 90 foot span and tearing up 500 feet of track, damaging another 1500 feet of track bed. The flood waters also destroyed the telegraph lines and railroad telephone wires along the tracks, and took out the high voltage lines along the highway, plunging the city into darkness as it would remain until the Montana-Dakota Power Company could reroute electricity into the city from the north hours later. Flood waters extinguished pilot lights in basement water heaters and furnaces allowing leaking gas to bubble to the surface posing countless explosion hazards. Over 7,000 gallons of gasoline were forced out of storage tanks at the Farmer Union Oil Company station, covering all water in the area with a quarter inch of gasoline just waiting for a discarded lit cigarette or even a spark to light an inferno.

Bernice Ullman was the only telephone operator on duty at Sidney's Mountain States Telephone office in the quiet hours of the graveyard shift. About 2:25 A.M., an anonymous caller, possibly Deputy John Collins, instructed Bernice to turn on the alarm and to warn all callers about the Vaux Dam failures and the flood. At first, she thought the caller was a prankster and the so-called emergency was a hoax. In the next few minutes, she heard several frantic callers screaming about water raging through the streets and getting deeper all the time, wanting to know what was going on. She immediately turned on the volunteer fire siren and called off-duty operators to come in and help her if they could. From that point on, Mrs. Ullman, alone at the switchboard, did not answer calls with the traditional, "Number, please". She abruptly greeted each caller with a curt, "Both Vaux Dams have broke! Leave town immediately!"

A number of residents who did receive the warning early enough made it to their cars and trucks and headed out of town. Some attempted to take the highway south to Glendive but had to turn around because the bridge was washed out. Highway 16 to Culbertson was impassable, jammed with huge blocks of ice. Several hundred fleeing citizens made it north to nearby Fairview, eleven miles away, while others were happy just to make it to higher ground above the floodwaters where they waited until the water receded. Hundreds of residents who failed to hear the fire sirens were awakened by the thundering roar of the water and ice, barely escaping with their lives, particularly those who lived in basement homes. Many terrified basement dwellers, soaking wet and clad only in robes and night clothes, shivered in the sub-freezing temperatures of the darkened city until they were rescued or taken in by nearby residents who were above water, though their own basements were flooded in most cases.

5:30 A.M., Monday, March 26: By the time dawn broke, the water was beginning to subside in most parts of the city, and only small streams ran along the gutters of mud covered streets in the higher northern half of town. Most basements were filled with silt and water, and the sound of small gasoline engines filled the air as water pumps of every size and description were put to work all over town. From high in the air, the area looked like so many ice cubes scattered over a drenched carpet of land as far as one could see. Tractors and heavy trucks with plows pushed and dragged the huge blocks of ice to clear obstructed roads and highways, or wherever they created a serious hazard.

6:00 A.M., Monday: Water still flowed heavily in some areas near Lone Tree Creek and a few other scattered locations, but most of the town was calmly recovering, already busily digging out of the muck and debris, searching for trapped victims. Along highway 16 on the west edge of town, a stair enclosure clad in gray tar paper protruded from the icy, muddy water like the conning tower of a partially submerged submarine. It stood as a lone sentinel atop a large, flat, rectangular structure that was under several inches of water, but discernable as the roof of what had recently been someone's basement home. It was a home no longer—just a flooded cistern, an underwater tomb for anyone who may have been in the house when the flood waters struck without warning in the darkness. Huge blocks of ice barricaded the only door and many of the small, submerged windows. More ice lounged on top of the basement roof amid debris and straw bales from the demolished fair grounds a short distance "upstream". Thirty yards to the west, a street sign stuck out of the water, its spindly metal post bent over, but surviving. It marked the corner of the sunken lot at the intersection of Sunset Boulevard and West Holly Street, otherwise known as Highway 16. The muddy street, inappropriately called a *boulevard*, was under at least three feet of water. Only Holly Street, appropriately called the *high* way, was now passable in the cold, gray dawn. An eerie, deathly silence hovered over the stark scene except for the soft murmur of running water. There were no signs of life here.

Saturday afternoon, March 31, 1951: In her second floor apartment nearly a thousand miles to the east of Sidney, Montana, Ruth opened the special delivery letter from her sister in Sidney with excitement and anticipation. The envelope was smudged with dirt and water stains, but it didn't matter to Ruth. Opening mail from Helen was always like opening a present. Helen's handwriting was so beautiful and legible, and the contents were more than just newsy; they were full of life. Perhaps Helen should have been the one writing the book, or perhaps she should have at least consulted with Helen as a collaborator. Ruth would give that some thought when she was ready to begin her first attempt at editing and rewriting her journal, transforming the manuscript into a book.

Thinking of her book, Ruth suddenly remembered that she had lent the carbon copy of her manuscript to Vivian Baker to read, and had forgotten to retrieve it from her before leaving Sidney. They had left town hurriedly, forsaking a lot of tearful goodbyes. Perhaps Helen could pick it up from Vivian and use it for reference as Ruth rewrote the story and compared notes with her sister. Yes, that would work out great. Some things happen just as they are meant to happen. It's amazing how life seems to work out sometimes, she mused. As she began to read, her smile disappeared; her hands turned cold and froze to the pages of Helen's letter. Ruth sat down, trembling, trying to hold the letter steady enough to read.

Monday PM
March 26, 1951
Dear Ruth,

I will try to write some kind of a letter. Like everyone else in Sidney, I am positively dazed from shock. Both of the big Vaux Dams went out between 2 and 3 o'clock this morning, and to say that Sidney is in the midst of a flood would be putting it mildly!! The first thing we knew about it was waking up at about 3 this morning to a continuous fire siren, and after we were up, seeing a stream of cars heading towards Fairview using the old lane east of us, the main highway, and the cemetery road... all with solid lines of cars, bumper to bumper, evacuating the town. I decided it must be a terrible fire, so I had the nerve to call the operator. All she said was, "The Vaux Dams have gone out! Leave town immediately!"

We did get the kids up and got into the car with a few important documents and extra clothes, but didn't go anywhere. We just sat out along the highway, ready to leave if necessary. The lights were all out in the town, and not until they went back on did I feel safe to come back to the house. Bill and Billy went on into town, and with all the tales they had to tell when they came back at 6 AM, I had to see for myself; so I've been riding around off and on since then.

Ruth, it is truly a blessing that you left when you did, and none too soon. Your basement is completely full, totally under water! Huge chunks of ice and bales of straw litter the top—no yards at all—silt halfway up the sides of the garage all the way around, to give you an idea of how deep the water got when it first hit your place. Lillys to the east of your house are ruined again, this time for good I'd say. There are blocks of ice all over the sugar beet field west of your place. The Fairgrounds are all wrecked, and huge (4' thick and as large as 10' square) chunks of ice cover the whole valley for miles and miles. I wish you could see the County Fairgrounds—hardly a building left, and all those big pieces of ice everywhere. I guess a huge wall of water came roaring down the hill this side of Doc Peterson's and the Lone Tree Inn, taking out cars, houses, wiping out the highway and bridge on the south side of town.

Newell's just got their two boys out of their basement in time just as the water took over... Security Building and Loan was filled to the top, and they finished pumping out the water just tonight. Now try to find anything. Osborn's Studio lost thousands of dollars worth of film he has stored in his basement. Practically every building in town that wasn't wiped out is sweeping out mud and pumping out water. The county yards are under water. Old Mrs. Beck's house (Eddie's folks) is under water, too. People are going around in boats. The greenhouse and Safeway, gone—and still the water comes.

We drove down to the south side of town when the water was down enough that we could get through with the Suburban, but you have to park about where the trailer court is and walk from there. From the Old Wagon Wheel, clear as far as you can see, are these huge chunks... thousands of tons of ice completely covering the fields, highway, everything. I've never seen the likes of this ever before in my entire life. Imagine, from the dam, clear through the fairgrounds and clear through town and south of town, all the way down to the Yellowstone River—this wide path of buildings and land just wiped out! It is like an unbelievable nightmare! And listen to this: as far as is known right now, there was no loss of life! Isn't that incredibly miraculous? When you look at that enormously wide swath of damage, I can't imagine how all these people escaped and lived to tell about it.

Thank God our new place sits on higher ground. From where I sit, I look across the highway right here to this huge lake so deep there are actually white caps on the water! They say it may run like this for weeks with all the snow yet to melt, and now all that ice to thaw, too. What a mess! Could be millions of dollars in damage. Had you folks still been here, you wouldn't have even saved an extra pair of shoes, never mind even saving your lives. It happened so fast you probably would have been asleep and couldn't have gotten out in time. Even if you managed to get out the door or climbed through a window before they all got blocked, the ice and water and debris would most likely have swept you away and you guys would have been the only fatalities in town. I shudder to even think about it! I guess some rescue workers were starting to pump water out of your basement to see if there were any bodies trapped in there. Bill happened to be driving past it, spotted them working and he told them you folks had moved back east just a couple weeks ago. If you had been here and lived through it, you would never be able to sell your basement. It isn't worth peanuts now. You told me you lost a lot of money selling it a couple weeks ago, and the buyer really took advantage of you because he knew you were in a hurry to leave. Guess what your buyer has now? Nothing! Even Ebersole's basement across from Verna Frost... buckled in, trashed. Lee's was flooded out, too. The whole town is in an awful state, and they say the drinking water situation is critical. We're supposed to boil our water before drinking it. Aren't you glad you sold out, even at a loss? You at least have some money... your slick buyer has a muddy, caved-in cistern.

So far, we are marvelously okay. We have water from our own deep well, lights, heat, etc. ... but the flood water is just across the road. The highway is acting like a dike for us... shielding us so far. I have been up since 3 AM so I am positively bleary-eyed and bewildered and I realize that we have a long siege ahead of us before things get even close to normal again. We'll keep you posted though and send you pictures of your old place, what's left of it.

Billy just came home with a huge board full of fish he took off the ice south of the golf course. The country club house didn't get any of the water—went right on past it. Billy got trout, bass and blue gills. I think he has about 40 fish in all. Now to figure out what to do with all of them. Too tired to think or write any more tonight. More later...

Tuesday, March 27...

Didn't get this mailed yet. Not sure if the post office is in business, so here are a couple more news items: your friends Johnny Smith and his wife lost everything!! Lucky to be alive! They got an advance warning Sunday night somehow, and managed to save a few personal things and stay at his mother's in town. I know you have been at their basement house on Lambert Road a few times. Well, three sides are caved in—total loss, just like your old place. And Mrs. Kitttleson would be gone if Pat Fitzgerald hadn't just happened to think of her. He literally saved her life. I'm sure there are many stories all over town like that, lots of people looking out for other people, helping out their neighbors and all. It is so heart warming! Makes a body feel good seeing that kind of thing going on. Oh, and Atkinson's basement out by your place went in... again! Mike Hansen's basement (Bach's old house next to Gerber's) filled up to the top and ran out the back door. Their basement is all buckled and shot. Haven't heard anything yet about your friends Don and Maxine Nutter, or should I say Senator Nutter. I'll try to find out about them and let you know.

Love to you all,
Helen

Ruth sat at the kitchen table feeling numb, stunned by what she had just read. She stared at Helen's letter again and reread small parts of it just to dispel her disbelief, because she wasn't sure if she was hallucinating or the letter was real. A hundred images flashed through her mind in rapid succession. She saw the cold little motel room with the kitchenette where the Foell family survived in cramped quarters for over four months—Herman and her dad finishing up the knotty pine wainscot in the living and dining rooms just before Christmas, a lovely space that would never become a gorgeous basement recreation room because it was now filled with mud, water and blocks of ice that had crashed through the roof—Bill carrying the Christmas tree down the stairs to save their first Christmas in Montana—Herman proudly turning on the new oil furnace that he had installed himself, including all the ductwork. So many images; so many experiences—many calamities and many miracles to learn from, all in such a short time. Tears welled up in her eyes, and she began to cry, sobbing uncontrollably for almost ten minutes. Her tears were not sorrowful for what was lost, but for what might have been lost.

She tried to picture Sidney in the tragic state it must be in right now. It made her shiver. She felt suddenly chilled and slipped into a sweater. Ruth's mind briefly touched that haunting question: What would it be like for the Foell family had they stayed there even two weeks longer? Again, her eyes filled with tears. Ruth thought about how they had splurged and bought that sleek, brand new car with part of the proceeds from selling the basement, knowing that "old faithful" would never make it back to Wisconsin. So, they returned to their home state in style, in a '51 Hudson Pacemaker, their first new car. She remembered how smoothly the return trip had gone across the Dakotas, Minnesota and crossing Wisconsin during the most unpredictable time to travel—winter. Although there were times when they could see nothing but snow banks towering high on both sides, creating a powdery white canyon flanking the narrow, plowed roads, God was watching over them. The weather behaved well, with clear, sunny skies; and they reached the old hometown without incident. Even the moving van with all their worldly goods arrived only two days later. No sooner were they comfortably settled in their new apartment than one of the worst blizzards of the season hit the Midwest. Hundreds of families were isolated on farms and marooned in small villages without electricity. Many motorists were stranded. The Foell family was again favored by God's grace.

Clutching Helen's letter, Ruth looked out the window as she had been doing frequently ever since they moved into the second floor apartment. A light snow was falling, and it was beautiful to watch as it fluttered gracefully to the ground below her. *The ground below her*... what a beautiful phrase. Her eyes brimmed with tears of gratitude as she offered her thanks to the Lord again, and yet again, for having her family together, safe, warm, dry and alive. How precious and priceless are those simple comforts. She loved her lofty perch, looking *down* on objects from the second floor level. What a delicious perspective to have. But she knew she would never stop looking upward, too; she had so much to be thankful for. The family that was feared lost was found.

THE END

LIFT YOUR EYES

Richard P. Foell
1978

If you're weary and tired of living
A life you have filled with despair,
Who can you blame if you weep all alone?
The life you have made is your own.

Never look downward; lift up your eyes;
Seek only pathways that climb.
Soar with your dreams like a great bird in the skies.
Never look downward; lift your eyes!

Take your eyes off the ground and take a look around;
Seek all the love you've been missing;
Reach your arms out; your spirit will rise;
Open your heart; lift your eyes.

Reach your arms out; your spirit will rise;
Look up to the heavens... lift your eyes!

EPILOGUE

Ruth intended to complete her journal and eventually rewrite the story in a format that would be more suitable for publication. She never completed the last chapter, or the proof-reading and editing, or the final re-writing of her manuscript. It remained in a desk drawer for several years while Herman's job during the Korean War moved the family from Wisconsin to New York, then to Ohio and back to Wisconsin again. Finally, when her life seemed to be settling down to a more tranquil pace so she could concentrate on completing her book, she became seriously ill and only the first four pages were rewritten. That prolonged illness was to be her last struggle. Cancer took Ruth Foell's life in September of 1960 at the age of 51. Herman's collapse on the basement floor described in Chapter 17 may have been a precursor to the three heart attacks he would sustain during the following ten years. Suffering from a "broken heart", his fourth and final heart attack took Herman's life, and he joined his beloved wife ten months later at age 52.

Ruth's sister, Helen, moved her family to Santa Barbara in the mid 50s, basking in the more hospitable winters of southern California after so many years in the Montana deep freeze. She was quite content to be surrounded by many shelves of wonderful books, working in a store that collected rare volumes.

Don Nutter, the good friend and unassuming, decorated war hero whose donated blood had saved Dick's life, became a state senator and was later elected Governor of Montana. During a fierce blizzard with 100 mile an hour winds on the night of January 25, 1962, Governor Nutter was killed with five others when wind shear ripped a wing from his plane, and it crashed in Wolf Creek Canyon just north of the state capital. During World War II, Don had survived 62 combat missions flying B-24 bombers and lived through the treacherous supply missions in C-47s crossing "the hump" in Burma for many months. Ironically, the aircraft that took his life in the Rocky Mountains of Montana was the same type aircraft he had piloted safely through the violent turbulence across the world's highest mountains where 1500 fellow aviators had perished. A tall bronze statue of Governor Nutter now stands in Veterans Memorial Park in Sidney.

The three Foell boys grew up, went to college, served in the military, got married and started families of their own. One of them eventually became a writer. The brothers didn't remain in Wisconsin. They ultimately fanned out to Orlando, Las Vegas, and Boston, but they remain close in spirit and keep in touch. Sadly, Ruth and Herman passed away even before their first grandchild was born, but they are survived by five grandchildren and eight great-grandchildren as of this writing, all of whom will now come to know the story of ***Calamities and Miracles... Family Feared Lost.***